S0-BFC-038

Chances Are

OTHER BOOKS AND AUDIO BOOKS
BY TRACI HUNTER ABRAMSON

Undercurrents

Ripple Effect

The Deep End

Freefall

Lockdown

Crossfire

Backlash

Smoke Screen

Code Word

Lock & Key

Obsession

Royal Target

Royal Secrets

Deep Cover

Chances Are

a novel

TRACI HUNTER ABRAMSON

Covenant Communications, Inc.

Cover image: *Couple Enjoying Outdoors* © Massimo Merlini & *Three Colors House Front* ©
Tobias Helbig, courtesy istockphoto.com

Cover design copyright © 2014 by Covenant Communications, Inc.

Published by Covenant Communications, Inc.
American Fork, Utah

Copyright © 2014 by Traci Hunter Abramson
All rights reserved. No part of this book may be reproduced in any format or in any medium without the written
permission of the publisher, Covenant Communications, Inc., P.O. Box 416, American Fork, UT 84003.
The views expressed within this work are the sole responsibility of the author and do not necessarily reflect
the position of Covenant Communications, Inc., or any other entity.

This is a work of fiction. The characters, names, incidents, places, and dialogue are either products of the
author's imagination, and are not to be construed as real, or are used fictitiously.

Printed in the United States of America
First Printing: March 2014

20 19 18 17 16 15 14   10 9 8 7 6 5 4 3 2 1

ISBN 978-1-62108-692-5

For all those who have fought the battle against cancer and for the people who love them through it.

Acknowledgments

MY HUMBLE THANKS TO REBECCA Cummings for sharing not only her editing talents but also her struggles, many of which helped with the accuracy contained within these pages.

Thank you to the Covenant family for supporting me in my many writing endeavors. A special thanks to Samantha Millburn for her incredible dedication and sacrifice to shepherd this book through the publication process and to Kathy Gordon and the rest of the publication committee for encouraging me to write the story that had to be written.

Thank you to Tanner Wilson and Jared Smith for letting me borrow your names, even though you evolved from missionaries to doctors. And thank you to Jessica and Ian Kearl for helping me name even more nameless characters.

My sincere appreciation to Jen Leigh, Amber Green, Darlene Sullivan, and Stephanie Read for carrying me through my crazy schedule and even providing chocolate chip cookies for breakfast when deadlines started crashing in. You're all amazing!

Finally, I want to thank my husband, Jonathan, and my children for their continued support. Thank you for encouraging me to follow my dreams.

Chapter 1

BEN EVANS STOOD IN HIS apartment living room, a bat in his hands, his eyes on the television across the room. He watched the recording again, trying to remember everything: the pitcher's release point, the spin on the ball, the way the catcher shifted behind him to the left. Then he watched the recorded image of himself cocking the bat above his head and chasing the low and outside pitch. That swing had ended the game and ended the Washington Nationals' brief journey through the play-offs.

His stomach clutched as he listened to the announcer's comments that had aired moments before he had strode to the plate, the questions the man had posed of whether the team's manager was making a mistake to leave Ben in. After all, rookie-of-the-year candidate or not, Ben Evans had never been in such a high-pressure situation before. Maybe it would be wiser to put someone with more experience in for that crucial moment. The commentator pointed out that Shawn Nills had a great history against this particular pitcher, and Lanski's bat had been hot for the past several weeks.

The comments weren't new to Ben. Hadn't Frank Petric suggested exactly the same thing when Ben had reached for his helmet and batting gloves? His manager, Jack Wheatley, had silenced the questions with a terse, "Go on, Evans. Grab a bat."

Ben remembered the anticipation of striding to the plate, the excitement of the fans. He also remembered the doubts. And he had let them matter.

The doubts and what-ifs rattled through his brain until he couldn't stand them any longer. He shut off the television and pulled on his shoes. Then he headed for the door and hoped that a long run would help him clear his head. Deep in his heart, though, he knew he would never forget.

* * *

Life wasn't fair. Maya thought she'd understood that simple statement when she'd been forced to run away from her home in India at the tender age of the thirteen and again when her grandmother had died two weeks after Maya finished her junior year of high school. Now she sat in her doctor's office and wondered if good luck really existed and, if so, why it never seemed to reach her.

She thought of the challenges of her senior year—being forced to move to a new town, leaving her old friends behind, and living with a foster family who wanted nothing to do with her, a family who cared only about the check they received each month from the county. Her foster mother's reaction had proven that when Maya had asked for money to restring her tennis racket. The woman had been cold and absolute, leaving no doubt that Maya wasn't going to get anything from them other than a roof over her head.

Her heart ached when she thought of the emerald ring her grandmother had left her, the one she had ultimately been forced to sell in order to provide for herself. She had started to think that just maybe the sacrifice had been worth it when the tennis coach from Vanderbilt took notice of her and offered her a full-ride scholarship.

Throughout her freshman year of college, she had finally started feeling like she could build a future for herself. Her schooling was going well, and between her roommate, Kari, and the tennis team, her social life had been full and rewarding. She had even managed to work her way into a starting position on the team only a few weeks into the season.

Her scholarship paid for her room and board, and a part-time job at the university bookstore kept spending money in her pocket.

Then came the headaches. Part of her wished she had never listened to Kari when she'd insisted six months ago that Maya go see the doctor.

At the time, she had expected some kind of prescription for migraines or maybe some allergy testing. Instead, she had been run through a gamut of tests, but none of them for allergies. An MRI, CT scans, the PET scan, and ultimately the scariest of them all—a biopsy. She knew enough about medicine to know that if the doctors were insisting on a biopsy *and* a PET scan, they pretty much already knew what they were dealing with. Cancer.

She didn't want to think about the bills piling up, her lack of adequate insurance, or the struggles with her family. At the moment, all she cared about was what she had to do to beat this thing.

The round of chemo had done little for her besides zap her energy and leave her in a daze. Now she was sitting here listening to the scan results after her first, and hopefully only, round of radiation.

Maya listened to the doctor speak, certain this must be another extension of her bad dream. He read through the technical jargon of the report while Maya waited for the bottom line: whether the treatments had succeeded in shrinking the tumor at the base of her skull, the tumor that threatened to leave her paralyzed or worse.

"The good news is that the cancer still appears to be contained to the primary tumor."

"You said the same thing six months ago," Maya said, her Indian accent still noticeable, even after six years in the United States. She drew a deep breath and forced herself to ask the question. "What's the bad news?"

"The growth of the tumor has slowed . . ." He trailed off.

"But you still can't operate," she finished for him.

He shook his head. "No. Unless we can figure out a way to shrink the tumor, we can't operate with any degree of success."

She gritted her teeth against the despair struggling to surface. She forced herself to draw a steadying breath and then asked, "What happens if we can't shrink the tumor?"

"Then the cancer will run its course."

"Meaning, I'm going to die." Tears formed in her eyes, and she tried to blink them back. "How long do I have?"

"Untreated, you'd be lucky to make it another year, but I'm not ready to give you an expiration date quite yet," Dr. Smith said gently. "There is one more option I think you should try. It's experimental, but the doctors running the trial have already had some success."

"Doctor, I'm only twenty years old. I want a chance to live, whatever it takes."

"That's what I wanted to hear."

* * *

Kari stood the moment Maya walked into the waiting room, and she searched her friend's face intently. They had become instant friends when Maya transferred to her high school during their senior year, both girls heavily involved with the tennis team. Maya's talent had outshined everyone else's, but Kari had appreciated her quiet confidence as well as her constant willingness to stay after practice to work with her.

Maya's dark eyes met hers now, but Kari was too impatient to try to read her expression. "Well? What did the doctor say?"

"I'll tell you when we get home."

Kari glanced at the handful of others in the waiting room. As Maya headed for the door, Kari couldn't help but notice that her friend had gone from petite to downright thin over the past few weeks. Her dark hair fell well past her shoulders, and even though Maya said it had thinned a bit from the chemo and at the spot where she'd had radiation, Kari still couldn't tell the difference.

Impatiently, Kari unlocked her car and waited for Maya to climb in before turning to her. "Okay, we're alone now. Tell me what he said."

Maya lifted her hands to cover her mouth, a gesture she often made when she was trying to settle her emotions so she wouldn't cry. This wasn't a good sign.

"Just tell me," Kari pressed.

"They still can't operate."

"Are they doing more chemo or radiation?"

"No. The chemo didn't work, and the radiation didn't work well enough."

"There has to be something the doctors can do," Kari insisted, panic lacing her voice.

Maya's shoulders lifted and fell with a sigh. "Dr. Smith said there is a developmental treatment they've had some good success with. . ."

"That's great!" Kari said with renewed enthusiasm. "What do you have to do to get into it?"

"Move to Washington, DC."

"What?"

"They're conducting the trial out of George Washington University Hospital in DC. Not only that—the treatments can last anywhere from three to six months." She shook her head. "We both know there's no way I can afford to live there for that long. I don't have the energy to work full-time anymore."

"You could take out a loan," Kari said desperately.

Maya shook her head. "I already tried that. Bankers are really funny about lending money to people they think are dying."

"Credit cards?"

Again, she shook her head. "I've already maxed out the three I have with my medical expenses. I can barely keep up with the minimum payments on those."

"We're going to figure something out," Kari insisted, already thinking about her brother's apartment in DC, the one that was currently sitting empty. She still wasn't sure if Ben had decided to live in LA during his off-season because he wanted to be closer to his girlfriend or because he wanted to get away from the memories of his last game in the play-offs. Regardless, she thought his decision could very well work in Maya's favor.

Kari slid the key into the ignition and drove to their apartment. As soon as they were inside, she said, "I'll be right back. I need to make a phone call."

Maya's only response was to lower herself onto the living room couch.

Kari pulled out her cell phone and headed for her bedroom, where she called her brother.

"Hey, Kar. What's up?" Ben asked in his typically relaxed voice.

"The usual: studying, preparing for a real career in life."

"Baseball is a real career," Ben said, and Kari could hear the humor in his voice. "It's just a fun career."

"Yeah, so you've said," Kari said, enjoying the familiar banter. "So how are things going in California? Are you really going to stay there for your whole off-season to train?"

"That's the current plan."

"In that case, I have a favor to ask you."

"What's that?"

"My roommate, Maya, and I were thinking about taking a trip to DC this weekend. Any chance we can crash at your place?"

He was quiet for a moment. "Yeah, I guess you could do that. When are you planning on leaving?"

"Probably Thursday or Friday."

"I'll go ahead and FedEx my spare key to you to make sure you have it by Wednesday."

"Thanks, Ben. I really appreciate it."

"Just don't go throwing any wild parties."

"Oh, all right," Kari said with mock exasperation. She heard his low chuckle as she hung up the phone, and she rubbed her hands together. That was almost too easy. She supposed eventually she might have to break down and tell her brother that Maya was staying longer, but she could give him those minor details later. One thing at a time.

* * *

Maya heard Kari's bedroom door open, but she kept her eyes closed in the hopes that Kari would think she was sleeping. She didn't want to face this latest reality, and she knew that if she had to face Kari's problem-solving personality, she was going to completely lose it.

"I've got it all planned out," Kari announced, clearly not buying her sleeping act.

Reluctantly, Maya opened her eyes. As always, Kari's green eyes were alive with enthusiasm, her tall, toned body the picture of health. "You've got what planned out?"

"How you're going to be able to afford to live in DC."

A little seed of hope sprouted. "How?"

"You know my brother, Ben, right?"

"Kind of. I met him when he came home for Christmas last year, and we went on a few runs together, but it's not like we exchanged phone numbers or anything. If you remember, his girlfriend kept him on a pretty short leash." Maya didn't add how disappointed she had been when she had discovered Ben had a girlfriend last Christmas. He was someone she would have loved spending more time with.

"That doesn't matter," Kari said briskly. "What matters is that my brother decided to spend his off-season working out in California."

"So?"

"So his apartment in Washington is going to be empty." Kari tucked a lock of her dark hair behind her ear. "I just talked to him, and he said we can stay there when we go to DC."

Maya looked at Kari blankly. "I think I'm missing something. Why would you be going to DC?"

"My accountant said I need some more business expenses this year."

"Kari, you're a student, and you do your own taxes."

"I know," Kari said without missing a beat. "What I'm telling you is that my brother is going to let you live in his apartment since it's just sitting there empty. That way you'll have a place to stay for the next three to four months."

"What happens if my treatments take the full six months?"

"I think you should apply for another credit card. I know it's not the ideal, but if you do need it, you can use a cash advance to pay for a place for the extra couple of months."

Maya stared at her, hope and possibilities bringing her back to life. "So I would be able to get the treatments?"

"Yes. You'll be able to get the treatments." Kari nodded. "I think you should call your doctor right now to see what you have to do to get into the trial. My brother is sending me his keys. We could be there as early as Friday."

"Friday? But what about school?"

"I think this is more important," Kari said, stating the obvious. "It won't be hard to withdraw from your classes, and the sooner you get started with treatments, the longer you'll have a free place to stay."

"I'll call right now."

"Hey, Maya," Kari said, interrupting her before she could dial. "You are going to beat this."

Maya drew a shaky breath. "I hope you're right."

Chapter 2

Kari paid the cab driver and then reached for Maya's largest suitcase.

"I can get that," Maya insisted.

Kari shot her a knowing look but didn't say anything. Instead, she grabbed her own bag with her free hand and led the way to the apartment building, pulling the two suitcases behind her. She reached the door and set one of the cases on its end so she could search for the key. She was still digging through her purse when the door opened.

A man in his early thirties emerged, his dark hair cut short, his goatee neatly trimmed. His dark eyebrows lifted, and he looked at Kari and Maya with a combination of curiosity and wariness. "Can I help you?"

"No, thanks. I'm just going to my brother's apartment."

"Who's your brother?"

Instantly guarded, Kari fumbled for an explanation. She didn't want to give her brother's name, fully aware of how private he was about keeping his address out of the public eye.

Apparently sensing her hesitation, he said, "I'm Ian Harris. I manage this complex."

Kari's shoulders relaxed slightly. "I'm Kari Evans."

"Oh, Ben's sister." Kari could tell Ian understood her dilemma. "Well, it's good to meet you. How long are you staying?"

"I'm only here until Sunday night, but Maya here will be staying for a few months." Kari noticed the skepticism on Ian's face and added, "Don't worry. Maya's not the type to throw wild parties."

"That's good to know." Ian dug out his wallet and grabbed a business card. "Here's my number in case you need anything."

"Thanks." Maya took the card he offered.

"No problem." He held the door and waited for them to pass through. Then, as an afterthought, he asked, "Hey, Maya. Do you have a car here?"

"No, I don't. Why?"

"I was going to make sure you knew the code to the garage," Ian said. "If you ever get in a bind and need a ride, let me know. My wife or I should usually be able to help you out."

"Thanks." Maya smiled. "I really appreciate that."

"It's not a problem." He gave a departing wave. "I'll see you later."

"Looks like you're making friends already." The elevator doors slid open, and Kari stepped inside. "It's nice to know you'll have someone who can help you out if you need it."

"Yeah." The word was barely louder than a whisper.

Kari looked over at her friend and noticed the white-knuckled grip she had on her suitcase. Kari wondered how she would feel if she was about to move into a place on her own, not knowing anyone, while facing a life-threatening illness. Then the simple fact hit her: she couldn't begin to imagine it.

* * *

Maya followed Kari down the L-shaped hallway and into the apartment. Immediately, she felt like a trespasser. The curtains to the windows across the room were open, with the Washington Monument visible in the distance.

Two long couches dominated the living room, and a large television hung over the fireplace. The kitchen was small and compact, tucked away from the rest of the living area, but the stainless-steel appliances appeared new. The entire apartment appeared to have been recently remodeled, but everything about it felt masculine, right down to the rack of baseball bats hanging on the wall and the lingering scent of aftershave in the air.

"Are you sure this is okay with your brother?" Maya asked from the edge of the living area.

"It's fine." Kari reached out and grabbed Maya's arm, pulling her farther inside. "Come on. My brother won't even notice you're here, much less care. Last time I talked to him, he was so wrapped up in his girlfriend that he barely remembered my name."

Maya let herself get pulled into the room. Curious, she crossed to the window, her heart lifting a little when she noticed the trees lining the street below, their leaves alive with fall colors. She loved this time of year.

"I'll show you around." Kari led the way to the cluster of doors on the far side of the room.

She opened the first door on the right to reveal a combination bathroom and laundry room. The large bedroom beside it held only a full-size bed and a dresser, and simple blinds covered the windows, with a glass door opening onto a balcony.

"This is your room." Kari set Maya's suitcase down inside the door.

"I didn't expect the guest room to be so big," Maya said, putting her smaller bag inside as well.

"The bedrooms are both around the same size, but my brother's room has the walk-in closet and private bath."

"There are two bathrooms?"

Kari nodded. "Ben wanted to make sure that when we came to visit he wouldn't have to wait for the bathroom."

"I'm surprised he even bothered with a two-bedroom. I would have thought it would be more economical to just put your family up in a hotel when you came to visit."

"Ben likes the idea of having friends and family stay with him. Of course, after his success last season, he's pretty much changed his tune and only lets family stay here now."

"Why's that?"

"A bunch of his high school buddies crashed here when he first got called up, and one of them made a copy of his house key. They came back when he was on the road and decided to stay here without asking. The apartment manager got complaints about the noise when their party got too loud, and when Ben got back a few days later, his place was trashed. He decided it was one thing to give free game tickets to his friends, but it was too much to open his home to them."

Uneasiness settled over Maya again. "Then why is he letting me stay here?"

"You're the exception." Kari smirked as she crossed the hall to Ben's bedroom. "Besides, it's not like he's even here right now, and you certainly aren't asking for tickets to his games."

Maya looked around Ben's room and once again felt like a trespasser. One of Ben's jerseys was mounted in a large shadow box that hung on the wall, along with several framed photographs. Maya stepped closer to look, recognizing one as the day Ben was drafted. Others were of him with various celebrities—an actress from a recent hit movie, the host from one of the night shows, the starting quarterback from the Redskins.

"It looks like your brother gets around."

"Yeah." Kari nodded. "After spending the last couple of years in the minor leagues, he's been enjoying the attention of being a star on his team."

"He's done well for himself," Maya said with a touch of regret hanging in her voice.

"Hey, don't start thinking like that."

"Like what?"

Kari cocked her head to one side. "I know you, remember? I know how hard it was on you when you had to stop playing tennis."

Maya shrugged. "That's all behind me now. There's no use dwelling on what might have been."

"Maybe not, but that doesn't change the fact that it's got to hurt," Kari told her. "Besides, you never know—you might start playing again after you get through these treatments."

"At this point, I'll be glad to make it to my twenty-first birthday."

"You're already twenty," Kari said pointedly. "Don't you think you might want to aim a little higher than that?"

Pain started at the base of Maya's skull. She put a hand against the wall and closed her eyes to help her brace against it. She bit back the moan that tried to escape, but she couldn't keep the sheen of sweat from appearing on her brow.

When the worst of the pain subsided, she opened her eyes to see Kari waiting patiently. "Are you due for another pain killer?"

She nearly shook her head before she spoke, but then she remembered how much the movement would hurt. "Not for another hour or so."

"Come on. Let's go into the living room. You can get comfortable while I figure out something for lunch."

"You don't have to wait on me, you know."

"I know, but you might as well let me since I'm only here for a couple days." She waited for Maya to sit down on the couch before heading into the kitchen. She opened one cabinet after another and let out a sigh. "Well, so much for my brother leaving any food here. I guess we can just order out or pick something up on our way to your appointment."

"I can go to the grocery store in a little bit," Maya offered. "I don't always do very well eating restaurant food."

"Oh, that's right." Kari grabbed her purse off the counter and fished out a small notepad and pen. She plopped down on the couch opposite Maya. "Help me make a list, and I'll go out now."

"Are you sure? After I take my next set of pills, I can go with you."

Kari shook her head. "You need food to take with your pills. Besides, this will give you a chance to rest a bit. Your appointment isn't until two. It's only eleven now."

Unable to argue with her logic, Maya nodded. They put together a basic grocery list, and then Kari left for the store.

As soon as Maya was alone, she curled her legs up under her on the couch and closed her eyes against the next wave of pain.

Chapter 3

"YOU'RE GOING TO PLAY BASEBALL with a bunch of eight-year-olds and their dads instead of coming with me to a party that will be crawling with movie stars?" Ben didn't miss the disbelief in Heather's voice. "You've got to be kidding."

"I promised my cousin David that I'd help with his son's practices while I'm here." Ben wasn't sure he could explain how much he was looking forward to the Little-League practice. He had to admit he enjoyed being recognized when he was out and about in town, but there was nothing better than hanging out with a bunch of adoring kids, especially ones who shared his love of baseball.

"Can't you miss it just this once?" Heather asked with an artful toss of her long black hair. She sidled up to Ben and slipped her arms around his waist. "Parties like this don't happen every day."

"From what I've heard, these parties tend to last all night," Ben countered. He acknowledged to himself that he was tempted. After just finishing his rookie year as a major leaguer, he certainly hadn't expected to be included in what was clearly an A-list event. In fact, he could hardly believe his life right now was real.

At only twenty-three years old, he was already a shoe-in to start next year at second base, money was plentiful, and he had a girlfriend who had already graced the cover of a magazine. It might have only been a small, local advertisement circular, but who was he to argue about whether the advertisement had made her a star?

One thing was certain: the stars would be out in Malibu tonight. But Ben knew that if he wanted his own star to continue to rise on the baseball diamond, he couldn't afford to get sidetracked. He really was looking forward to the Little-League practice, but that wasn't the only reason for his decision. He had a job to do, and that included following his workout schedule to the letter, right down to the 5:00 a.m. start time. When he went back to DC, he wanted to prove he was more than the guy who had made the last out in the play-offs.

He wasn't sure he was ready for this kind of party anyway. He'd heard the rumors. The drugs and drinking. The complete lack of morals. He might not always be the best about religious stuff, but he knew he didn't want the kind of temptation and pressure he would likely have to deal with at the party.

Besides, he had a reputation to protect. Throughout his childhood, his parents had taken him to church every week and taught him good Christian values. As a teenager, he had made the conscious choice to live by certain standards—standards that would prevent him from having any skeletons left behind to haunt him later. When he had been drafted right out of high school, the one thing he had promised his parents was that he would always strive to be the kind of person kids could look up to. He wasn't about to break that promise after only one year in the majors.

"Oh, come on. It'll be fun." Heather gave him a little pout. "I thought now that the season was over we were going to have more time to spend together."

"We are spending more time together," he insisted. "We went out to dinner last night. We were out at the beach this afternoon."

"And we can go to this amazing party tonight," Heather finished for him.

"Look, if you want to go to the party that bad, then go," Ben said, not really expecting her to agree.

Ben could tell she was disappointed and annoyed when she said, "That would be weird if I went by myself."

He shifted so his hands were loosely around her waist. "Then stay here. After I finish with the kids' practice, we can hang out, maybe catch a movie."

"You want to go to a movie instead of to the party?" she asked sarcastically.

Now irritation rippled through him. "Like I said, if you want to go to the party so bad, then go." He waved at the kitchen table. "The invitation is over there. It'll get you in."

Her entire countenance changed in an instant. The irritation was gone, and he saw a glimpse of the girl he had fallen for nearly six months before. Her voice was all honey and sugar now. "Are you sure?"

Ben hesitated. He considered convincing her not to go, already worried that she was getting too caught up in the world he had landed in.

When he and Heather had met, she had been a breath of fresh air. He had been halfway through his first road trip when they had crossed paths in a restaurant in LA while he and the team were waiting for a table after their game. She had been so at ease with everyone that he'd forgotten to be in awe of the players he now called teammates. She and her friend had joined them that evening, and over the next few weeks, they had started talking and texting often.

Girlfriends had always been easy to come by for him, but now he was beginning to wonder if she was as interested in him personally as she was in his social status. Early on, he hadn't really cared one way or the other. As a rookie, it was easier to have someone calling herself his girlfriend than to have others constantly offering to take the title. Maybe now that the season was over, he needed to reconsider the reasons he and Heather were together and decide what he really wanted in a girlfriend.

His cell phone rang, and his sister's name illuminated the screen. He nearly ignored her call so he could finish his conversation with Heather but then remembered that Kari was in DC this weekend.

"I'm sorry, but I've got to get this." Ben hit the talk button. "Hey, Kari. What's up? Did you get into my place okay?"

"Yeah. I'm just heading to the store right now to pick up some groceries. I didn't expect the cupboards to be completely bare. You were just here a couple weeks ago."

"Sorry. The cleaning lady probably threw everything out."

"Ben, there wasn't even a can of soup in your place."

He heard the sarcasm in his sister's voice, and his mood lifted a little. "I usually ate out or ordered in."

"Wait," Kari said, taking a step back in the conversation. "You have a cleaning lady?"

"I did," Ben told her. "She came in once a month while I was there, and I asked her to do another cleaning after I left."

"Is she going to show up unexpectedly while we're here?"

"No," Ben said. "I'm not planning on having anyone come in until I get back in April. So that means you need to clean up after yourself."

"Don't I always?" she asked sweetly.

"No, you don't," he said without hesitation. "If I come back to my place and find dirty dishes all over the apartment, I'm going to have to hurt you."

"Yeah, yeah," Kari said and changed the subject once more. "So when are you coming back to DC?"

"I don't know. I report for spring training in February, but I'll probably go straight to Florida. Most likely, I won't make it back to DC until late March when the team comes back to get ready for opening day."

"You know, if you can score me a ticket, maybe I'll come for the season opener."

"You'll still be in school."

"Yeah, but I can take a day or two off. Besides, I'd love for my friend Maya to see you play."

"I suppose you want me to get her a ticket too."

"You do make the big bucks."

"I'll see what I can do." Ben chuckled. He hung up the phone and tried to remember the last time he had laughed. He looked over at Heather, who now held the party invitation in her hand and was staring at it raptly. They certainly hadn't laughed together since he'd moved to Los Angeles two weeks ago.

Heather held up the invitation. "Are you sure you don't want to come with me?"

"I'm sure." He didn't draw her closer when she leaned in and gave him a quick kiss. Instead, he found himself relieved when she crossed the room and the door closed behind her.

Why was it that he was annoyed with Heather because she wanted to take advantage of an invitation he didn't want anyway, yet he didn't mind the fact that his sister had asked for an extra ticket for her friend? Feeling used but surprisingly liberated by the prospect of having a free evening, he headed for his room to get ready for Little-League practice.

* * *

Kari hung up with her brother and grinned. *That was almost too easy*, she thought to herself. She still considered the idea of having Maya move into her brother's apartment to be inspired. She also knew Maya would never agree to live there unless she believed she had Ben's permission. Kari wasn't about to risk the possibility that her brother might say no. After all, what was the likelihood that he would agree to let someone he'd only met once move into his apartment for the next three to six months, even with his sister's prodding?

She'd keep this arrangement a secret from both of them. It would never hurt Ben, and it could only help Maya. She had to keep them both in the dark to give Maya a fighting chance.

Pocketing her phone, Kari headed into the local market and grabbed a basket. She considered for a moment what to make for dinner, quickly adjusting her idea of what was appetizing to what Maya would be able to eat. The only things on Maya's list were vegetable broth and saltine crackers. After watching her go through chemo and radiation over the past few months, Kari could understand why those two items were the staples of her menu. But she also knew Maya was wasting away and needed to expand her diet to keep from losing any more weight.

Fifteen minutes later, she paid for the things Maya had asked for, as well as a deli sandwich for herself and a few other items that would last them through the weekend. She hated that she couldn't stay longer to make sure Maya would be okay, but she couldn't afford to fall behind in her classes.

With the groceries in hand, she made her way back to her brother's apartment to find Maya curled up on the couch, sound asleep. Kari's heart ached when she saw the too-pale skin stretched over hollow cheeks and the clothes that were now several sizes too big. Maya looked almost childlike . . . and so dreadfully alone.

Maya hadn't told her much about her family, except that she and her grandmother had converted to Christianity before moving to the United States. When she had pressed for more information, Maya had refused to discuss it, always insisting she couldn't fully explain the cultural differences between her childhood and her life now. Kari surmised that something in her past had been unpleasant enough for her or her parents to have cut off all contact, but whatever it was, Maya refused to talk about it.

They had been halfway through their senior year before Kari had realized Maya had never invited her to her house. Sensing Maya didn't have much support at home, it had been natural for Kari to include her in many of her family events. Going to college together had been yet another step along their budding friendship. When they had decided to room together during their freshman year, Kari realized for the first time that she hadn't ever seen anyone from Maya's past reach out to her in any way.

Kari had thought things would change between Maya and her family after Maya found out about the cancer, but as far as Kari knew, she hadn't even told them about the disease or the possibility that her life could be cut short. Kari couldn't imagine what it would be like to not have her family to lean on. Sure, her brother could be obnoxious sometimes and her older sister was forever stealing her shoes, but she didn't doubt for a minute that if she needed something, they would be there for her.

Kari started putting the groceries away and debated whether she should make Maya some soup. She heard movement and poked her head into the living room to see Maya struggling to sit up on the couch.

"What time is it?"

Kari glanced at her watch. "Almost one. Did you want me to make you some soup? Or I have some apples and bananas."

"I'll just have a banana." Maya pushed off of the couch and crossed into the kitchen.

"How about a piece of toast or something to go with it?"

She shook her head. "This is fine, thanks."

"You know, you're going to have to start eating more, or you'll waste away."

"I will eat more," Maya promised. "The doctor said it might take a few weeks to get my appetite back."

"It's been a few weeks," Kari countered.

"I'll eat something else when we get back from the doctor's office."

Kari unwrapped her sandwich. "Okay, but I'm going to hold you to that."

Maya took a small bite of her banana. "We should probably leave soon. Didn't you say the hospital is about a five-minute walk?"

"I'll call for a cab," Kari offered.

Maya shook her head. "That's nice of you to offer, but I need to figure out my way around on foot since I don't have a car. Besides, maybe the walk will help me work up an appetite."

"Okay, but if you aren't feeling up to it, we're getting a cab to bring us back."

"Deal."

Chapter 4

MAYA CLASPED HER HANDS TIGHTLY together as she sat watching Dr. Schuster read her file. He was maybe in his early thirties, much younger than she'd expected for someone running a clinical trial. Dr. Smith had already talked to Dr. Schuster about including her in this trial, but Maya knew things could change if this initial screening didn't go her way. If the doctor told her no, she might as well pick out her tombstone now.

He took off his reading glasses and leaned back in his chair to look at her. "It says here you live in Nashville, Tennessee. You do realize you'll have to move here to DC in order to participate in the trial."

Before Maya could respond, Kari spoke for her. "She already has an apartment to live in while she's here."

"I'm sorry to be blunt, but how are you going to pay for that? For the first three months, you can't expect to work."

"She won't have to pay rent," Kari told him, her voice protective. "My brother has an apartment here that he doesn't use except during baseball season. He won't be back until late March or early April."

Dr. Schuster looked pleased. "In that case, it looks like you will fit this trial nicely, especially since you already have a medical port."

"What's a medical port?" Kari interrupted.

"You know, the port below my collar bone where the nurses gave me my infusions when I was having chemo," Maya told her.

"Oh, that." Kari nodded.

The doctor shifted some papers on his desk and handed Maya a packet of information. "Look over all of this information, and if you're still interested after you read it, get back in touch with me by next Friday."

She accepted the thick envelope and took a deep breath. "I'll read through everything, but I can tell you now I want into this program. You've read through my file. We both know this is my last chance to beat this thing."

He gave her a curt nod. "In that case, get all of the paperwork filled out. If you're ready now, we'll start you this week. You'll need to be back here Monday morning at 9:00 a.m."

"Thank you," she said with a relieved sigh.

"Oh, and, Maya?"

"Yes?"

"Do yourself a favor and go to the grocery store between now and then."

"We just went."

"There's a pretty specific diet in the information there. You'll want to make sure you have everything you need for the next few weeks. Your energy level will be really low until your body gets used to it."

"We'll make sure she has everything she needs," Kari promised.

* * *

Ben read the early morning text message from Heather and shook his head. He hadn't seen her since she'd walked out of David's house on Friday with the party invitation in her hand. She had texted him once on Saturday to let him know she wasn't going to make it to dinner with David and his family. This latest text said she wasn't feeling well enough to make it to the Sunday dinner David's wife, Wendy, had planned.

"What's going on?" David asked when he walked into kitchen, where Ben was still staring at his phone.

"Heather said she can't make it to dinner tonight."

"Does she not like us or something?" David asked. "This is your third week here, but she hasn't made it to Sunday supper once."

Ben raked his fingers through his hair. "I don't know what her problem is. She had a great time when we all went out to dinner together last week."

"Maybe she doesn't like Wendy's cooking."

"How would she know? She's never tried it," Ben said with a shake of his head. "I'm starting to think we're not a very good match."

David gave Ben a sympathetic look. "It's never easy to get to know someone when you try to date long distance."

"We saw each other quite a bit during the season."

"Yeah, but I'll bet it was mostly going to games and then out to dinner or parties afterward."

Ben nodded.

"Unless you've totally changed, you've never been much of a party guy unless it's an after-game celebration."

"Yeah, I guess that's true," Ben mused. "I thought I knew her better than I obviously do, but honestly, I don't think she knows me very well either."

* * *

"Kari, Maya, this is my wife, Jessica."

"Nice to meet you," Maya said to the petite blonde before sliding into the backseat. "We really appreciate you offering to drive us to the store."

"It's not a problem," Ian insisted. "We needed to go ourselves anyway."

"Ian said you don't have a car here. I know there's a market around the corner, but if you ever want to go to one of the bigger grocery stores, let me know. I'm always running out of something."

"Thanks," Maya said, praying that the dull ache in the back of her head wouldn't explode before they completed their shopping spree.

"You look like you're in pain," Kari said perceptively. "Did you take your medicine this morning?"

"Yeah."

"Are you okay?" Jessica asked with concern in her voice.

"It's just a headache," Maya said.

"I have some Tylenol if you need it."

"That's okay, but thanks." Maya tried to follow the conversation as it continued around her, but little by little, the headache spread, and her stomach started churning, the apple she had eaten an hour before now making her nauseated.

Realizing that the lingering effects of the radiation and the tumor weren't going to hold off the way she wanted them to, Maya found herself hoping she could at least make it to the grocery store before her stomach protested completely.

She closed her eyes and tried not to think about how she was feeling. When Ian pulled into the parking lot, she stepped out and slowly followed the others toward the building. As soon as they stepped inside, she asked Jessica, "Do you know where the restroom is?"

Jessica pointed to the corner of the store. "Yeah, it's over there on the left."

"Thanks." She turned to Kari. "I'll catch up with you."

Before Kari could say anything, Maya made her way to the bathroom and rushed inside.

* * *

"Is she okay?" Jessica asked Kari. "She looked really pale."

"Her stomach must be bothering her again."

"If you need me to take her back home, I can do that," Ian offered.

"Thanks, but hopefully she'll be okay. This is probably the last time she'll be able to come to the store for the next few weeks."

"How come? We can still bring her even after you leave."

"Yeah, but she's going to be undergoing treatments, and she probably won't have the strength to do any shopping for a while."

"What kind of treatments?" Jessica asked, concern showing rather than morbid curiosity.

Kari hesitated. She didn't want to betray her friend's confidence, but Ian and Jessica would be the only people Maya knew here in DC. "She has a tumor at the base of her skull. We're hoping this new treatment will shrink it enough for the doctors to remove it."

"Cancer?"

"Yeah." Kari pressed her lips together and fought against her own rising emotions. "This is pretty much her last chance."

"That's tough," Ian said.

"Look, I know we just met, but anything you can do to help her out would be great. These first few months aren't going to be easy on her."

Jessica nodded, and her mind seemed to be processing everything. "We'll definitely check in on her."

"Thanks. She's not very good at asking for help."

"Then we'll try to make sure she doesn't have to ask."

The three of them went about their shopping, and Kari wasn't surprised that Maya didn't reappear from the bathroom until they were waiting in the checkout line. As soon as Maya joined them, Kari asked, "Are you okay?"

"I'm fine."

Kari could tell by the way Maya stood so rigidly that the pain was pushing toward unbearable, but she didn't challenge her friend. Instead, she stood silently and tried to force positive thoughts into her mind.

* * *

Maya followed Kari onto the sidewalk in front of the apartment building, where a cab was waiting, a sense of dread coming over her.

"I wish you could stay longer," Maya said as she embraced her friend. Everything had happened so fast over the past week that she hadn't really taken time to foresee this moment when Kari would leave and she would find herself completely alone in a strange city. Nothing was familiar here, and she didn't know anyone besides her doctor and the Harrises.

After their trip together to the store, Ian and Jessica had offered repeatedly to give Maya a ride or help out anytime she needed. It didn't take much to realize Kari had told them about her illness.

Maya appreciated the fact that they were so sweet about offering to help her, but that wasn't the same as having Kari there to support her through these next treatments. Looking back now, she was still amazed at how willing Kari had always been to reorganize her schedule to go with her to the various chemo treatments and drive her to radiation. She couldn't count how many school assignments Kari must have done sitting in a waiting room.

"I'll call you as soon as I land," Kari promised.

Maya sighed. "I'm really going to miss you."

"I'll miss you too." Kari stepped back and handed her suitcase to the cab driver. "I'll figure out a way to come visit you during Christmas break."

"That would be great, but you don't have to do that. You'll want to spend the holidays with your family."

"What about your family?" Kari asked. "Are you sure you don't want to let them know what's going on?"

Maya instantly stiffened. "My family isn't like yours."

"I'm sure they would want to know what you're dealing with," Kari said gently.

"Sometimes it's best to leave the past behind you and face the future alone." Maya gave Kari another hug and changed the subject. "Don't forget to call when you get home."

"I won't. And you don't forget to eat." Kari climbed into the cab and gave her a last wave. Then the taxi pulled away from the curb, the image blurring through the tears that filled Maya's eyes. Her throat closed, and an emptiness swept through her as the cab disappeared into the Sunday afternoon traffic.

Chapter 5

MAYA TOOK THE SEAT THE nurse indicated and gripped her purse. She didn't know why she was nervous. The doctor had already admitted her into the trial. She looked around the room, where six lounge chairs were positioned in a wide half circle. Two of the other chairs were already occupied, IV stands stationed nearby to hold the medicine being infused into the patients. Each of the other two participants had a friend or family member sitting beside them, and they were chatting quietly.

"Do you have anyone here with you?" the nurse asked gently.

"Not right now," Maya told her.

"But you'll have someone to drive you home, right?" she asked. Before Maya could answer, she added, "Dr. Schuster doesn't want anyone in this trial using public transportation."

"I noticed that in the informational packet he gave me, but the place I'm staying is only a couple blocks away."

The nurse looked at her. "It could be next door, and you'd probably still need someone to drive you home. This treatment isn't always easy on patients."

"I read about the side effects, but it didn't say much more than fatigue, muscle soreness, and nausea."

"The good news is that the nausea usually only lasts for the first two weeks or so while you're adjusting to the treatments. Unfortunately, the fatigue and soreness can be pretty extreme, especially during those first few hours after an infusion."

"Would I be able to get more pain meds to help with that? I'm nearly out of what my doctor back home prescribed."

"I'll talk to the doctor to see what we can do for you, but if you were thinking about walking home today, I would reconsider."

"That's good to know," Maya said, her voice neutral. She supposed she could call Jessica for a ride, but she hated the idea of inconveniencing someone else. This week would be the worst because she would have to be here every day for various tests, blood work, and infusions.

According to the doctor, after the first week, she would still have to come to the hospital four days a week: two days for infusions, one for a shot, and another for her routine blood work. She looked away when the nurse hooked the infusion to her port.

As soon as the nurse was finished, she asked, "Can I get you anything? Some water or something to read?"

"I'm fine, thanks," Maya told her, retrieving her water bottle from her bag. "How long do these infusions take?"

"Between three and four hours." The nurse stepped back and added, "I'll be back in a little bit to check on you."

"Thanks." Maya took a sip of her water and watched the nurse move over to help the patient two chairs over. Even though Maya had a paperback Kari had specifically given her to read during her treatments, she closed her eyes and let memories of her family and of the beautiful home where she had spent her childhood wash over her.

She had been one of the fortunate ones in India, with a family of wealth, one that expected the children to learn to read and write and pursue other interests. Tennis had been her love and the one thing she had taken with her when the time had come to make her escape to avoid becoming a child bride.

The premarriage ceremony had taken her completely by surprise, as had the fact that the man her father intended her to marry was three times her age. But Rishi was a powerful businessman in the nearby village, one with whom her father had hoped for some time to join forces.

Maya had been terrified that Rishi would come back and claim her as his bride long before she reached the legal age of eighteen. Her tennis competitions had given her exposure to areas outside of her village, and she had gained an understanding that arranged marriages were rarely forced. But she had seen it happen so many times before—when what was supposed to be an introduction between the prospective couple turned into a forced marriage.

Unfortunately, her father and Rishi didn't care what people in other parts of the country did. They simply wanted the marriage contract to be upheld. Even at thirteen years old, Maya understood she was supposed to have some say about the man she married and when. Still, in her village, traditions often prevailed, particularly when the groom had money or influence. Rishi had both.

Her pillow was wet with tears when her grandmother came to her in the middle of the night. She whispered words to her in Hindi, saying simply, "If you want to escape this marriage, you must come with me now."

As if in a dream, saying nothing, asking no questions, together they quickly packed as many of Maya's belongings as she could carry. Just as they were slipping out a side door, Maya saw her mother standing down the hall. Tears glistened in her eyes, but the moment Maya took a step toward her, her mother turned and walked away.

Brokenhearted and confused, Maya had let her grandmother lead her outside to the car she had hired to take them to the airport. The struggles that had followed, first living in a tiny, one-room flat in London and then immigrating to the United States, were memories she rarely let herself dwell on.

"Are you doing okay?" The nurse asked, breaking into her thoughts.

Maya opened her eyes. "Yes, thank you."

"Okay. Let me know if you need anything."

Maya watched her walk to the next patient and listened to her chat with him and the woman who had accompanied him. Loneliness overwhelmed her, and she closed her eyes once more. This time, when the memories tried to form, she pushed them back and willed herself to sleep.

* * *

Ben held the phone to his ear with one hand and used the other to load marshmallows, graham crackers, and chocolate bars into a grocery bag.

Heather's voice answered with a sultry "Hello."

"Hey, are you already on your way? We're heading over to the beach in a few minutes."

"The beach?"

"Yeah. We're going out with my cousins tonight. Don't you remember? Sand, campfire, s'mores?"

"You may have said something about a campfire and s'mores, but you didn't tell me we were going with your cousins."

"That was the whole point of going, to spend time with them."

"I thought you came to LA so you could spend more time with me, not with them."

"Actually, it was a bit of both."

"Can't we do something tonight, just the two of us? I haven't seen you all weekend."

"Whose fault is that?" Ben asked. "You're the one who kept canceling on all of our plans."

"I told you I wasn't feeling well."

"Is it really that big of a deal to come hang out and have a barbecue with David's family?"

"You know I'm not good around kids."

"Fine." Ben couldn't deny that David's children hadn't really hit it off with Heather. Now that he thought about it, Ben had rather enjoyed a peaceful weekend without having to worry about Heather and the drama that often surrounded her.

"How about if we meet for lunch tomorrow?" Heather suggested. "I just heard of this new place in Beverly Hills. It's supposed to be amazing."

Ben closed his eyes. He knew he had no future with Heather, and it was silly for him to keep postponing the inevitable. This wasn't the first time something like this had happened, but he had tried to fight against the annoying feeling that Heather really was with him only because of his fame and money. Disgusted by the image and his newfound certainty that it was true, he knew what he had to do. "Fine. Go ahead and make a reservation for one o'clock. We can talk then."

"Okay. I'll see you tomorrow."

Ben hung up and saw David standing at the edge of the room.

"I gather Heather isn't coming tonight?"

"You guessed it."

"You know, Wendy will understand if you can't make it."

"Heather's not worth missing out on spending time with you guys. I've always loved the whole campfire-on-the-beach bit."

"Are things okay with you two?"

"I'm pretty sure we're over. She just doesn't know it yet."

Chapter 6

THE PAIN WAS EVEN WORSE than she had anticipated. The doctor had already called in a new prescription for pain medication at a local pharmacy, but unfortunately, it was over two miles away.

"Here's the address." The nurse held out a slip of paper.

Maya took it from her, even that little bit of effort weighing on her. "Thanks."

Concern shone in the woman's warm, brown eyes. Maya read the name tag on her scrubs: Betsy. "Do you need me to call a ride for you?"

Maya wanted to say no, but she didn't know how she was going to make it all the way to the front door, much less the quarter mile to her home. Quietly, she looked through her purse and pulled out her cell phone and Jessica's phone number.

She made the call, relieved when Jessica answered and agreed to come get her.

"Let me get you a wheelchair, and I'll have someone take you outside," Betsy said.

"I think I can make it," Maya told her, though she knew the words weren't true.

"We both know better than that," Betsy said gently. "It will get better after the first few treatments. I promise."

She motioned to a dark-skinned man who appeared to be in his late sixties. He wheeled a chair to her.

"This is Henry," Betsy told her. "He'll make sure you get out front to find your ride."

"Thank you." Maya lowered herself into the wheelchair.

"So, Maya, where are you from?"

"Ohio."

Henry smiled. "Honey, that accent is not from Ohio."

"I'm from India originally."

"Ahhh. The land of curry and spice," he said, the simplistic description invoking images of her family gathered together to share a meal of pilau rice and kadai lamb. "Do you know how to make curry chicken?"

Delighted despite her exhaustion, she offered him a warm smile. "Of course. It's one of my favorite foods."

"Maybe one day after you're better, I'll talk you into making that for me. My wife never has been able to get it quite right."

"Is your wife from India?"

"No. New Jersey."

"New Jersey?"

He chuckled. "But she knows I love anything with curry in it; my favorite's curry chicken."

"Then as soon as I'm better, I will teach her if she wishes to learn."

"We'll look forward to that day."

The automatic doors opened, and Henry pushed Maya outside. A moment later, she saw Jessica pull into the parking lot.

"That's my ride there."

Henry pushed her closer to the curb and waved a hand to get Jessica's attention. Then he helped Maya into the car, gave her an encouraging look, and closed the door.

Maya shifted to face Jessica. "Thank you so much for the ride. I really appreciate it."

"I'm happy to help. I'm just glad you caught me. Normally I work during the day, but it just so happened that I had a dentist appointment and decided to take the rest of the day off."

Maya tried to hide her disappointment. She hadn't really wanted to ask Jessica to drive her every day, but she had hoped the possibility would exist if she needed it. "Would you mind terribly if we stopped by the pharmacy? I need to pick up a prescription, and I'm afraid it might be a little too far to walk."

"Sure. Which pharmacy?"

Maya gave her the address, and Jessica pulled out of the parking lot. Twenty minutes later, Jessica said good-bye to Maya at the elevator and left her to make it the rest of the way to Ben's apartment on her own.

Maya had managed to fight back the worst of the pain while struggling through the tedious process of collecting and paying for her prescription, but as soon as she made it inside, she headed for the kitchen and fumbled for a glass of water. She was barely able to open the pill bottle, but somehow, she managed to twist it open and pop two pills into her mouth.

Swallowing, she limped to the couch and gently lowered herself onto the plush cushions. Slowly, she leaned back and closed her eyes, praying that this pain would ultimately be worth it.

* * *

Ben laced up his running shoes and pulled a hoodie over his head. His early morning workout session with David had gone well, but now he was ready to work off some extra energy without confining himself to a weight room. He had considered driving down to the beach to run but had instead decided to spend more time ambling through the local neighborhoods.

He set out at an easy pace, giving his muscles time to loosen for the first mile or so. He passed a high school, noticing the variety of cars in the student parking lot. He remembered all too well what it was like to be one of the few who couldn't afford a car of his own, always relying on others to take him where he wanted to go.

Looking back, he was grateful his parents hadn't been in the position to give him everything he'd wanted growing up. Even though it had been tough at the time, wishing he had the latest cell phone and a form of transportation that didn't involve two wheels and pedals, he was astute enough to know that the lack in his childhood and teenage years made him appreciate what he had today.

His mind continued to wander as he pounded past the school and into the adjoining neighborhood. He thought of his impending lunch date with Heather and found himself pondering the future. He was only twenty-three, young enough that he hadn't worried a lot about marriage yet but old enough for the idea to have entered his mind.

Undoubtedly, the recent engagements of several teammates had been the catalyst to such thoughts and had left him pondering what he wanted in his future. He couldn't deny that over the past few weeks he'd found himself comparing his relationship with Heather to what his friends had.

He supposed he had always known Heather wasn't going to be the woman in his future. As much as he appreciated how she had helped him transition into his life as a big leaguer, they had little to talk about when they were alone.

He hadn't been completely honest with her last night when he'd said he had come to California partly to be with her and partly to be closer to his cousins. The convenience of staying with David and his family had worked out great, but even if they hadn't lived near Heather, he probably would have figured out a way to stay in LA during the off-season. Besides wanting to see where this relationship with Heather would take him, the climate was great, and he was ready to live away from his parents' home.

Now he found himself grateful that he hadn't rented a place of his own. His expectations and Heather's were obviously very different. Heather apparently expected that they would spend all of their time together going from one social event to another. He had envisioned spending his days working out, preparing for next season, and having the convenience of living close enough that they could go out most evenings.

He had held firm about getting in his workouts each day, but until this past weekend, he had let Heather largely dictate what they did when they had time together. The more he thought about it now, the more he wondered if he really enjoyed spending time with her or if he just enjoyed the novelty of having someone who clearly enjoyed being around him.

The incident with the party last weekend, though, made him doubt if it was even him she was interested in or if it was just the perks of his profession. Deep down, he already knew the answer. He turned a corner and headed back home. As much as he dreaded it, he knew lunch today would be the perfect time to end things with Heather so he could move on to follow his own dreams without anyone holding him back.

* * *

"My friend must be running behind," Maya told Henry when he wheeled her outside after her second treatment. "I can just wait over there on the bench."

"I don't mind waiting for a few minutes."

"Oh, it's okay. She said she wasn't sure when she'd be able to get away from work."

"All right. If you're sure." He wheeled her over to one of the benches along the building and helped her from the chair. "You're sure you're okay?"

"I'll be fine," Maya lied. She didn't know how she was going to manage walking the quarter mile to Ben's apartment, but she couldn't very well sit in the hospital all day. At least Henry had gotten her out the front door.

"Okay. I'll see you tomorrow."

"Thank you, Henry."

He nodded and pushed the empty wheelchair back inside.

Maya waited until she was sure he was gone. Then, gathering all of her strength, she stood and slowly walked toward the parking lot and the intersection beyond.

She managed only a handful of steps before she started looking ahead for someplace she could rest along the way. A tree in a grassy median in the parking lot became her first target, and she hated that something less than thirty yards away could seem so far. She hadn't even made half that distance before a familiar voice sounded behind her.

"Did your ride not show up, or were you lying to me?" Henry asked.

Maya didn't answer.

He motioned to the wheelchair in front of him. "Sit down."

"I can make it. It's only a few blocks."

"Maya, I said sit down," he demanded, taking her arm and helping her into the chair.

Her heart sank. Logically, she knew she wasn't going to make it all the way to the apartment without help, but she kept hoping that somehow the Lord would give her the strength she needed. Expecting Henry to take her back to the hospital, she calculated whether she might have enough cash in her wallet to pay for a cab. But to her surprise, he pushed the chair forward in the direction she had been heading.

"Okay. Where are we going?"

"What?"

"You said it was only a few blocks. I'm taking you home."

"I can't ask you to do that," Maya insisted. "I don't want you to get in trouble for being gone too long."

"I'm taking my lunch break," Henry told her. "Besides, I'll let you repay me by making me some Indian food once your treatments are over."

Maya's eyes teared up at the kindness of the gesture. She blinked several times and managed to say, "Thank you."

"You're welcome." He wheeled her to the intersection and waved a hand. "Now, which way are we going?"

Chapter 7

Ben didn't know where he was going. The address Heather gave him for the restaurant was actually to some fashion boutique. When he finally managed to find a parking space off of Rodeo Drive, he stopped to ask for directions, only to end up at a hotel. Thinking that perhaps the restaurant was inside, Ben went in and met a family of five from the Washington, DC, area, who happened to be huge Nationals fans.

Ten minutes, a nice chat, and several autographs later, Ben gave up looking for the restaurant and pulled out his cell phone to call Heather.

"Ben, I was just getting ready to call you."

"Sorry I'm running late. The address you gave me wasn't right. Where is the restaurant?"

"Actually, I can't make it today."

"What?"

"My agent called a little while ago to tell me about a movie audition. He said the part was made for me."

"I didn't know you were trying to get into acting."

"I've been toying with the idea for a while now."

"Why didn't you call me sooner?"

"My agent only called me an hour ago. I had to get ready," she told him unapologetically. "How about if we do lunch tomorrow instead?"

"Whatever," Ben mumbled.

"Great," she said, clearly either unaware or unconcerned about his frustration. "I'll talk to you later."

"Yeah," Ben said under his breath as he pocketed his phone. "Much later."

* * *

Maya passed through each day very much like she did the one before. With her strength faltering, she forced herself to ask Jessica for a ride to the hospital each morning. Jessica dropped her off early on her way to work, and then after the infusion, Maya waited in the doctor's office until Henry took his lunch break.

As he had on that first Tuesday, Henry wheeled her the several blocks to her apartment, depositing her at the elevator door before going back to the hospital. Each day, she tried to focus on the blessings of having people who were so willing to help her in this strange city instead of thinking about the constant pain and her complete lack of energy.

For two weeks now, she had been living off the food Kari had bought her. She had already run out of bananas and a few other items from their trip to the store, and she was now down to the last of her yogurt, oranges, and apples. The diet Dr. Schuster had given her was simple enough, including lean meats, fish, fruit, certain vegetables, and whole grains. Unfortunately, many of the items were a bit pricey, and others still weren't sitting well with her.

She knew from past experience with cancer treatments that it was best to try to concentrate on the positives in life. Though simple, she enjoyed her new routine. When she wasn't at the hospital getting infusions, she spent what little energy she had reading the books she had brought with her and sitting out on the balcony so she could watch the bustle of traffic on the street below.

Now that she had survived the first couple weeks of treatments, she hoped she could regain a little more energy to do more around the apartment and even outside. At least her meals since moving here had been largely disposable, so except for the trash that was starting to overflow in the kitchen, the apartment looked pretty much as it had when she got there.

A knock sounded at the door. She hesitated, wondering who could be coming over first thing on a Saturday morning.

Concerned that it might be someone looking for Ben, her mind raced with explanations of why she was living in his apartment, certain Ben wouldn't appreciate the potential rumors her presence might invoke. Hesitantly, she made her way to the door and looked out the peephole. She relaxed when she saw Jessica standing in the hall.

Maya pulled the door open, her eyes narrowing when she saw the vacuum cleaner in her hand. "What are you doing here?"

"I've come to clean your apartment." She walked past Maya into the apartment and started unwinding the vacuum cord.

"You don't have to do this."

"I know, but I thought I should probably help you out while I can." She plugged the cord into the wall.

"What do you mean?"

Jessica turned to her. "Ian has a job interview on Tuesday in Philadelphia. He wants me to drive up with him so we can house shop in case he gets the job."

"Really?"

She nodded. "The interview is at one in the afternoon, so we can drop you off at the hospital for your treatment before we leave."

Maya pressed her lips together, overwhelmed by Jessica's kindness. "I don't know what I would have done these past couple of weeks without your help."

"I'm glad we were able to do something for you. I'm just worried about what will happen if Ian gets this job. We'd probably have to move right away."

"Things are supposed to get a lot easier now that my body's getting used to the treatments." Her legs shaking, she lowered herself onto the couch. "I'm sure I'll be able to walk to the hospital if I need to. Worst case, I'll take a cab."

"I wish I knew someone else who could help out. Unfortunately, just about everyone around here works during the day."

"It'll be fine," Maya assured her. "You and Ian concentrate on what's best for the two of you."

Jessica motioned to the hall. "Why don't you go sit out on the balcony while I vacuum. You probably shouldn't be in here while I'm cleaning."

"Okay." Maya mustered her energy, stood, and made her way through her bedroom and out onto the balcony. Her body aching, she lowered herself into one of the two padded chairs Kari had found stashed in her brother's closet and looked down at the street below. A young couple walked along the sidewalk, the woman pushing a stroller, a toddler in his father's arms.

Longing swept through Maya. What would it be like to have a life such as that? The woman appeared to be only a few years younger than her husband, and the way she looked at him made Maya wonder if she had chosen this marriage for herself rather than being matched by her family. Even after spending the past seven years outside of India, she was still amazed at the personal freedoms people had here in this country.

For a moment, she let herself imagine what it would be like if she managed to beat this cancer. Would she too find love someday? Or would the day eventually come when her family would find her and take her back to marry Rishi? In less than a year, she would be able to apply for US citizenship and guarantee her freedom from the arranged marriage. But first, she had to survive that long.

The hum of the vacuum cleaner sounded through the open balcony door. She continued to watch the couple below, letting herself believe her future still held possibilities.

* * *

Ben walked into the Beverly Hills restaurant and immediately saw Heather waiting for him at a center table. He wondered if she had deliberately asked for a table where she was sure to be seen by everyone coming and going. Regardless, he wasn't thrilled with the idea of enduring a meal with her when all he wanted to do was end this relationship.

This lunch had been rescheduled four times over the past two weeks, three of which resulted from him finding excuses to delay the inevitable. He supposed he had been the superficial one in their relationship by putting off breaking up with Heather so they could attend a movie premier together, but he had wanted to go, and he hadn't wanted to go alone.

He had to admit, Heather had looked stunning in her silver gown, her hair swept up into some complicated hairstyle. All evening, she had been attentive, and it had reminded him of her easygoing way with people and the reasons he had started dating her in the first place. Then he had driven her home and found himself bored as he'd listened to her ramble on about the people they had met.

Heather was great when they were going somewhere exclusive or would be with people she considered celebrities. She made Ben feel like he had the same social status as everyone else, even when they were surrounded by starlets and sports legends. The more time he spent around his family, though, the more he realized she wasn't as eager to engage with people who worked more ordinary jobs.

Heather spotted him and gave him a beaming smile. She waited until he sat beside her before saying, "I'm so glad you made it. I have so much to tell you."

She launched into a one-sided dialogue about the auditions her agent had arranged, dropping several hints about how Ben should talk to a few of the actors he had met over the past few months to help her chances. Already dreading the confrontation looming between them, he picked up his menu and put it off a little longer. "Do you have any idea what's good here?"

"I don't know." She opened her menu as well, taking her time to make a selection. As soon as the waitress took their order, Heather shifted the conversation to a safe topic. She asked all of the right questions about how his workouts were going, and Ben fell into the familiar routine of small talk.

When they finally finished and walked outside together, Ben asked, "Where did you park?"

"Oh, actually, I had a friend drop me off. You do have time to take me home, don't you?"

"Yeah, sure." Ben led the way down the street to his car, fighting the urge to pull away when she slipped her arm through his. When they reached the car, he unlocked the door, waited for her to slide in, and mentally prepared for the twenty-minute drive to her apartment.

They rode in silence for the first few minutes. Then, finally, Heather said, "I heard Shawn Nills is getting married in DC soon. Are you going back for that?"

"I was thinking about it," Ben said noncommittally, a little surprised that Heather even knew about his teammate's wedding. Shawn had been pretty adamant about keeping the event private, and he couldn't remember mentioning it to Heather.

"I guess all of your teammates will be there," Heather continued.

"Probably."

She shifted in her seat and gave him a hopeful smile. "It would be great to see all of them again."

"Yeah. I'm looking forward to it."

She let out a little sigh and, apparently, decided to take a more direct approach. "Don't you want to have a date for the wedding? That'll be so awkward if you go by yourself."

"Not really." Ben gave a slight shake of his head. "It's not like I don't hang out with these guys all the time during baseball season. Besides, you seem to be enjoying the social scene here in LA."

"That's true, but I wouldn't mind a quick trip back East."

"As long as I pay for it," Ben said, instantly regretting his words.

Heather glared at him. "You think I'm only with you for your money?"

"No," Ben proceeded cautiously, even though she had pretty much just voiced his suspicions. "But I do think we don't have nearly as much in common as I thought we did."

Her expression softened, and she put a hand on his arm. "What are you talking about? Of course we do."

"Look. I just think it may be time for us to take a break for a while."

"You want to take a break now? When we're finally living in the same city?"

"Actually, I'm moving back to DC." Ben's response surprised him as much as it did her.

The carefully controlled mask Heather had been wearing dropped away. "What? Why?"

"Like I said, I think we need a break from each other, and I need to get refocused on preparing for next season."

She waited several heartbeats, apparently taking the time to regain her composure. She seemed understanding once more when she said, "You can work out anywhere. Besides, the weather is so much better here than in DC during the winter months."

"To some extent, that's true," Ben agreed. "But I've decided I want to get back to my place in DC and work out there."

"Oh." Apparently at a loss for words, Heather remained silent for the rest of the drive to her apartment. To Ben's surprise, when he pulled into the parking lot, she leaned over and kissed him. "So when are you planning on leaving for DC? Maybe we can go out tonight or tomorrow."

"I have a lot of packing to do," Ben told her, not sure why he wasn't quite able to voice the words that things were completely over between them.

"Well, if you change your mind, you know where to find me." She gave him a sultry smile and leaned in to kiss him again. He turned his head so she kissed his cheek instead of her intended target. Then he got out of the car and circled to open the door for her. It wasn't so much that his mother had taught him how he was supposed to treat a woman as he just wanted Heather to get out of his car.

"Good luck with all of those auditions," Ben told her, slamming the car door shut. Leaving her standing on the sidewalk, he hurried back to the driver's side. "See you later."

Quickly, he started the car and pulled away. The moment he was clear of the parking lot, he let himself relax and breathe a sigh of relief.

Chapter 8

"Maya, I'm all finished in here," Jessica told her, stepping out onto the balcony, where Maya had dozed for the past twenty minutes. "I have to run out to the grocery store. Do you need anything?"

"Actually, that would be great. Can you hand me my purse there? I'll get you some cash."

"Sure." Jessica handed the purse to her and asked, "What all do you need?"

"Just some yogurt." Careful not to move too quickly, Maya retrieved her wallet from her purse and opened it. When she saw that she had only thirteen dollars inside, she hesitated. Not sure if she might need a cab to get to the hospital on Friday, she pulled out the three ones. "It doesn't really matter what kind of yogurt you get. Whatever is cheapest is fine."

"How many do you want?"

"Whatever that will buy. I have some other stuff in the pantry, but yogurt is the one thing I ran out of."

"Okay. I should be back in an hour or two."

"Thank you so much for everything. I really appreciate all you've done."

"I'm happy to help." Jessica stuffed the cash in her pocket. "Do you want me to help you back inside?"

"No, that's okay. It's so nice out; I think I'll enjoy the weather a bit longer. I imagine once it turns cold, I won't get the opportunity very often."

"That's true. We've been really lucky that it's been so mild for the past few weeks." She stepped back inside. "I'll see you later."

"Okay. Thanks." Maya tucked her wallet back into place, leaving the purse on her lap rather than expending the effort to put it away. With the fall leaves swirling on the ground below, she once again tried to find the positives in her life and fight the fear that this might be one of the last opportunities she would have to enjoy moments like this.

* * *

Ben pulled into the parking garage beneath his building shortly after ten on Tuesday morning. He wasn't sure what possessed him to drive across the country instead of fly and have his car shipped. Maybe he just realized he needed some time alone to sort out his feelings.

When he left DC the month before, he hadn't wanted to admit that he'd been running away, that he'd needed to get out of the shadows of that last play-off game for a while. Instead, he had let himself go where his newfound fame was the thing that people cared most about. He supposed he could hardly blame Heather for seeing him that way. Regardless of why he'd left, he was back now, his car stuffed full of his belongings and a bag full of trash on the passenger side floor.

The news that he had placed second for rookie of the year had come when he was halfway across Indiana. At least he'd had a little time to come to grips with that news. When he'd first been nominated, he hadn't really thought he had a chance to win. Then he'd let himself start believing the hype. He really did have to stop letting the media influence his emotions.

He stepped out of the car, pressing a fist against the kink in his back as he arched and proceeded to stretch. Deciding to leave his unpacking for later, he popped the trunk and retrieved the suitcase that held most of his clothes before heading for the elevator. Realizing that he should probably stop to check his mail, he hit the button for the main floor.

When he reached the mailboxes, he heard his name. "Hey, Ben. Welcome back."

Ben turned. "Hey, Ian. Good to see you." He motioned to the suitcase in Ian's hand. "Where are you headed?"

"Philadelphia. Job interview."

"Good luck, then."

"Thanks," Ian said. He took a step toward the door and turned back to add, "By the way, I'm sorry about what's going on with your girlfriend. I really hope everything works out okay."

Ben's brow furrowed. How could his apartment manager in DC possibly know that he and Heather had broken up? Heather was still refusing to acknowledge it, and the only person he had told about the breakup was his cousin. Afraid to know what might already be floating around in the news, he muttered, "Uh, thanks."

Ben made his way upstairs to his apartment and unlocked the door. He stepped inside, pleased to see that his sister had apparently taken his threats seriously. The floors appeared to be freshly vacuumed and the end tables surprisingly free of dust.

He walked through the living room to see that it looked just as he would have expected after a visit from the cleaning lady. The guest bedroom door was closed, but he didn't have the energy to look inside. Instead, he hauled his suitcase into his room and dumped it in his closet. He would worry about unpacking and laundry later. First, he needed food.

His sister apparently hadn't cleaned everything out of the kitchen like she had the rest of the house. Two sorry-looking apples and three even sorrier-looking oranges were in a ceramic bowl on the kitchen counter, and half a loaf of bread was tucked into the breadbox beside the toaster. He didn't want to think about the mold that might be growing inside after three weeks. Without peeking at the expected science experiment, he picked up the bread and tossed it in the garbage can.

Hopeful that his sister had left something still edible behind, he opened the door to the cabinet where he normally kept his food. His eyes narrowed. Cans of vegetable broth, a six pack of ginger ale, and three boxes of saltine crackers occupied one shelf. The rest of the cabinet was completely bare, just as he'd left it. Since when did his sister eat broth? She was famous for saying that if she was going to take in calories, she wanted to chew them.

A little curious, he moved to the refrigerator and opened it to find it empty, except for three yogurts and an open box of baking soda. Deciding beggars couldn't be choosers, he checked the expiration date on one of the yogurts to see that it was indeed still good. Then he grabbed a spoon and plopped down on the couch to eat his impromptu snack.

* * *

Maya walked into the apartment, grateful that she was starting to regain some of her strength. Henry still insisted on bringing her home in the wheelchair, but if she continued to improve at the rate she had over the past few days, she hoped she could walk to the hospital for her treatment on Friday rather than spend the last of her cash on a cab.

Thinking that maybe her stomach could handle toast, she headed for the kitchen and set her purse on the counter. Then she stared at the empty breadbox. She could have sworn she still had the better part of a loaf left, and she was sure she had seen it after Jessica had come over to clean.

Her eyebrows furrowed. Had memory loss been one of the side effects of this treatment? She didn't remember that on the list. Then again, if memory loss *was* one of the side effects, maybe she had forgotten about it.

Realizing toast wasn't an option on her limited menu, she pulled open the refrigerator to get a yogurt. Again, she found herself staring. She could have sworn there were still three left. She remembered distinctly that Jessica had bought her five yogurts. She had eaten one yesterday and another on Sunday. Memory or not, the side effects of her treatment hadn't changed the basic fact that five minus two equaled three.

Now convinced that she must be suffering from some kind of memory loss, she retrieved a yogurt and pulled open the drawer to get a spoon. A sound at the front door caught her attention. Then she heard the doorknob turn.

Heart pounding, she grabbed the skillet hanging on the wall. Ignoring the pain the movement caused her, she held it above her head, arms trembling but poised to strike.

She heard the jingle of keys, saw the imposing figure in the backwash of the hall light, and heard the thud of a bag dropping to the floor. Then the figure turned and must have seen her when she edged her way into the living room. Both hands went up defensively. "Whoa!"

The surprise in the voice and the weakness in her arms caused Maya to rest the skillet on her shoulder rather than try to swing it. Though the curtains were drawn and the only light in the room came from the kitchen, Maya was able to make out the face. She'd thought about this particular face often enough over the past ten months. "Ben?"

He flipped on the light. "Who are you? And what are you doing here?"

"I'm Maya," she told him, a little surprised he didn't remember her. When he continued to stare at her blankly, she added, "Kari's friend."

His eyes narrowed. "Maya? You were at my house last Christmas. We went running together."

She nodded.

Ben looked farther into the apartment. "Where's Kari?"

Maya stared at him, not quite sure why he was so confused. Kari had assured her that Ben said she could stay here. The weight of the skillet became too much to bear, and she took a step into the kitchen to set it on the counter before turning back to face Ben. "Kari's back in Tennessee at school."

"And the reason you're here is . . . ?"

"She didn't talk to you." Maya said it more as a statement than a question. "Kari said it was okay if I stayed here for a few months."

"A few *months*?" He instantly shook his head. "You've got to be kidding me."

"I'm afraid not," Maya said. "She said she talked to you three weeks ago."

He looked at her skeptically. "I would have remembered that conversation."

Maya's cheeks colored, dread and embarrassment seeping through her. "I can't believe Kari did this."

"I don't know what she was thinking." Ben looked equally embarrassed, and his voice was apologetic when he said, "I'm really sorry, but there's no way you can stay here, at least not while I'm here."

Mortified that she had been living in this man's apartment without his permission, she managed to ask, "How long are you in town for?"

"I'm back for good." He glanced down at his watch, a sense of urgency now emanating from him. "And unfortunately, I agreed to do an interview with a local reporter this afternoon. If the press finds out a woman is staying here—"

"You don't have to explain," Maya interrupted. "Kari has told me how hard you work to make sure you're the kind of person kids can look up to. The last think I want to do is ruin your reputation."

Ben looked relieved that she understood. He glanced at the door and dug his wallet out of his pocket. "Do you have somewhere else you can stay? I can pay to get you a hotel room until you figure something else out."

Maya thought of Ian and Jessica, remembering that they were out of town. She wasn't sure where else she could go, but she couldn't bring herself to accept Ben's money, especially since she had been living in his apartment for free for the past few weeks. "That's kind of you to offer, but I'll be fine."

Still looking uneasy, Ben said, "I'm sure there must be someone around here who could use a roommate."

"Right." Maya couldn't bring herself to tell him she couldn't afford to pay rent. Even if she could, finding a roommate would take time. At the moment, the only two people she knew who didn't work at the hospital were the ones who were not only out of town right now but who were also hoping to move permanently within the next few weeks. Thoroughly humiliated, she motioned to the guest room. "I'd better go pack."

She sensed his immense relief in the way he held himself. Quickly, she turned away so he couldn't see the despair on her face and made her way to the room that had been hers until a few minutes ago. Then she closed the door and prayed that she could keep her emotions from overflowing in front of Kari's brother.

Using every bit of energy she had, she set her suitcase on the bed and started packing her belongings, her mind racing for where she could stay now.

She thought of the lobby area in the hospital and was pretty sure she could blend in with the various patients in the waiting room during the day. The problem would be the increased probability of her getting sick if she tried that.

As Kari had suggested, Maya had already applied for another credit card to help pay for her living expenses, but she hadn't received it yet. Even if she managed to apply for another, she would need an address before she could try again.

She couldn't very well insist on staying, even though she was sure Ben was likely to spend much of his time in the weight room. Her hands stilled when she finished packing her jeans. In addition to the weight room, this apartment building had a large clubhouse downstairs, complete with several couches.

With a short-term destination in mind, Maya finished packing, her breathing labored from performing what should have been a simple task. She could hear Ben pacing in the living room, clearly impatient to have her gone. Mustering all of her strength, she managed to set her carry-on suitcase upright, pain shooting along her spine. She closed her eyes a moment until the worst of the pain subsided. Then she stared at the larger suitcase, wondering how in the world she was going to lift it off her bed, much less take it downstairs.

Avoiding the seemingly minor problem in comparison to now being homeless, she opened the bedroom door and went into the bathroom. Her hands trembling, she gathered all of her medications and put them into her purse.

Trying to ignore her unspeakable embarrassment, she took her time to make sure she had everything and to let her breathing steady. When she was sure she had left no trace that she'd ever been there, she pulled her small suitcase into the living room.

Ben had his cell phone pressed against his ear, the sound of a phone ringing audible from across the room. As soon as he saw her, he ended whatever call he had been trying to make and asked, "Is that all you have?"

"No, there's another suitcase in the bedroom."

"I'll get that for you." While he headed for the bedroom, Maya went into the kitchen. She opened the cabinet under the kitchen sink and retrieved a grocery bag she had tucked there. She then took two of the three boxes of saltine crackers and loaded them into the bag.

Ben appeared in the kitchen doorway and set her bag down. "I really am sorry about this, but I'm sure you understand."

"I understand," Maya said quietly.

"Can I at least help you take your bags downstairs?"

She wanted to say no, but necessity didn't permit her that luxury. "Actually, that would be great, if you wouldn't mind."

He hefted the two suitcases effortlessly and headed for the door. Even though Maya was carrying only the bag of crackers and her purse, she struggled to keep up with Ben's long strides. She followed him out into the hall and then into the elevator. Both of them stared straight ahead and remained silent on the ride down. When they reached the lobby, he asked, "Where is your car parked?"

"Actually, I'm going to have a friend come pick me up. If you could just take those into the clubhouse, I'll wait in there."

"Sure," Ben said without hesitation. "No problem."

He shifted her bags and led the way past the weight room and through a wide archway into the clubhouse. Maya followed him inside, looking around for someplace she could tuck her suitcases where they might not be noticed. She motioned to the huge entertainment armoire in the corner. "Maybe you could set them down over there so they're out of the way."

"Don't you want me to leave them by the entrance?"

"My friend said she might be a few minutes," Maya told him.

"Okay." Ben set the bags down on the far side of the room. When he turned back to face her, he ran his fingers through his hair and awkwardly crossed back to the door. "You know, if you want, I can call you a cab so you don't have to wait. It's really the least I can do."

"You don't have to do that." Maya straightened her shoulders. "I really am sorry about the misunderstanding."

"Hey, I know my sister. I'm sure she figured I wouldn't even notice," Ben said. "I'm afraid we're both victims of her best intentions."

"Kari means well. Please don't be upset with her."

"I'm sure someday we'll all look back on this and laugh." Ben grinned at her, but Maya could tell it was forced. "At least you didn't actually hit me with the skillet."

"That's one way to look on the bright side." Maya returned his smile with an attempted one of her own. She hoped she could find a bright side for herself.

"I guess I'll see you later." Ben moved to the door. He turned back and looked at her, hesitating briefly as though he was going to say something else. Instead of speaking, he headed through the doorway and disappeared back the way they had come.

Chapter 9

BEN LET OUT A GUILTY sigh as soon as he walked back into his apartment. He felt like a heel for kicking Maya out like that, but he couldn't be expected to let some girl he'd met only once stay at his apartment. Besides, it wasn't like she couldn't find somewhere else to go.

The fact that she roomed with his sister and attended Vanderbilt practically ensured that she came from money. Like most private schools, tuition there was outrageous, and Ben knew Kari and Maya had become friends during high school. Not to mention that Maya's clothes weren't exactly out of a thrift store. The jacket she had been wearing was over three hundred dollars. He knew that for a fact since he had bought one exactly like it for his sister.

He heard a phone ring, the unfamiliar tone sounding from the other end of the apartment. Instinctively, he patted his pocket to confirm that his own phone was where he normally kept it. He followed the sound to the guest bedroom, but the ringing stopped as soon as he stepped through the door.

A moment later, the phone started ringing again. It didn't take long for him to find it on the far side of the bed, plugged into a charger, where Maya must have left it. He picked it up to see a DC number on the screen. Wondering if perhaps her ride was calling, Ben answered the phone. "Hello?"

"Yes, I'm trying to reach Maya Gupta."

"She can't come to the phone right now, but can I get a message to her or have her call you back?"

"This is Betsy from George Washington University Hospital. Can you please let her know Henry is on his way over to pick her up? There's a problem the doctor needs to discuss with her."

"Um, sure. I'll make sure she gets the message," Ben said awkwardly.

"I appreciate it," Betsy told him. "Tell her Henry already left, so he'll be waiting for her in the lobby."

"I'll let her know." Ben's curiosity heightened. He had never been one to have much exposure to hospitals, except for the occasional emergency room visit for various injuries over the years. Still, he knew enough to realize that medical professionals didn't usually send a car for someone and certainly not when they were located practically next door.

Afraid that whomever she was going to be staying with might pick her up before he could pass along the message and give Maya her phone back, Ben grabbed the charger and phone and jogged toward the door.

* * *

Maya waited until she was sure the clubhouse was completely empty before she leaned into her large suitcase and knocked it onto its side so it would be hidden from sight behind the couch. If someone sat down beside it, they might notice it, but otherwise, she was pretty sure it would go unseen.

Worst case, if someone stole her clothes, she would have to manage with the few in her overnight bag. Nearly everything she owned was a hand-me-down from Kari or purchased from a thrift store anyway. As soon as she was satisfied that her larger bag was as safe as she could make it, she squatted down and slid both the crackers and her other suitcase under the couch, pushing both items back far enough that they too wouldn't be seen.

She put a hand on the couch in front of her and pulled herself up enough to slide onto it. Little flecks of light sparked in front of her with a sudden rush as she shifted her body too quickly. She closed her eyes against the stars she didn't want to see and tried to settle on the couch in the hope that she could rest for a few minutes and regain some of her strength.

She knew she needed to call Kari to tell her what happened, but her emotions were so torn she wasn't sure she could talk to her quite yet. She knew Kari had meant well. She also knew her friend well enough to know that Kari must have realized her brother wouldn't agree to let her stay, or she would have asked first.

The door to the clubhouse opened, and Maya looked up, surprised to see Henry walk inside pushing a wheelchair.

"What are you doing in here? I thought I was going to pick you up in the lobby."

"What do you mean?"

"Didn't Betsy call you?" Henry closed the distance between them.
"No."

"Dr. Schuster wants to see you. Betsy asked me to come pick you up. We knew your friends probably wouldn't be able to give you a ride over this time of day." He leaned over and put the footrests up and then reached down to help her shift over into the chair.

Worry creased her brow. "Did he say what he wants to see me about?"

"Nope. Just said to call and have you come in."

"That doesn't sound good."

"Now, don't you start worrying yourself prematurely. Let's get you over there, and you can find out if there really is something to worry about."

"Okay." Maya shifted back in the chair. "Thanks for coming to get me."

"That's what friends are for."

She looked up at Henry, realizing for the first time that she did have a friend. But the sinking feeling in her stomach quickly overshadowed that thought. She hoped the worst thing she would have to face today was the loss of a place to stay, but with her health already fighting to regain its balance, she was afraid the question of *where* she was going to live was about to fall in importance to the question of *if* she was going to live.

* * *

Ben reached the clubhouse to find it already empty. Hoping that maybe Maya had just moved outside to wait for her ride, he jogged out the doors and looked around. At first glance, he focused on the cars parked along the curb, searching for anyone who might be coming or going. When he didn't notice anything, he expanded his focus to the pedestrians on the street.

A couple of girls were walking along the opposite sidewalk, and there was an older gentleman pushing a wheelchair about a block away. Convinced that he'd missed her, he looked down at the phone in his hand.

"She'll figure out she's missing it eventually," he said to himself. He headed back inside and pulled his own phone from his pocket to call his sister. It was about time he laid down some ground rules when it came to lending out his stuff. When the call went straight to voice mail, he sighed in frustration.

He glanced down at his watch to see that it was almost one o'clock. Kari was probably in class.

Hoping to put this awkward situation behind him, Ben headed back upstairs. As soon as his interview was over, he'd hit the weight room. Maybe after a good workout he would be able to relax and settle back into life in DC.

* * *

Maya took the seat across from Dr. Schuster. She wasn't sure if it was a good sign or a bad one that they were meeting in his office instead of an examining room.

He looked at her, a serious expression on his face, and Maya struggled not to squirm in her seat.

"Maya, I was looking over your file this morning, and I'm afraid there's a critical piece of information our administrative staff missed when you were first admitted to this program."

"What was that?"

"I didn't realize you don't have insurance."

"I have student insurance at Vanderbilt. I think it's good through the rest of the semester even though I had to withdraw."

Dr. Schuster nodded. "One of our administrators called about that this morning. You are correct that your student insurance policy is good through December. Unfortunately, it only covers expenses incurred within their service area."

"I'm still not sure I understand the problem. I was told that this clinical trial wouldn't cost me anything. Why does it matter if my insurance covers me here or not?"

"The clinical trial is covered here. Assuming we are successful in shrinking the tumor, we would then need to operate to remove it. The cost of the surgery is not covered by the trial."

"Can't I just go back to Nashville to have the surgery?"

He shook his head. "As I said, your policy covers you through December. The earliest we can expect that you could have the surgery is late January."

Maya swallowed hard. "How much will the surgery cost?"

"Anywhere from thirty thousand to a quarter of a million."

"A quarter of a million *dollars*?"

"That's typically the high end," he told her. "Looking at your situation, my best guess is that you'd be looking at around seventy-five thousand. That would include a week's stay in the hospital. If you end up needing additional rehabilitation after you're released, that would increase the cost."

"Will the hospital work with me on some kind of finance plan?"

"There's only so much they can do. They can let you pay off a portion of the expenses over time, but you would have to come up with half of the money up front. I can work the numbers for you so we put the estimated costs on the low end of thirty thousand, but that still means you'd have to come up with fifteen thousand dollars before we can operate."

She blinked hard against the tears that threatened. "I understand."

"Do you have any family who can help you with the expenses?"

Maya's heart sank. For seven years, she hadn't spoken a single word to her family, with the exception of her grandmother. Now that her grandmother was gone, she had a choice to make. She could give up this fight and let the cancer win, or she could stop fighting the traditions of her family and hope her father would help her.

"I'll talk to my parents."

"Good." His shoulders relaxed slightly, but his voice remained somber. "Because if we can't be sure you can have the surgery at the end of this trial, we will have to release you from it."

"My father has done very well for himself. I don't think coming up with fifteen thousand will be a problem for him."

"Great." Relief sounded in his voice. The doctor nudged the phone on his desk closer to her. "Do you want to call him now?"

"I don't think you'd want to pay for that phone call. Besides, it's the middle of the night where my family lives."

"Where do they live?"

Maya drew in a deep breath and let it out. "India."

Chapter 10

"ARE YOU SURE YOU DON'T need me to take you home?" Henry asked doubtfully.

"I'm sure. I have a few errands to run, so I'll just take a cab today."

"Okay." Hesitation filled his voice. "If you're sure."

Maya could tell he wasn't quite sure if he should trust that she was telling the truth. "I will take a ride down to the curb though, if you're offering. And if you could hail me a cab, I'd appreciate it."

"Well, that's easy enough." Henry helped her into the chair and headed for the elevators. "Did everything go okay with the doctor?"

"Yeah. There was just some confusion about my insurance. We got it all figured out."

"That's good. It always makes me nervous when they send for patients like that."

"Yeah," Maya said on a sigh. "Me too."

Henry wheeled her outside and flagged down a cab for her. As soon as Maya was situated in the backseat, Henry waved and headed back toward the entrance.

"Where to, miss?" the driver asked.

Maya rattled off the address for the closest pharmacy. When the driver pulled up in the parking lot a few minutes later, Maya pushed open the door. "Can you just wait for me? I won't be long."

"I'll be here."

She walked inside and headed for the counter where she had seen a display for prepaid cell phones during a previous visit. She had a good deal on the contract for her regular cell phone, but it didn't include international calling. Quickly browsing through the phones in front of her, she selected the cheapest one that would suit her needs. Then she took it to the counter, choosing to pay for it with the one credit card she thought might still be below its limit.

Ten minutes later, she handed over the last of the cash in her wallet to the cab driver, stuffed her new purchase into her purse, and walked into Ben's apartment building. She lowered herself onto the couch in the clubhouse and uttered a quiet prayer.

The thought that her parents probably still didn't know her grandmother had passed away surfaced. When her grandmother became ill during Maya's junior year of high school, her primary concern had been to make sure Maya wouldn't be taken back to India and forced into marriage. With that in mind, she had made Maya promise not to make contact with her family under any circumstances. Now, for the first time since leaving her home, Maya knew she had to break that promise.

Her grandmother would have understood her reasons, but she also would have shared the same concerns Maya faced now. What if Rishi still intend to go through with the marriage contract Maya's parents had agreed to? Surely, after all these years, he would have found another girl to take to wife.

Exhausted, she leaned back on the couch, hoping no one would notice her sitting there. She couldn't make the call to her parents for another seven or eight hours, but maybe, if they were willing to help her with the costs of the surgery, they might also be willing to give her some money for rent for the next month. Though she already knew her family's support was questionable at best, Maya clung to the hope that they would help her— because her life literally depended on it.

A couple came through the door and walked past her, both of them sending curious glances her way. While some residents used the main entrance by the mailboxes, she knew a good number preferred to cut through the clubhouse on the way to a side entrance, which was closer to the nearest subway station and the outdoor parking spaces.

Realizing she might look more natural if she had a phone or a book in her hand, she opened her purse to retrieve her cell phone. When it wasn't in the inside pocket where she normally kept it, she pulled the prepaid phone she'd just purchased out and started digging through her purse.

Certain that she'd put it in her purse that morning, she searched through the bag again, only to confirm that it wasn't there. "Great," she muttered under her breath. Between the hospital waiting room, the doctor's office, the cab, and the drugstore, she could have lost it anywhere.

Grateful to have the prepaid phone, she removed it from its packaging and activated it. She called the international operator and got the country code for India, knowing she should prepare for the inevitable. After jotting the number down on the back of her credit card receipt, she slipped her arm through the strap of her purse, leaned back on the couch, and let her eyes droop closed.

* * *

Ben heard his phone ring and dug it out of his pocket, hoping his sister was finally calling him back. He had called a couple of times but hadn't been able to reach her. He had ultimately resorted to sending her a text message with a request to call him.

When he saw that it was Heather's name on his screen instead, he silenced the phone and put it back into his pocket. She was consistent. He'd give her that. Every day around eight o'clock her time, she tried to call him.

Only once had he actually answered, and that had happened only because he'd been on another call and hadn't checked the caller ID before answering. He had tried to explain during their most recent conversation that when he had suggested they take a break, he meant from each other. He still wasn't quite sure she understood what that entailed.

There was no doubt that Heather was beautiful and often the life of the party, but he was done investing time in a relationship that wasn't going anywhere. Besides, he suspected Heather would only stay interested in him as long as his star was on the rise. He had little doubt that she would bail on him the minute he was out of the news. Even flying low on everyone's radar after the season ended had left her a little restless.

A little part of him wished someone would have caught a glimpse of him with Maya in his apartment building, if nothing else but to show Heather he was moving on. Admittedly, when he'd first spotted Maya in his place, for a brief moment, he had thought that maybe Heather had flown to DC to surprise him. It hadn't taken long to see beyond their similar builds and hair color and focus on the differences. While Heather probably should have bought stock in several cosmetic companies, Maya didn't appear to wear any makeup.

Pushing aside thoughts of the two women who had recently complicated his life, Ben took the elevator down to his car and debated whether he should finish unpacking or head out to grab some dinner. He quickly decided in favor of a hot meal and headed for one of the local sports bars he had frequented during the baseball season.

Not surprisingly, the hostess greeted him by name. "Ben, welcome back. I thought you left town for the off-season."

"I'm back for a while," Ben told her. "Can you set me up with a table, Abby?"

"Of course." She picked up a menu and led him away from the bar and toward the tables in the back, where he normally sat.

Ben followed her, raising a hand in greeting as they passed one of the waiters he had come to know over the past few months. He took the seat against the wall, the basketball game on the television monitors closest to him immediately capturing his attention.

A minute later, a waitress put a glass of ice water down in front of him and proceeded to take his order. Feeling very much at home, Ben stretched his legs out, leaned back, and let himself enjoy the game.

* * *

Maya jolted awake, her heart pounding as she tried to identify her surroundings. It took her a moment to remember that she wasn't in Ben's apartment upstairs but, rather, was restricted to the common areas of the building. She looked around to find the source of the sound that had woken her and was surprised to find herself alone.

She had managed to stay awake through most of the afternoon, only dozing a few times. During the early evening hours, the building had come alive with activity as people had come home from work and gone out with various friends. Feeling awkward with so many people passing through the clubhouse, Maya had gone outside to sit on one of the benches in front of the building. When the sun disappeared beyond the horizon and the chill of the evening had become too much for her, she'd taken refuge in the locker room that adjoined the weight room.

The crackers she had taken from Ben's apartment had provided her with a semblance of dinner, and she now had a sleeve of saltines tucked away in her purse so she wouldn't have to dig them out from under the couch every time she needed to eat something.

After darkness had fallen and the building had quieted, she'd returned to the couch in the clubhouse and given in to her fatigue.

She looked outside now to see the darkness of night was complete. A glance at her watch showed her the time had come. While the sun wasn't up in Washington, DC, right now, it was shining brightly over her home in India.

Drawing up her courage, Maya located the country code she had found earlier and proceeded to dial the phone number for her parents' home from memory. Her father's voice sounded in greeting, and Maya felt an ache in her heart.

"Pita?"

He hesitated briefly before speaking sternly in Hindi. "You must have the wrong number."

"Pita, it's me, Maya."

"The only Maya I know is dead to me. She left, disgracing herself and her family."

Tears welled up in her eyes, and she nearly hung up. Reminding herself that she didn't have any other options, she forced herself to continue. "I'm sorry to bother you, but I need your help. I'm sick."

Silence hummed through the phone.

She took his silence as a good sign. "I am going through treatments for cancer, but I will need to have an operation." Maya drew another steadying breath. "The hospital won't allow the doctors to operate unless I can pay some of the money up front."

More silence. Then her father spoke, and she thought she could hear anguish in his voice. "What hospital? What doctor?"

After so many years of hiding her location from her family, it took a moment for her to respond. She reminded herself that if her father did agree to help with the money, she would have to give him enough information to send it to her or the hospital. "I'm being treated at George Washington University Hospital in Washington, DC. My doctor is Dr. Schuster."

"And this doctor thinks he can cure you?"

"We hope so." She swallowed hard and offered him the truth that she hated to face. "It's my last chance."

Again, it took him a moment to respond, as though he was trying to control his emotions. "I see."

"I'm not asking you to give me the money. I will pay you back. I just need some time to get better first."

"If I do this, will you honor the marriage contract between you and Rishi?"

Disappointment engulfed her. She had so hoped that after all these years Rishi would already be married. She closed her eyes, praying that her father would forgive her for running away, for choosing Christianity and freedom over her family.

"Please don't ask me that," Maya pleaded. What would she do if she had to choose between a life as Rishi's wife or death as a free woman?

"It sounds as though little has changed over the years." A combination of hurt and regret sounded in his voice, only to be replaced by anger. "I never should have allowed my mother to meet with those missionaries. They ruined her, and now she has ruined you."

"No, Pita. She saved me."

"Then why are you calling me? Talk to her."

"Grandmother is gone."

Uncertainty and something else sounded in her father's voice when he asked, "My mother is dead?"

"Yes, Pita. I'm sorry." Her heart squeezed in her chest. "I hope time has helped heal the difficulties between us."

Now his anger and grief seemed to erase the compassion she'd heard a moment before. "There is no difficulty if you will remember your heritage."

Maya closed her eyes. She wanted to live. Truly she did, but a sense of panic came over her at the thought of agreeing to her father's terms. "I'm sorry, Pita, but I can't do that."

"Then I can't help you."

She bit back a sob and tried to hide the tears in her voice. "Please give my mother and my brothers my love."

Her father's only response was to hang up the phone, leaving Maya alone with her fears and an overwhelming sense of loss.

Chapter 11

Maya held her book in her hands, staring blindly at the pages. She couldn't believe she didn't have any place to live, anyone here who cared about her. The years struggling to make ends meet with her grandmother and then the year feeling so alone while in foster care seemed like paradise compared to this.

The phone call with her father had plummeted her hopes of finding a quick solution to her problems. She repeated the conversation over and over in her mind, reminding herself that it was no more than what she should have expected. For seven years, she had lived without her family, and they were obviously doing fine without her.

A tear trickled down her cheek, and she brushed it away. She turned her eyes upward and wondered why God was letting this happen to her. No matter how hard she prayed, it seemed like every desired answer was being denied almost as quickly as she could utter a request. What had she done to make God want to reject her so completely?

She knew she probably should have accepted the money Ben offered her to get a hotel room for the night, but she hadn't been able to do it. At first she had been so shocked by the offer that she had turned it down instinctively. Then she had seen the pity in his eyes and had been too embarrassed to recant her refusal.

Maya waited until the morning rush of residents departed before she made her way into the locker room, a change of clothes and her toiletry bag tucked into her oversized purse. She was lucky that no one had come in while she showered and changed, but she had learned one thing over the past twenty-four hours. Being homeless was exhausting.

After returning to the clubhouse, she slipped her dirty clothes into her suitcase, trading them for a baseball cap Kari had given her. She pulled it on now, feeding her long hair through the hole in the back.

When Ian and Jessica told her they were going to be gone for a few days, she had been relieved when they'd left on a Tuesday, since Wednesday was one day she never had to go into the hospital, but today, she would have welcomed the diversion.

Sitting around the clubhouse rereading an old book normally wouldn't have bothered her, but between the treatments and the early morning exchange with her father, all she wanted was a quiet, private place to curl up and hide. She also wouldn't mind something to eat to break up the monotony. Saltines weren't exactly appetizing when eaten for four meals straight.

Maya heard footsteps and looked up to see Ben down the hall, heading for the weight room. She quickly tugged down her baseball cap, bowed her head, and lifted her book so her face wasn't visible in case he happened to glance past the weight room and into the clubhouse area where she was sitting. As soon as she heard the weight room door close, she peeked out from beneath the bill of her cap.

She knew it was a gamble to hide out in Ben's building, but until she found a better option, this was the only place she could stay warm and dry. Not to mention that she still had Ben's key, so she could get into the building and access a reasonably clean bathroom.

The problem now was not just that someone might notice her camped out in the clubhouse but also that she was flat broke. The credit card she had applied for hadn't come yet, and at this point, she had no way of knowing when it might show up.

She remembered her childhood home, where servants took care of every need and food was always plentiful. She could have that life again, she reminded herself. All she had to do was agree to marry a man she didn't love, a man who would treat her like a piece of property and likely forbid her from following her religious beliefs.

She continued to stare at the same page for nearly an hour, the words blurring before her as her doubts and fears plagued her. Another door opened, and Maya looked up, this time to see Ian and Jessica heading right for her.

"Maya, what are you doing down here?" Ian asked, obviously surprised.

Maya ignored his question and asked one of her own. "What are you doing back so soon? I thought you were going to be gone for a few days."

He grinned. "I got the job."

"We came back early so we can start packing. He starts a week from Monday."

"So soon?" Maya asked.

"Yeah. I can hardly believe everything is happening so fast."

"Who's going to take over managing here for you?"

"Actually, that's already all worked out. The owner of the building has been wanting his nephew to take over for me for a while. That was the main reason I was looking for a new job."

"Oh." The weight room door opened again, and Maya glanced over to see Ben emerge. She quickly ducked her head in case he headed for the front of the building instead of back toward the elevator. She was relieved to hear his footsteps head away from her.

When Maya heard the elevator ding, she looked up to see Jessica staring at her suspiciously. "Is something wrong between Ben and you?"

"Just a little misunderstanding." Maya sighed. She wasn't sure if it was her loneliness or Ian and Jessica's kindness that made her willing to confide in them. "I was supposed to stay in his apartment for the next few months while he was living in California. Now that he's back, I'm without a place to stay."

"He kicked you out?"Jessica asked incredulously.

"It wasn't really his fault. He didn't know I was still staying there, and I didn't expect him to come home for a few more months."

"Wait, what?" Jessica looked confused. "Why didn't he know you were here?"

"Honestly, I'm not sure. I thought Kari had worked it out with him, but now I'm having my doubts. Ben's acting like Kari never told him I was coming here at all."

"Oh, wow." Ian shook his head. "What are you going to do now? Are you moving back to Nashville?"

"I can't." Maya's lower lip quivered. All of the exhaustion and turmoil of emotions welled up inside her, and she tried to fight back the flood that was trying to get out. "These treatments are my last chance."

Jessica sat down beside her and put a hand on hers. "Is the cancer that advanced?"

Tears spilled out onto her cheeks. "If they can't shrink the tumor, it'll eventually kill me. I found out yesterday that even if they do shrink it, I can't afford the surgery to remove it." Her hands lifted and fell in a helpless gesture, tears now streaming down her face. "And now I don't have any place to live."

"Well, you can't just stay down here," Jessica told her. "Where are your things?"

Color rose to Maya's cheeks. "There's one over there and another under the couch."

"Ian, can you get her stuff? We'll bring it into our place until we can work something out."

"Sure."

"Come on, Maya." Taking Maya by the arm, Jessica helped her up and led her down the hall to their apartment.

* * *

Ben rubbed a towel over his wet hair, feeling much better now that he'd worked out and showered. His interview had gone well, and he'd already called his teammate Gavin and made plans to get in some batting practice with him the next day. He'd also made a trip to the grocery store so he could have a glass of juice if he wanted to without having to go out to a restaurant. He supposed he should have put a little more effort into his grocery shopping so he could fix a meal or two himself, but he figured he could deal with that after he figured out a routine and knew if he really would have the time or inclination to cook.

After tugging on a pair of worn Levi's and a long-sleeved Washington Nationals T-shirt, he padded barefoot into the living room. He'd just picked up the remote control when someone knocked on the door. Dropping the remote back on the couch, he headed for the door and pulled it open.

"Hey, Ian. Come on in."

Ian followed Ben inside and sat down in the living room across from the seat Ben chose for himself. Ian leaned back only to shift forward again to rest his elbows on his knees. Restlessly, he tapped his fingers together.

Sensing his uneasiness, Ben asked, "Is something wrong?"

"Actually, yeah. I've got this situation that I have no idea how to solve."

"What's the problem?"

"Look, I don't want to get into your personal business, and I have no idea what the deal is with you and Maya, but she's staying at our place now." Accusation laced his tone as he continued. "Jessica and I are moving to Philadelphia next Friday. I can let her stay in our empty apartment until the new manager moves in the following weekend, but I don't know what to do after that. I don't want to throw her out on the street, but I have no idea where she can go."

Ben's eyebrows narrowed in confusion. He still hadn't heard from his sister, but he was quite certain this shouldn't be his problem. And he really didn't know what he had done for Ian to think it was. Still, he couldn't help but remember the vulnerable look on Maya's face when she had found him at home, nor could he deny that he felt guilty that his arrival had forced her to change her plans. "I thought she was staying with a friend."

"She is. She's staying with us, but like I said, we're moving, and she has to stay here in DC."

"Why doesn't she have anywhere to go?"

"I don't think she can afford a place of her own."

Uneasy with where this conversation was going and the unexpected and unwanted feeling of responsibility, Ben asked, "Isn't there another friend she can stay with?"

"As far as I know, we're the only friends she's got here. Besides, she needs to stay within walking distance of the hospital."

His confusion hiked up another notch. "If she's working at the hospital, why can't she afford a place of her own?"

Ian's eyes narrowed. "She isn't working at the hospital. She's undergoing treatments there."

"Treatments for what?"

"Cancer." Ian looked at him, bewildered. "I thought you knew."

Ben remembered the call from the doctor and thought of the expression on Maya's face when he had told her she had to move out: a flash of sick panic followed by a mask of acceptance. Slowly, Ben shook his head. "I didn't know anything about it. My sister never told me she was sick."

"I don't know a whole lot about what's going on, but from what little Kari and Maya have told me, it's pretty bad. She has to stay here in DC because she's in one of those clinical trials." Ian shrugged. "Of course, all of that might not matter anyway if she can't come up with the money for the surgery after the trial is over."

"What are you talking about?"

Ian looked at Ben awkwardly. He dismissed the topic with a wave of his hand. "That's not important right now. The real question is, what do we do about Maya now that we're leaving?"

Ben dragged a hand over his face. "Why didn't she tell me what was going on?"

Ian cocked an eyebrow but remained silent. He didn't have to voice the answer to his question when it was obvious. Ben had wanted Maya out of his apartment and out of his life, and Maya had obliged.

Ben let out a heavy sigh. "Let me give my sister a call to see if she has any ideas."

"Thanks, Ben. I appreciate it."

"Yeah." Ben stood, feeling about two inches tall. He crossed to the end table and opened the drawer where he had stashed Maya's cell phone. "By the way, can you give this back to Maya? She left it here."

"Sure. No problem." Ian headed for the door. "I'll talk to you later."

"Yeah," Ben said. "Later."

Chapter 12

KARI CLIMBED INTO HER CAR and immediately pulled her new cell phone out of the box. She still couldn't believe her old phone had been stolen—and in her ethics class of all places. Someone definitely deserved a failing grade. She just wished she knew who it was so she could get all of her phone numbers out of her old phone.

Her phone rang, and she glanced down to see her brother's number on the screen.

"Hello?"

"Where have you been?" Ben sounded irritated.

"My phone got stolen," she told him defensively. "What's your problem?"

"My problem is that I showed up at my apartment and found your friend living there."

"Oh." She winced. "That."

"Yes, that," Ben said sharply. "Kari, how could you do that without even talking to me about it?"

"Ben, I'm sorry. I just didn't know what else to do."

"You could have asked."

"I was afraid you'd say no."

"Of course I would have said no," Ben shot back. "You know how ruthless the press can be. Can you imagine what would happen if some reporter started saying that I had a girl living with me? Not to mention I don't appreciate being taken advantage of. I thought I could at least trust my own family."

Kari glossed over the insult. "Ben, you said you weren't going to be in DC until after spring training. Your apartment was just sitting there empty."

"That didn't mean you could just hand my house key over to some stranger!"

Kari's voice softened. "I love Maya like a sister. I couldn't just sit back and wait for her to die. Not when there was a chance she could get better."

Some of the anger faded from Ben's voice. "Look, I know you were just trying to help your friend, but you've put me in one heck of a bind. I can't let her stay here, but now she doesn't have anywhere else to go."

"I've got a few hundred dollars saved. Maybe I can pay for a hotel or something for her."

"Kari, a few hundred dollars will only pay for one night around here."

"I've got to do something," she said in frustration. She thought for a moment, and slowly, logic caught up with her. "Wait a minute. Why are you in DC? I thought you were going to spend the off-season in LA so you could be closer to Heather."

"Things weren't working out with Heather."

"Oh. Sorry to hear that."

"I'm sure you are," he said sarcastically. "You're sorry that I got in the way of your plans."

"Yeah, I am sorry about that," Kari admitted, "but I know you really liked Heather."

"That doesn't matter. What matters now is what I'm supposed to do about Maya. She's got a place to stay for the next week or so, but after that, she'll literally be out on the street."

"I'll try calling her. Maybe we can find one of those programs like the Ronald McDonald House where she can stay while going through treatments," Kari suggested. "There is one favor I need though."

"What's that?"

"Can you go get her phone number for me? I lost all of my contact numbers when my phone was stolen."

"Maya's your best friend. Don't you already know her number?"

"Not by heart. I always just hit her name on my favorites list."

"You're going to owe me for this," Ben said, his voice resigned. "I already feel lousy for kicking her out of my place."

"I'm sure Maya understands. I'm the one she's going to be furious with."

"With good reason," Ben muttered. "All right. I'll go track down her number for you, but you have got to figure something out for Maya that doesn't include using my apartment."

Kari stiffened at his tone. "You know, it's not like Maya asked for this. All she wants is to make this cancer go away so she won't feel like a burden anymore and so she'll actually have a chance at life."

Ben fell silent for a moment. "Kari, I'm sorry your friend has to deal with this. Really, I am. But it isn't fair for you to dump all of this on me. I hardly know her."

"Don't worry, Ben," Kari said edgily. "I'll take care of it."

* * *

Maya hated feeling like a burden. Absolutely hated it. She still couldn't believe she had broken down and told Ian and Jessica so much about what was going on. At least she hadn't told them about her family or the conditions her father had put on the help she needed.

As Americans, she doubted they could begin to understand the culture she'd come from. Of course, she knew some believed Indian children didn't have a choice when parents arranged a marriage, but now that she was older, she knew her situation was an unusual one. Normally, if one of the parties involved didn't want to go through with the marriage, the families would honor the child's wishes. Her father was an exception to the norm.

For the past two nights, she had slept on the Harrises' couch, and on Thursday, she had lingered at the hospital after her treatment to try to stay out of their way for as long as possible. Their apartment had turned into a frenzy of packing and cleaning. Maya wished she had the energy to help more. Other than sitting on the couch and folding laundry, she'd hardly had the strength to do anything.

Jessica still gave her rides in the morning, and Henry continued to insist on taking her home each day, even though Maya really thought she would be able to walk the short distance on her own now.

She looked around the living room at the packing boxes and scattered belongings, a new sense of determination working through her. If Ian and Jessica could uproot and change their lives so quickly, there had to be a way for her to do the same.

She dreaded talking to Ben, but she knew she was going to have to in order to check on the credit card application. She had to imagine he wasn't going to be thrilled with her name being associated with his address, but she had already thought of a solution to that. Kari would let her use her address for another round of credit card applications, and she could change the new one to Kari's address as well.

She shuddered to think of the amount of interest she would end up paying before this was all over, not to mention the late fees that would start piling up within the next month or two.

A knock sounded at the door, and it took Maya a minute to remember that the Harrises had gone out to buy more boxes and she was alone in the apartment.

She pushed off the couch to answer the door. Her face immediately paled when she saw Ben standing in the hall.

"Hi. Do you have a minute?"

"Sure." Maya stepped back and let him inside.

Ben looked around the apartment. "Where are Ian and Jessica?"

"Out looking for more boxes." Maya moved back to the couch and sat down, hoping Ben wouldn't notice how weak she was. "Did you want to sit down?"

"Yeah. Sure." Ben looked around at the chairs piled high with boxes and opted to sit on the other end of the couch. "I talked to my sister a little while ago."

"Is she okay? I've been trying to call her for days, but she hasn't been answering."

"I had the same problem. Apparently, her phone was stolen."

"Oh. That's too bad."

"Look, I wanted to apologize about everything that's happened. I had no idea you were staying at my place or why you came to DC."

"I don't need your pity," Maya blurted. Then she forced herself to relax her shoulders. "I'm sorry. It's just that I don't want you to feel responsible for me. None of this is your fault."

"Still, I feel lousy knowing I made a bad situation worse."

"Again, it's not your fault." She noticed the way he tensed, but she didn't understand why. She drew a deep breath and forced herself to press on. "I actually did want to talk to you though. I applied for a credit card, and I used your address. If you could let me know when it arrives, I'd really appreciate it." She rushed on before he could protest. "I promise I'll change the address on it as soon as it arrives."

Ben sat in silence for a moment. "Do you have any idea when it's supposed to get here?"

"It should be any day. I'm kind of surprised it hasn't shown up yet."

"I'll let you know. Which reminds me, Kari asked me to get your phone number from you so she could call you. She lost all of her contact information when her phone was stolen."

"Sure." Maya took his phone when he offered it to her, and she plugged her name and number into his directory.

"Ian said you're going to stay here through next week. What are you going to do then?"

"As soon as I get my new credit card, I'll use it to get a place nearby. Once I finish the first round of treatments, I should be able to get a job so I can support myself."

"I might be able to ask around for you when you start looking for jobs," Ben offered, even though he wanted nothing more than to walk away from the situation and not look back. Sick people made him uncomfortable.

"I appreciate that."

Ben stood. "Well, I'd better get going. I'll give you a call when that mail shows up for you."

"Thanks." Maya stayed seated. She was pretty sure she could stand but decided not to risk it. She waited until he was gone before she retrieved her own cell phone and called Kari's number once more.

Kari answered in an uncharacteristically timid voice. "Hello?"

Maya's voice was weary when she said, "Kari, how could you?"

Kari shifted from timid to resigned. "Here we go again."

* * *

Ben sat beside his teammate Liam Bailey and listened to the conversation swirling around him. For the first time since leaving California, he found himself thinking that maybe Heather had been right—not about her expectations that he stay in a relationship with her but about going to a wedding dateless.

As one of the youngest players on his team, he was quickly realizing he didn't have a lot to talk about with his teammates when baseball wasn't the main topic of conversation.

With this being the first of three weddings this off-season, he was starting to wonder if perhaps he should try to bow out of the others.

As though reading his thoughts, Liam said, "I can't believe we have two more weddings in the next couple of months."

Rachelle, Liam's fiancée, spoke up. "I just hope I'm not limping down the aisle. I swear, if I twist my knee one more time, I'm going to scream."

"I thought you were going to have surgery on your knee last month," Ben said.

"I was, but my insurance company was being such a pain about everything that Liam and I decided it would be easier to wait until after we're married so I can use his insurance."

"Will it make that big of a difference?"

She nodded. "My insurance company didn't approve the surgeon I want."

Ben thought of his earlier conversation with Maya. She was struggling to find a way to put a roof over her head, and not once had he heard her complain about her lack of insurance. From what Ian had said though, it sounded like she was either trying to fight this cancer without it or with a policy that wasn't giving her what she needed.

When Rachelle and one of the other women at the table started talking about wedding colors, Ben picked up his water glass and wondered how soon he could say his good-byes without offending the bride and groom.

Chapter 13

Maya walked into Ian and Jessica's apartment on Friday afternoon, amazed at the work they had done during the four hours she had been at the hospital for her latest round of scans. For more than a week, they had cleaned, packed, and organized in preparation for this day.

She'd known the movers were due anytime when she left that morning, and Jessica had made sure to give Maya the key to the apartment just in case they were gone before she returned home, but Maya hadn't really thought that would happen. She had been wrong. The furniture and boxes were all gone except for a box in the corner that held the air mattress Jessica had offered to lend Maya. Maya's suitcases were stacked neatly beside it, and the floors appeared to have just been vacuumed.

She set her purse down by the door and crossed into the kitchen, a small smile lighting her face when she saw a box of plastic spoons and a stack of half a dozen plastic cups on the counter. Beside them was a folded note. She opened it, surprised to see two ten dollar bills folded inside.

Maya,
Sorry this couldn't be more, but hopefully this will help tide you over for now. Keep the faith.
Jessica

Maya blinked back tears that threatened, touched by the thoughtful gesture. Too tired to cross the room to her purse, she put the folded bills in her pocket. Then she opened the refrigerator to see a dozen cartons of yogurt, a package of string cheese, and some apple juice.

She retrieved a yogurt and a spoon, looking longingly at the dinette area where the kitchen table had been. What she wouldn't give for a chair right now. She tried to boost herself onto the counter but wasn't quite tall enough or strong enough to achieve that feat. Even though she didn't look forward to getting up again, she let herself slide down against the kitchen cabinet until she was sitting on the floor.

She had only eaten two bites when her phone rang from the other side of the room. "Great."

She set the yogurt down on the floor and struggled to stand. By the time she made her way across the room, the phone had stopped ringing.

Pulling it free from her purse, she checked the log for missed calls. Whoever had called her wasn't in her directory, nor was the prefix from the DC area. She was debating calling the number back when her phone rang again, the same number illuminating her screen.

"Hello?"

"Maya? It's Ben Evans."

"Oh, hi."

"Hey, I wanted to let you know you have some mail here."

Relief flowed through her. A full week had passed since she had asked Ben to keep an eye out for her new credit card, and she was starting to wonder if it would ever arrive. "Great. Is it okay if I come up to get it right now?"

"Sure. I'll be here."

"Thanks. I'll be right up." Maya went back into the kitchen and picked up her yogurt off the floor. Not wanting to waste it, she took the time to finish eating, though she was anxious to see how high her new credit card limit would be. If she could get one that was fifteen thousand, she might be able to swing all of these expenses she was about to face.

She took the time to rinse off the plastic spoon, not willing to throw away anything she might need again in the future. Realizing she didn't have a garbage can, she rinsed out the yogurt container as well and set it on the counter.

After making sure she had her keys, she left the apartment and crossed through the lobby toward the elevator. She glanced down at her keychain and felt a little guilty that she hadn't given Ben his key back yet. He probably didn't even realize she had it.

She really did plan to figure out someplace else to live before she had to move out of Jessica's apartment, but Ben's key gave her a sense of security in knowing that if nothing else, she could go back to staying in the apartment building's clubhouse if she needed to for a few days.

She saw someone rush toward the elevator doors as they slid closed, but her reflexes weren't quick enough to hit the door open button. "Sorry," she mumbled under her breath, though there was no one to hear her.

She exited on Ben's floor but made it only a few steps before she was overcome with a wave of dizziness. She reached out and put her hand against the wall to steady herself. It took a minute before the floor once again looked flat and she felt strong enough to put one foot in front of the other.

She was nearly to Ben's door when she heard the elevator doors chime open. Instinctively, she glanced behind her to see who was getting off on this floor.

Maya's heart stopped when she looked up and saw the man coming down the hall. He was older now, and he appeared to have gained about twenty pounds around his middle, but she couldn't miss the familiar arrogance in his bearing. She also remembered well the way he looked at her as though she was a piece of property.

She couldn't believe after all these years of hiding that the man her father had promised her to was here, only a few yards away.

Her face pale, her palms sweaty, she knocked on Ben's door, praying he would answer quickly. She looked over her shoulder and saw the recognition in Rishi's eyes. What was he doing here? How had he found her?

The telephone call with her father replayed in her mind, and she knew in an instant she had made a mistake in asking for help.

Rishi continued toward her with a determined stride. Maya pressed her ear to the door, listening for footsteps. Ben said he would be here.

Quickly, Maya dug the key to Ben's apartment out of her purse. With only a moment to spare, she slid the key into the lock, flipped it open, and slipped inside, quickly locking it again behind her.

She leaned back against the door and saw Ben coming down the hall toward her. He looked rather indignant when he asked, "What are you doing in here?"

Before she could answer, Rishi pounded on the door.

"Don't answer that," Maya begged him. "Please don't answer it."

"Who is it?"

An angry voice called out from the other side of the door. The words were in English, the voice heavily accented. "Maya, I know you're in there."

Ben stepped forward and yanked the door open before Maya could stop him. "Who are you? And what do you want with Maya?"

"Who are you?" he countered and turned to glare at Maya. "And what are you doing here in a man's apartment? You have been promised to me."

Maya took a step back, the room spinning out of control.

"What's he talking about?" Ben asked, looking completely bewildered.

"Maya is my fiancée."

"Is that true?"

Maya shook her head, the gesture causing a burst of pain to shoot through her. "I never agreed to marry him. My father . . . It was my father who promised to give me to him."

Rishi edged forward. "She must come with me now."

Ben's eyebrows drew together, and he looked from Maya to Rishi, clearly contemplating what to do. Finally, he said, "I don't think Maya is ready to come with you right now."

"She doesn't have a choice," he said and took a step forward

"No!" Maya jerked back to stay out of his reach, stumbling in the process. The next thing she knew, she was falling backward. Her head connected with the wall behind her, and then all she remembered was sliding weakly to the floor.

* * *

"She must be here," the man named Rishi said insistently to the woman sitting behind the hospital information desk. Two other men stood to his left and clearly accompanied Rishi. Ben lingered behind them, still not quite sure what to think about this man Maya had been running from.

"I'm sorry, sir, but I don't have a patient under that name."

Rishi straightened, and his irritation was evident when he continued. "She was brought by ambulance just a few minutes ago."

"It's possible that she is still in the ER. Let me call down there and check for you." The woman picked up the phone and made the call. After a brief conversation, she hung up and shook her head. "I'm sorry, but they don't have anyone by that name down there either."

Unexpectedly protective of his sister's friend and well aware that hospital patients could request their name to be unlisted, Ben stepped forward and said, "They probably took her to Georgetown Hospital. It's just down the road."

Rishi turned and gave Ben a disdainful look. The man had yet to speak to Ben and was clearly irritated that he too had come to check on Maya.

"He could be right," the hospital volunteer agreed. She then proceeded to give the directions.

To make it look like he too bought the woman's story, Ben followed the man outside. He waited for Rishi and his associates to disappear into a long black limo and then followed behind them as though he too was headed for the other hospital. Deliberately, he let himself get caught at a red light to put some distance between them. As soon as the limo made its first turn, Ben circled back to George Washington University Hospital.

This time, he bypassed the information desk and looked at the directory on the wall. After locating which floor the cancer center was on, he headed for the stairs. He approached the reception desk at the cancer center, not sure where else to go to find out which room Maya was in.

Unwilling to be stonewalled, he approached the receptionist.

"Can I help you, sir?"

"I'm here with Maya. She was brought in a few minutes ago by ambulance, and I need to know which room she's in."

"Maya?" Surprise filled her voice.

"That's right."

She hesitated for several seconds. "I'm sorry, but can I have your name?"

"I'm Ben Evans. My sister Kari was letting Maya stay at my apartment while I was out of town."

An older man standing to the side of the room with a wheelchair stepped forward. "Where do you live?"

Ben rattled off his address, including his apartment number.

The man's eyes narrowed for a moment. "Wait a minute. I know you. You're the second baseman for the Nationals."

"That's right." Ben nodded, now a little uncomfortable that he'd just given these people his address. He shifted so he could speak to the man and to the receptionist at the same time. "Look, I know why she isn't being listed as a patient here. I was there when that guy tried to get her to go with him." He spoke with sincerity when he added, "I just want to make sure she's okay. My sister will never forgive me if I don't do at least that much."

The receptionist and the man looked at each other and seemed to carry on a silent dialogue. Finally, the woman motioned to the man. "Henry can show you where she is."

"Thanks. I really appreciate it." Ben followed Henry out of the waiting area and back out into the hall. They got onto the elevator, and Henry pressed the button for the fourth floor.

"I'm not sure she'll be awake yet. The doctor gave her some pain meds when she first got here, and those usually wipe her out."

"She only came in about fifteen minutes ago. How did she get treated and admitted so quickly?"

"I was helping a patient outside when the ambulance pulled up. When I saw the paramedics wheeling her in, I called the doctor to let him know. Dr. Schuster had her admitted right away."

Ben fell silent, not quite sure what to think of the quick treatment and the fact that the hospital staff was clearly so familiar with Maya.

"She's a nice girl, that Maya. Said she's going to make me curry chicken when she gets stronger." Henry became a bit wistful. "I sure hope that happens soon. It's hard to see anyone lose the cancer battle, but it really hits home when it's someone sweet like her."

Henry's cell phone sounded. He pulled it out of the little clip attached to his belt loop. "Excuse me for a minute." He took the call, then said, "I've got to go help someone else. She's just down this hall. Room 412."

"Thanks."

"No problem. You let Maya know I'll stop in on her after I get off work, will you?"

"Yeah. I'll do that."

Chapter 14

MAYA OPENED HER EYES AND saw Dr. Schuster standing at the side of her bed. Then she remembered Rishi, and a sick sense of panic washed through her.

Her emotions must have shone on her face because Dr. Schuster spoke gently. "Your fiancé isn't here."

"He isn't my fiancé. Not really."

"Henry said he was pretty convincing when he stopped by the clinic looking for you."

"He was at the clinic?" Maya asked, panic seeping into her voice.

The doctor nodded. "Apparently, he told the staff he was here to surprise you. He had enough of your personal information to be convincing."

"My father said I would marry him. I never agreed."

"I spoke with your father a couple of days ago," Dr. Schuster told her.

"I figured as much. He probably called to check up on me to make sure I wasn't lying to him when I called. He must have told Rishi where I was." She sighed and winced when a sharp pain pulsed through her.

The doctor lowered himself into the chair beside her. "You hit your head when you fell. It doesn't look like you have a concussion, but we're going to keep you here overnight for observation. Your white blood cell count was a bit higher than I like, and I want to make sure you aren't getting an infection."

Maya thought of the air mattress she had expected to sleep on and immediately decided this might not be such a bad thing, especially if the hospital could keep Rishi from visiting her.

"There's one more thing," Dr. Schuster said. "I just got the preliminary results of your scans."

Her heartbeat quickened. "And?"

"We're seeing moderate success."

"What does that mean?"

"It means the drugs do appear to be working. We've seen some shrinkage of the tumor, but it isn't as much as we had hoped. At this rate, it looks like you would have to go through a second round of treatments before you could have surgery."

A wave of conflicting emotions crashed over her—a surge of optimism that her cancer could be beaten, desperate despair about how she could possibly afford to live without any means of income for another five months, and an overwhelming sensation of loneliness at the thought of continuing here with only the hospital staff to interact with.

For the briefest moment, she even considered agreeing to the arranged marriage in order to solve her money problems, but she knew she couldn't really do it.

"There is one more thing I'm reluctant to bring up."

Maya caught a glimpse of movement in the doorway, but she kept her focus on the doctor. "What's that?"

"Maya, I spoke with your father again today." Dr. Schuster took a deep breath and blew it out as though trying to steel himself against the words he was about to say. "I'm sorry, but if you have no means of paying for your surgery, I don't have any choice but to drop you from the trial."

Maya didn't try to fight back the tears that instantly sprang to her eyes. "Doctor, please. Please give me a little more time. I can come up with the money. I only need another week or so."

Dr. Schuster sighed heavily. "I've already talked to the board, and they aren't budging on this." Before Maya could protest further, he added, "Since it's the weekend, I can delay the paperwork, but if you can't come up with some proof that you'll be able to continue treatment after this trial by Monday morning, I'll have to cancel your infusion."

Maya lifted her hands to cover her mouth as she bit back a sob. Her mind raced with possibilities, but she knew that even if the credit card came through with a high limit, she would need at least one more to afford the additional living expenses to make it through an extra three months here.

Dr. Schuster clenched his teeth for a moment and then shook his head. "I'm sorry, Maya. I really am."

"If I can't come up with the money now, would I be able to get into the trial again in a few months?"

She sensed the doctor's discomfort as he shook his head again. "If you were responding more quickly, I might be able to get you in, but the truth is that your cancer is probably more aggressive than we first thought for the results to be so slow. If you have to stop now, medically speaking, your survival rate wouldn't be high enough to readmit you to the trial."

Tears continued to run freely down Maya's cheeks, and she could no longer form words. The doctor put his hand on her shoulder and then took a step back. "I'll check back on you in the morning. The nurse will be in to give you something for the pain in about an hour."

Maya watched him make a quick exit and swiped at the tears on her cheeks. Sliding farther down into the hospital bed, she curled up beneath the blankets, silently praying that somehow God would give her a glimmer of hope, some indication that her life might still have meaning.

* * *

Ben's throat closed as he thought of his first conversation with Maya in his apartment. Guilt gouged through him, piercing even deeper now that he had overheard the doctor talking to her a few minutes ago.

How could he have known his sister had handed over his apartment to Maya in an effort to save her life? He kind of caught the gist that it was because of her illness that Kari had helped her, but he hadn't fully comprehended that without the help, she might actually *die*.

After hearing the conversation between Maya and her doctor, Ben hadn't been able to bring himself to go into her hospital room, so he'd returned home. Even if he had been brave enough to face her tears, he didn't think he could handle his own conflicting emotions. He had always worked so hard to keep his body in top shape, recognizing that his career depended on maintaining his health. Listening to the doctor give Maya what appeared to be a death sentence hit Ben low in the gut and left him floundering to understand exactly what he was feeling.

He remembered what Maya had been like less than a year ago. She too had been an athlete, with aspirations of going professional.

It could have been him, he realized suddenly. Maya had been just as diligent as he'd been last Christmas about staying in shape, and he suspected she had been equally determined to succeed. More than once, they had gone on their morning runs together, and he remembered being impressed that she hadn't scoffed at the five-mile distance he went each morning. Admittedly, he had slowed his pace to match hers at the time, but it had seemed a minor trade-off to have someone to keep him company during his workouts.

He let himself remember the time he had spent with Maya now, suddenly realizing his time with her had been one of the factors that had prompted him to break up with Cassie, his old high school girlfriend. The easy camaraderie during those morning runs had made him notice the lack of such a friendship with Cassie, despite the fact that they had dated for more than three years.

He looked around his apartment and wondered what would have happened if he hadn't come back to DC. If things had worked out with Heather, he would still be living in LA, oblivious to Maya's struggles, and she would be living in his apartment pretending everything was all right. Or at least she would have been, right up until Rishi showed up to claim her as his bride.

Ben shuddered at that. The idea of a forty-plus-year-old man with a girl less than half his age was positively creepy in his mind. It didn't take a genius to figure out that this was clearly a one-sided arrangement. Just the thought of Maya marrying Rishi made Ben feel sick.

He fingered the letter that had come for Maya, knowing he really needed to go back to the hospital to give it to her. He needed a little time first to make sure he had his own emotions under control before he had to face her.

Someone knocked on his door, and he braced at the idea that Rishi might have returned in search of Maya. Half tempted to give the guy a piece of his mind, Ben dropped Maya's mail onto the coffee table and strode to the door. His jaw dropped when he yanked it open and saw Heather standing on the other side.

"Surprise!"

He was so stunned by her presence that he didn't think to stop her when she leaned in and kissed him in greeting and then breezed through the door.

"What are you doing here?"

"I had planned to surprise you so you'd have a date for Shawn's wedding—"

"The wedding was yesterday," Ben interrupted.

"I know. I was supposed to get here yesterday morning, but my flight was canceled, and I couldn't get another one until this morning. I'm so sorry I missed it." She dropped onto the couch, and the mail on the coffee table caught her attention. She picked up the letter Ben had just been holding. Instantly, her cheerful smile disappeared, and accusation filled her voice. "Who is this Maya Gupta? And why does she have mail coming to your apartment?"

"She's a friend," Ben answered automatically before he remembered he didn't need to explain himself to her.

Heather's face reddened, and her voice lowered in anger. "Have you been cheating on me?"

Ben crossed his arms and prepared to make sure Heather understood exactly where their relationship stood. "We'd have to still be a couple for me to be cheating on you, but for the record, I'm not dating Maya."

"Who is she?" Heather asked, completely glossing over Ben's insistence that they were through.

"She's one of my sister's friends." Ben shook his head and forced himself to get the conversation back on topic. "Heather, I don't think you are hearing me. I've tried to be a gentleman about this, but the truth is, I don't want to date you anymore."

Heather batted her eyelashes in what he considered her innocent look. "You can't possibly mean that. I just flew all the way across the country for you."

"No, you came across the country to get what you wanted. I never invited you here, and now you need to go."

"You're kicking me out?" Heather's voice rose to an uncomfortably high pitch. "I don't have anywhere else to stay."

Her words resonated through him, the fact that she would use them when she had an apartment in California and clearly had the means and resources to buy a plane ticket to DC grating on him. Maya truly hadn't had anyplace to go when he had kicked her out, and she hadn't said a word, nor had she accepted his offer of money to help her.

Ben glanced down at his watch to see that it was already three in the afternoon, probably too late for Heather to catch a flight back to LA tonight. His voice was stern when he spoke. "You knew perfectly well that you wouldn't be able to stay here when you got on the plane in LA."

She looked at him sheepishly. "I just figured you'd get me a hotel room like you did the last time I came to visit."

"Last time, I invited you, and we were still dating." Ben dug through his wallet and pulled out some bills. "This should be enough to pay for a room at one of the hotels by the airport." He held it up and added, "But understand that this is the last thing you're ever going to get from me. We are through."

"Well, you don't have to be so cruel," she said shrilly. Annoyed, she stood and snatched the money from his hand.

Ben moved to the door and yanked it open. He stood rigid and silent as she blew past him. As soon as she was in the hall, he gave in to the anger bubbling up inside him and slammed the door.

Chapter 15

MAYA PRESSED A COLD WASHCLOTH against her eyes, knowing there wasn't anything she could do to hide the fact that she'd been crying. She wasn't sure what hurt worse, understanding this cancer was going to kill her before she had a chance to really experience life or realizing her father considered her life of less importance than his agreement with Rishi.

At least the nurses had assured her they wouldn't let Rishi know what room she was in. The last thing she needed was to have to face him right now. She heard someone enter the room, and she looked up quickly to see it was Ben. A flush of embarrassment crept into her cheeks.

"How are you doing?" he asked and then winced. "I'm sorry. That's probably a stupid question to ask someone with cancer."

Maya pressed her lips together, fighting against her current reality. "I'm so sorry about what happened at your apartment."

"I'm sorry I kicked you out when I first got here." Ben moved closer to the bed. "I had no idea what you were dealing with."

"It doesn't matter now." Her lower lip quivered, and she blinked quickly to fight back the tears that once again threatened.

Ben shifted his weight and held up the letter with her name on it. "Here. I thought you might want this."

Maya took the envelope from him, concerned when she didn't feel the telltale spot inside it where the credit card would normally be. She ripped it open and only had to read the first line for the tears to start flowing again.

"What is it? I thought that was what you were waiting for."

Her pride completely shattered, she held out the letter so he could read it himself. *Denied.*

Ben read through the letter and then looked at her and asked, "How much money do you need?"

"A lot."

"Maya, I make a lot of money. I might be able to help."

She looked up at him, a little spurt of hope surging through her before logic caught up with it. "Ben, that's generous of you to offer, but I can't ask you to do that. Even if I could find someplace cheap to live for the next six months, I'd still need at least fifteen or twenty thousand dollars for the surgery."

"Surgery costs that much?" Ben asked, realizing he had never thought about the cost of medical care before. Until today, his only thought regarding hospitals was that he wanted to avoid them.

"Actually, that's just the part I'd need up front."

"How have you been paying for treatments?" Ben asked, realizing immediately that he probably shouldn't have asked such a personal question.

"After my grandmother died, I sold her emerald ring just to survive. I had a little money left over and was able to pay for my first treatments with that." Regret hung in her voice. She drew a breath and spelled out her reality. "It's not just the money though. Now that my family knows where I live, it's only a matter of time before my visa is revoked."

"What are you talking about?"

"Rishi is a very powerful man in India. If he still plans to go through with this marriage after seven years, I have to think he'll go the extra step to pay off whoever he needs to in order to send me back to India."

"Seven years? How old were you when you got engaged?"

"I was thirteen when I was promised to him. The day after the arrangement was made, my grandmother helped me run away."

Ben shook his head in disbelief. "Where is your grandmother now?"

"She died over two years ago."

"I'm sorry." Ben offered the simple condolences with sincerity. When Maya didn't speak, he continued. "I still don't understand why Rishi would go to such lengths to get you back to India."

She spoke but barely louder than a whisper. "Once I'm back home, I won't have a choice but to go through with the wedding."

"After all this time, I'm surprised this guy hasn't given up."

"Me too," Maya agreed. "My grandmother told me once that my father agreed to the marriage contract partially to ally himself with Rishi. My father is in shipping, and Rishi owns several manufacturing companies. A family connection would strengthen both of their businesses."

"Surely they could form a business alliance without involving you."

"They could. Maybe Rishi needs the dowry my father promised him. I'm sure it was considerable."

"I didn't think people paid dowries anymore."

"Actually, they're illegal in India, but so is marriage before the age of eighteen. Rishi doesn't follow those laws," Maya told him. "Whatever his reasons, if he's here in the United States, it's obvious he isn't going to let this go."

Ben recognized the truth in her words. And the regret. "What are you going to do?"

"If Kari will let me, I'll move back to Nashville with her. I'll try to get my old job back and start saving money for my . . ." She couldn't say the last word, *funeral*, but it vibrated through the room as though it had been said.

Ben fell silent, obviously at a loss for words.

A nurse walked in, her attention on Maya. "I'm sorry to interrupt, but we need to take you downstairs to run a few more tests."

Maya didn't respond but looked at Ben once more. "Thanks for stopping by."

"You're welcome." Ben hesitated. "Would it be okay if I come back to see you again later?"

He could see the surprise in her face when she said, "I'd like that."

Ben moved to the doorway and gave her an awkward wave. Then he disappeared back the way he had come.

* * *

Less than three hours after saying good-bye to Maya, Ben once again walked down the hospital hallway toward her room, the smell of disinfectant and hospital food lingering in the air. He stepped around a hospital cart, still trying to figure out why he had told Maya he'd come back to see her. He supposed it was out of loyalty to his sister. After all, Maya had been her best friend for a couple of years. Even though he hadn't personally met Maya until the previous Christmas, he had heard her name with regularity since Kari's senior year of high school.

He entered Maya's room to find her dozing, her dark eyelashes thick against her dusky skin. She was much paler than she had been last winter. Thinner too. When they had first met, he had struggled to reconcile the petite woman with the accomplished athlete his sister had claimed her to be. Though he had never seen Maya play tennis, Kari had described her as tenacious and ruthless. The woman lying before him didn't appear to be either of those things.

He wasn't sure whether to wake her. Luckily, her eyes opened before he had to decide what to do. He took a tentative step forward and greeted her. "Hey there."

A combination of surprise and pleasure flitted over her face. "You came back."

"I told you I would."

"Yes, you did." Maya motioned to the seat beside her. "Did you want to sit down?"

"Sure." He lowered himself onto the chair and watched her adjust her bed so she was sitting up rather than lying down. He sat there for several awkward seconds, wondering what in the world he was supposed to say to her. Finally, he gave in to asking the one question that mattered most. "Are you really going to give up your treatments and go back to Tennessee?"

A flash of temper flared in her voice. "What choice do I have? I don't have a place to live; I'm being dropped from the trial; I don't have a job. I don't even have any friends here, except the people I know at the hospital."

Her temper lit his frustration. Logically, he understood she was out of options, but the idea of her just accepting her fate ate at him. He raked a hand through his hair. "There's got to be something you can do."

"There is. I can marry Rishi." Maya's voice was even and filled with contempt. She shook her head as though refusing that possibility. "Even if I could bring myself to agree to that, I don't think he'd let me stay here and finish my treatments. He just wants to save face with everyone in his village back home and link his companies to my father's."

Though he was disgusted with the idea of Maya marrying Rishi, let alone the idea that her future husband would let her die without remorse, Ben forced himself to ask, "Are you sure?"

"I'm sure I can't agree to marry him. At least he won't know where I am if I leave DC. Besides, Kari's been like a sister." Emotion clogged her voice when she added, "It might be selfish of me, but I don't want to die alone."

Maya's words, spoken so softly, crashed over him. Marriage might be able to save Maya's life, but after meeting Rishi, Ben found himself agreeing with Maya's assumption that the man didn't have any interest in helping her, particularly if it included Maya staying in the US.

Words repeated through his mind, both Maya's and his own: *Marriage could save her life. Kari's been like a sister.*

Ben swallowed hard as an improbable solution started working its way into his mind.

He repeated her problems: She didn't have a place to live. She was being dropped from the trial. A man who didn't care about her was trying to get her deported.

He could fix that. He could fix all of that with one simple act.

His stomach churned fiercely with nerves as he contemplated the gravity of where his thoughts had taken him. *Marriage could save her life.* The words repeated in his mind again. His hands started to sweat, his emotions tying him in more knots than if he'd stepped into the batter's box at the bottom of the ninth inning with two outs.

The flash of clarity shot through him, undeniable and clear. Never before had he felt such a jolt when faced with a problem, nor had he ever found himself the answer to someone else's unspoken prayers. The solution was so obvious, yet he resisted it despite the absolute certainty that seeped into his very being.

He couldn't speak for a moment, so shocked by the images in his mind. Then all he could do was stare at the woman he was going to marry.

* * *

Maya wasn't sure what to think of the odd expression on Ben's face. She felt bad that she had let her temper flare, but she felt like she was entitled to let some of her emotions spill over. After all, she now knew this battle with cancer was really entering its final chapter. He had to understand that.

With his steady gaze on her, she found herself feeling suddenly awkward and decided it might be best to nudge him on his way. "I should probably try to get some rest. Thanks again for coming."

Ben's words burst from him as though he couldn't quite contain them. "I think I know how you can stay in the trial."

She looked up, confused. "The panel already made its decision. It's over."

"Let me ask you something." Ben stood and paced across the room before turning back to face her. "What would have happened if you had already gotten married before Rishi found you?"

"Actually, that's what I was hoping would happen," Maya admitted. "If I had already married, he would have lost his claim over me, especially now that I live in the United States."

Ben fell silent and seemed to be deep in thought. Then he seemed to draw up all of his energy. "I think you should marry me."

Maya's jaw dropped. She couldn't have heard him correctly. "Excuse me?"

"I know it sounds crazy, but just hear me out." Ben reclaimed his seat, leaned forward, and rested his elbows on his thighs. "If you marry me, you wouldn't have to worry about Rishi anymore, and as my wife, you would have medical insurance so your surgery would be only a fraction of the cost."

The details he was laying out made sense, but she still couldn't wrap her brain around the idea. "You can't be serious."

"I am serious. It would be a marriage"—he paused for a moment as though searching for the right word—"a marriage of convenience. It will help you out, and you can move back into my guest room."

"I thought you had a girlfriend."

"We broke up," Ben told her with a grimace that made her think the breakup wasn't an amicable one. "Since the breakup was so recent, I wouldn't want to go out and broadcast that I'm married, but we should be able to go down to the courthouse and get a civil marriage to help you out."

"Ben, people shouldn't get married on a whim, and I wouldn't feel right about marrying you just to get health insurance. It wouldn't be honest."

"The insurance is a side benefit," Ben said. "The real issue is making sure Rishi can't bother you anymore. I mean, we get along okay, right?"

"I suppose so . . ." she managed. She stared at him. "I still don't understand why you would tie yourself to me like this. Marriage is a big deal."

"Marriage is a big deal," Ben repeated in agreement.

"Then how can you possibly want to marry someone you barely know?"

He fell silent as though debating whether he could trust her with the truth. Finally, he said, "Because it feels like the right thing to do."

The burning sensation that bloomed in her chest was sudden and unexpected. She stared at Ben, wondering if he could feel it too. This didn't make any sense, but she couldn't deny the unmistakable feeling of hope that swamped through her. She struggled to grasp at logic. "What happens if someone finds out about the marriage?"

"If someone finds out we're married, I'll let the team's publicist deal with it," Ben told her. "The biggest reason I was worried about you living in my apartment was that I didn't want to take a chance of any negative press. If someone finds out you're there, at least we'll have a marriage certificate to protect my reputation and yours."

"What happens after my treatments are over?"

"We'll cross that bridge when we come to it."

Maya fell silent for a moment. "What you're suggesting all sounds too good to be true. Are you really sure about this?" she asked. "Maybe you should take some time to think about it."

"I think we both already know this is the only answer." Abruptly, Ben changed the subject. "When are you supposed to get released from here?"

"Tomorrow morning."

"Since tomorrow's Sunday, we won't be able to do anything about getting married until Monday morning."

"Actually, I have my infusions on Monday mornings."

"We'll go Monday afternoon, then," Ben told her. "I know it's not the best scenario, but you can still stay at Ian and Jessica's place tomorrow night. I really don't feel comfortable having you move back into my apartment until we're married."

"You're talking like this is already a done deal. It's a lot to think about."

"Take the next day or two to think about it. You have my number. Regardless of what you decide, call me when you're getting released, and I'll come pick you up."

"What if Rishi is watching for me?" Maya asked timidly. She hated to admit her fears, but she found herself compelled to share them. "Ben, I'm afraid of Rishi. I'm afraid he'll make me go with him if he gets the chance, and I'm not strong enough anymore to run away."

"He doesn't know you've been staying at the Harrises' apartment. I think if I drive you home, we can get you inside without him seeing you."

"Kari has always talked a lot about you. I'm beginning to understand why she is so proud of you."

Ben looked a little embarrassed, and he stood up. "Try to get some rest. I'll see you tomorrow."

Maya watched him leave, immediately replaying their conversation. He didn't really plan to go through with marrying her, right? But if he did . . . The possibilities were almost too good to be true. A place to stay, health insurance, protection from Rishi. She would have a chance to fight again. She would have a chance to live.

The thought that the Lord had given her a miracle crossed her mind, but then the light of hope waned. Maybe He wasn't putting Ben in her life to help her live. Maybe it was because He knew this was the end. Maybe this was God's way of making sure she would be safe until the end.

She closed her eyes and clasped her hands together, afraid to question the reasons. Quietly, she let herself consider the possibilities and found herself praying that Ben wouldn't change his mind.

Chapter 16

BEN WAS ALREADY SECOND-GUESSING himself by the time he got back to his apartment. Maya was right. He supposed he did need to spend some time thinking about marrying her before he followed through with his suggestion. Still, it wasn't like he was *really* going to marry her. It was more like the justice of the peace would give them permission to room together without damaging either of their reputations. Then he laughed at the ridiculous justification. He was losing it.

He picked up the baseball glove he had left on the table and slipped it onto his hand. He pulled the ball from the webbing and tossed it from his bare hand into his mitt, repeating the process as he paced across his apartment. In his mind, he went through the logic he had laid out to Maya. He had to admit that he was a little relieved that he had sensed hesitation in her too.

He knew the idea was as left field as it could get, but he would benefit from it too. After all, if he was a married man, the baseball groupies were much more likely to leave him alone. He didn't mind the fans. In fact, he enjoyed talking to his fans. He just didn't want to let another Heather into his close circle of friends.

Figuring he really should make sure it was legally possible to get married on Monday, Ben wandered into his bedroom and sat down at his computer. He tugged his glove off his hand, tossing it onto his bed so he could have both hands free to search the Internet. His first search revealed a required three-day waiting period in DC before they could get married. He tried Maryland next to find that it was a little better, only requiring a forty-eight-hour waiting period.

His final search gave him the instant gratification he was looking for— Virginia marriage licenses didn't have waiting periods or residency restrictions.

He looked down through the requirements, pleased to see that the process seemed pretty straightforward.

He was still reading through the website when his phone rang and he answered it to find his sister on the other end.

"Have you talked to Maya?" Kari asked, not bothering with a greeting. "I can't get ahold of her."

"Actually, I just got back from visiting her in the hospital."

Kari's voice sharpened. "What's she doing at the hospital at this time of night? Is she okay?"

"She just had a little accident." Ben went on to explain the events of the day, including the fiancé who had come to take Maya back to India.

Kari was uncharacteristically quiet for a moment. Then she said, "I knew Maya moved to the US with her grandmother, but she never said anything about an arranged marriage."

"After meeting this guy, I can see why her grandmother helped her run away. It's not just that he's so much older than her. There's something creepy about him."

"I can't believe she's having to deal with this on top of everything else. What is she planning to do?"

"She's going to marry me," Ben said, the words sounding foreign even to his own ears.

"*What?*" Kari's shock shot through the phone. "I'm sorry, but did you just say you and Maya are getting *married?*"

"Well, it won't be like a *real* marriage," he admitted sheepishly.

"You're going to have a fake marriage?" Kari asked. "Good luck explaining that to Mom and Dad."

"Oh man. I hadn't even thought about what Mom and Dad might say." Ben groaned.

"Ben, why are you doing this?"

"It just makes sense. I like her. She likes me. We get along fine," Ben said. "If she marries me, she'll have health insurance and she can stay here without me getting into some PR nightmare about living with a girlfriend. Plus, her father and fiancé won't be able to force her to go back to India if she's already married to a US citizen. Besides, if the surgery isn't successful . . ."

Kari was silent for a moment, clearly understanding the words he didn't say. Her next question came out of the blue. "Are you in love with her?"

"Of course not. I hardly know her."

"Ben, it's great that you're trying to help Maya, but I never meant to put you in this kind of bind. Not to mention I'm definitely not seeing Mom and Dad being thrilled with this idea."

"Maybe I don't need to tell them, at least not until afterward."

"You'd better make sure they hear it from you and not some reporter," Kari said, sounding more supportive now that she understood his logic.

"I'm hoping I can keep it out of the press."

"Ben, you were second in the voting for rookie of the year. You know you're going to stay in the spotlight during the off-season."

"Yeah, but we're going to get married at the courthouse with the justice of the peace. The chances of a leak are minimal."

"As long as no one sees you arrive or leave together. Just seeing Ben Evans walking into a courthouse is enough to make the papers right now. Add a woman arriving with you, and the press will have a field day."

"Yeah, you're right. Maybe we should come in different cars."

"That might be a good idea," Kari said. "When is all of this going to happen?"

"We are planning on going Monday afternoon, right after she gets done with her treatment at the hospital."

Kari made a few suggestions, and with her help, Ben decided it would be best if he hired a car to take Maya from the hospital to the courthouse in Virginia. He could meet her there to get their marriage license and perform the required civil ceremony. Afterward, he would have the car bring her back to his apartment building, and he would go meet Gavin for their afternoon batting practice.

"You know, you probably should think of another reason to go to the courthouse, just in case someone does see you there."

"Any suggestions?"

"I don't know. Maybe you should look on the courthouse website to see if that gives you any ideas."

"Thanks, Kari," Ben said, reaching for his computer mouse. "I assume I can trust you not to tell anyone about this."

"I'll keep your secret," Kari promised. "And, Ben, I hope you know you could be saving Maya's life."

Oddly embarrassed, Ben said, "I don't know if it's really that extreme. Let's just hope it doesn't backfire."

"I'll pray that it doesn't."

* * *

Ben walked toward his illegally parked car, looking for the slip of paper under his windshield wiper, irritated to find none. This was the third time he had parked in a no-parking zone in an attempt to get a ticket, and he still hadn't succeeded.

Why was it that when he wanted to get a ticket, he couldn't do it? He bet that if he really had an emergency and forgot to put money in the meter under normal circumstances, it'd take a cop five minutes, tops, to notice.

He had liked Kari's idea to find another reason to go to the courthouse so he would have an excuse for being there on Monday. A personal appearance to pay a parking ticket and offer an apology had seemed the simplest excuse. If only he could get someone to write him the darn ticket.

He saw a traffic cop walk around the corner, a ticket book in hand. The man was the epitome of the middle-aged cop who stopped at the donut shop each morning.

Instantly, Ben's spirits lifted. He turned back the way he had come, lingering in the entrance of the restaurant, where he had just eaten breakfast. He watched the policeman ticket two cars where the meters had expired. The cop then approached Ben's car, looked down at the license plate, and continued past it.

Ben stared in confusion. The policeman was obviously here to write parking tickets, and the meter beside his car was clearly expired. Why in the world would he pass on the opportunity to write him one?

Ben stepped forward. "Excuse me."

"Yes?" The cop turned around, and recognition dawned. "I thought you must be around here somewhere." He motioned to Ben's car. "You really need to move your car before someone who doesn't know you comes through here and gives you a ticket."

"Wait a minute. Are you saying you didn't give me a ticket because of who I am?"

"Well, yeah. I mean, that was a tough break last month, losing in the fifth game of the first series in the play-offs. I didn't want to kick you while you were down."

"How did you even know this was my car?"

The officer cocked one eyebrow. "The license plate does say EVANS32. Everyone who follows the Nats probably knows what you drive or could figure it out with your name and jersey number right in front of them."

Now his failed efforts were starting to make sense. He searched for the right words, finally saying, "I really appreciate your kindness, but I don't feel right about not getting a ticket after I did something wrong."

The cop's voice was incredulous. "You *want* me to give you a ticket?"

Ben nearly said yes. Deciding to play it cool, he said instead, "No one ever wants a ticket, but it's only fair that I get one too."

The policeman stared at him as though he was still trying to figure out if Ben was serious. "Okay. If that's how you feel."

Ben watched the man write out the ticket and then accepted it when the cop handed it over. "I assume I can just pay this at the courthouse?"

"If you want, or you can mail it in. The address is on the back there."

"Okay." Ben unlocked his car and opened the passenger door to put the ticket inside.

"Good luck with next season," the policeman told him. "I'll be rooting for you."

"Thanks." Ben motioned to his pen. "Can I borrow that for a minute?"

"Sure." Ben took the pen from him and pulled a baseball out of his duffel bag. He scribbled his signature on it and handed it and the pen to the officer. "Have a nice day, Officer."

The man's face lit up with pleasure. "Hey, thanks. My son will go nuts when he sees this."

"Just tell him I appreciate the hard work you do," Ben told him. "And I'll pay more attention to how much time I have on the meter next time."

With a friendly wave, Ben climbed into his car and started it up. Now that he had the parking ticket in his possession, he thought he might actually be ready for Monday. Maybe.

Chapter 17

MAYA'S MIND HADN'T STOPPED RACING since Ben had talked to her the night before. She supposed she was still in shock over the idea of getting married in two days, but she couldn't deny that for the first time in months, she felt like she was looking forward. The idea of being free of Rishi gave her such a liberated feeling.

What a contrast, she thought to herself. Marriage to Rishi would have been akin to slavery, while marriage to Ben would ensure her freedom. Two more days, and for the first time in her life, her future would belong entirely to her. Just knowing that possibilities existed for her made the treatments seem more bearable.

"How are you feeling this morning?" Dr. Schuster asked as he entered her doorway.

"Good, actually."

His eyebrows lifted at her answer. "I'm glad to hear it." He approached her bed. "Let's take a look at that bump on the back of your head."

Maya shifted in her bed and turned away from him so he could see where her head had connected with the wall in Ben's apartment. He pressed two fingers against the welt, and Maya squirmed slightly.

"It looks like the swelling is going down, and your color is much better." The doctor stepped back and waited for her to lean back against the pillow before he continued. "I hate to bring it up, but have you managed to convince your family to help pay for your surgery at the end of this trial?"

"Not exactly, but I do have a friend who figured out a way to help out."

"You have a friend who is going to give you fifteen thousand dollars?"

Maya was struck with the fact that Ben's offer was in essence giving her that much money and more. "Actually, he's my fiancé."

Now Dr. Schuster looked at her suspiciously. "I thought running away from your fiancé was what landed you in here."

"That was someone else."

"How many fiancés do you have?"

"Technically, I have two. The one I said yes to and the one my father said yes to."

"Ahhh." He nodded in understanding. "So exactly how is your fiancé planning to help?"

"I guess you could say I'm getting married earlier than I'd planned," Maya said, hoping her words were still true and that Ben wasn't already getting cold feet. "Once we're married, I'll be covered by his insurance, and we'll be able to come up with the money for the surgery."

He studied her. "If that's the case, I'll approve your continuance in the program for another week. By the end of the week though, I'll need you to get me the insurance information, even if you aren't covered by it yet."

Maya felt a little guilty at the thought that maybe it wasn't completely honest to get married to gain insurance coverage. Then she remembered Ben's words. The insurance was a side benefit, not the primary reason for getting married. She also couldn't deny that the more she pondered this decision, the more she felt an overwhelming peace. She turned her attention back to the doctor. "Thank you, Doctor. I really appreciate everything you've done for me."

"I'm just doing my job." He scribbled something on her chart. "I'll put in the order to have you released. It will probably be around eleven, in case you need to call someone to give you a ride home."

Maya retrieved her phone as soon as he left. Feeling really awkward, she forced herself to dial Ben's number.

Ben sounded out of breath when he answered.

"Hi, Ben. It's Maya."

Instantly, his tone changed, and she sensed that her voice made him uncomfortable. "Oh, hi."

"I'm sorry to bother you." Maya fumbled, reminding herself that he'd told her to call. "You said you wanted me to let you know when I was getting released from the hospital."

"Yeah. Have you already seen the doctor?"

"He just left. He said I should be able to leave around eleven."

Now she heard his hesitation. "Eleven?"

"Yes, but if you aren't able to pick me up like you planned, I can work something else out."

"I was just planning on going for a run, but that's okay. I can wait until after I pick you up."

"Thank you. I really appreciate it."

"I'll be over there in a little while," he told her and hung up.

Maya set her phone down and tried to chase away her doubts. She would find out soon enough if Ben was going to back out on the crazy proposal he had given her. Footsteps sounded outside her door, and she looked up to see Henry standing there.

"Hey there, little girl. Do you mind if I come in?"

"Of course not." Maya lifted a hand and weakly waved him in. "What are you doing here on a Saturday?"

"I wanted to make sure you were okay. My wife also sent you this." He held up a loaf of banana bread covered in plastic wrap.

"That is so sweet. Please tell her thank you for me."

"I will." He moved farther into the room and set the offering on the tray in front of her. "Have you talked to the doctor yet today?"

"Yes. He just left."

"And?"

"And it looks like everything is going okay," Maya told him. "He said my tumor isn't shrinking as fast as they'd hoped, so it will probably take a couple of extra months in the trial until they can operate, but overall, it looks promising."

"Well, that's what I like to hear." He sat down in the chair beside her bed. "Now, what are we going to do about that Indian guy who keeps coming here looking for you?"

"What?"

"You know I don't like to pry, but I'm not falling for that man's tricks a second time."

"What do you mean?"

Henry described how Rishi had come into the cancer center looking for her, giving enough information about her to slip past some of the privacy protocols.

A feeling of dread started threading its way into her thoughts, overshadowing the possibilities she had been looking forward to. "When was the last time you saw him here?"

"He was down at the information desk when I got here."

"Great." She let out a heavy sigh and glanced down at her watch. What would happen if Ben showed up to get her while Rishi was downstairs?

"What?"

"My friend Ben was heading over here to pick me up. I'd better call him and tell him not to come over until we're sure Rishi has left."

"Honey, he's not going anywhere. From what I can tell, he or one of his buddies has been camped out downstairs since six o'clock this morning."

Maya's anxiety increased. "I can't let him find me. He'll ruin everything."

"When's your friend coming to get you?"

"I just talked to him. He said he'd be over in a little while."

"In that case, I'd better get downstairs," Henry told her.

"What are you going to do?"

"You just leave everything to me."

Chapter 18

POTENTIAL CONVERSATIONS WITH HIS MOTHER played in Ben's mind as he headed for his car. Last night when he had talked to Maya, everything had seemed so clear. His conversation with Kari had helped him work through a lot of the little details, but the idea of telling his parents had started eating at him as soon as he'd hung up the phone.

What would his mother think if she knew he was about to marry someone he didn't love, that he would likely be a widower while still in his twenties?

He'd spent a great deal of time over the past fifteen hours pondering whether he should really go through with this fake marriage. Even though he found himself feeling anxious and uneasy about the possible leaks to the press and the thought of living with a woman he barely knew, every time he started to back out, he thought of that moment of clarity that had come over him when he was in Maya's hospital room.

Ben tried to focus on that feeling now in an effort to calm his turmoil of emotions. He drove the short distance to the hospital and pulled into the parking lot. Immediately, he slowed when he saw the limousine parked near the front entrance. He was pretty sure it was the same limousine Rishi had arrived in the night before when he'd shown up looking for Maya.

Ben circled through the parking lot, trying to decide whether he should risk going into the hospital through the emergency room entrance. He parked on the far side of the lot and pulled out his phone. He didn't want to alarm Maya by telling her Rishi was camped out in front of the hospital, but he thought maybe the doctor could push back her release time in the hope that the guy would leave.

That thought had barely crossed his mind when he saw Rishi and another man get in the limo. Ben waited, relieved when the sleek black car pulled away from the curb. As soon as it left the parking lot and disappeared into traffic, Ben got out of his car and headed for the main entrance. He saw Henry, the man who had shown him to Maya's room the day before, and gave him a friendly wave.

"That guy looking for Maya didn't see you, did he?" Henry asked, concern in his voice.

"No. I waited until they pulled away to get out of my car."

"Good." He gave a satisfied nod.

The woman at the desk let out a chuckle, and Ben looked at her, confused. "Am I missing something here?"

"Not really," Henry told him. "I just came and told Evelyn here that Dr. Schuster wanted her to call Georgetown University Hospital to check on Maya. We figured if that guy thought she was at Georgetown instead of here, he would get out of Maya's way."

"I guess he fell for it."

"Hook, line, and sinker." Henry smirked and motioned toward the elevator. "Come on. Let's get her out of here in case he decides to come back."

"Sounds like a plan." The two men fell into step together, and Ben asked, "So how well do you know Maya?"

"Well enough to know that she's too smart to get treated like someone's property," Henry told him. "It's good to see that she has a friend here in town now. I've been worried about her being alone these past few weeks."

Ben didn't know what to say.

"Most people fighting cancer have someone to help them through their treatments, you know, give emotional support and such," Henry continued. "Maya's been quite a trooper going through this alone."

"I didn't even realize she had cancer when I ran into her here," Ben admitted, the slice of guilt resurfacing.

"She's a gem, that one." Henry clearly held respect and admiration for Maya. "I've been doing this for a while now. You get to know the different types who come through here. Some are angry, some are in denial, and then there are those like Maya who accept their luck and concentrate all of their energy on fighting their way back to health."

"She does seem pretty frail."

"She's actually gotten a lot better over the past week or so. I still can't believe she tried to walk home after her second treatment." He shook his head in disbelief. "The girl could barely walk two steps, and she tried to make me think she had a ride coming. She couldn't have made it fifty feet before I caught up to her."

"How did she get home?"

"I took her," Henry told him matter-of-factly. "After that, she started waiting in the doctor's office after her treatments so I could help her on my lunch break. The hospital lets me borrow a wheelchair to get her home every day."

They reached Maya's floor, and Henry took a step toward the nurse's station. "I'll make sure the paperwork is all taken care of and get a chair for her. I'll meet you in her room in a minute."

Still trying to visualize the scene Henry had painted, Ben headed to Maya's room. He noted the alarm on her face when he knocked on the door and the relief that followed when she saw that it was him. "Don't worry. It's just me. You're buddy Henry sent Rishi on a wild goose chase."

"The nurse said I should be all set to go," Maya told him. "I'm just waiting on a wheelchair."

"Is somebody looking for me?"

Maya's face instantly brightened as Henry stepped in from behind Ben, and for the first time, Ben heard humor in her voice. "I thought today was your day off."

"Some patients deserve special treatment." Henry winked at her. "Come on. Let's get you out of here."

He pushed the chair closer and locked the brakes so he could help her into the chair. Maya struggled to stand and shift around so she could sit down. Surprised by how much weaker she seemed since she had walked into his apartment yesterday, Ben looked around the room. "Do you have everything?"

"Yes. Thank you."

That was all Henry needed to hear before unlocking the brakes and wheeling her out of the room.

* * *

On Monday afternoon, the car was waiting right where Ben said it would be, a uniformed driver standing beside it. Maya smoothed her cream-colored dress over her knees and wished she could smooth her nerves away as easily.

Not wanting to bother Ben for a ride this morning, she had splurged and taken a cab to the hospital, knowing she didn't have the strength to walk that far yet. The doctor had told her to take it easy for the next few days, and having a car waiting for her was certainly going to make it easier to take that advice.

"I wonder who that's for," Henry said as he pushed her forward.

"Actually, I think it's for me." She looked up at him to see the surprise on his face. "I'm meeting Ben for lunch, and he said he was going to send a car for me."

"Well, the boy has class. I'll say that for him." Henry wheeled her closer and spoke to the driver. "Is this for Maya?"

"Yes, Maya Gupta."

"That's me," Maya said, butterflies fluttering in her stomach.

Yesterday, when Ben had dropped her off at Ian and Jessica's apartment, he had outlined his plan for the two of them to arrive at the courthouse separately and then leave separately to keep the press from seeing them together. She understood his reasoning, but she kind of wished she would have had a little more time to get to know Ben before saying "I do."

It's just make-believe, Maya reminded herself.

She let Henry help her into the back of the car, and then she settled back against the smooth leather seats. "Thank you, Henry."

He nodded. "I'll see you tomorrow."

"I'll see you then."

Henry closed the door for her, and the driver got in and started the car.

Maya took a deep breath, still not quite sure what to think about the fact that she was using one marriage to protect her against another. Throughout her infusion this morning, she had tried to relax, but as the hours passed, the tension had continued to build through her shoulders.

She looked out the window, watching the buildings pass until they gave way to the Potomac River. The crystal blue sky reflected off of the water, and she could see the Lincoln Memorial in the distance.

She had read about the many monuments of this historic city and wondered now if perhaps she might one day feel well enough to see them all. Some of her tension faded at the simplicity of that thought.

When they arrived at the courthouse, the driver dropped her off at the entrance. The climb up the handful of stairs was taxing, and by the time Maya reached the door, she was struggling to catch her breath and praying she wouldn't have far to walk.

Using the elevator, she made it upstairs and was halfway to the clerk's office before she had to stop and sit down. She glanced down at her watch, seeing that she still had ten minutes before she was supposed to meet Ben. Taking advantage of the extra time, she let herself lean back against the wall, hoping to regain her strength.

* * *

Ben parked in a parking garage down the street from the courthouse. His long strides ate up the sidewalk, his sunglasses in place so that, at least for now, he was avoiding getting noticed by strangers. This morning he had been forced to deal with a more pressing problem when he discovered one of Rishi's associates in the lobby of his building.

Luckily, Ben had been on the elevator heading downstairs to the parking garage when he had noticed the man. As far as Ben knew, he hadn't been seen.

He jogged up the courthouse steps, thinking that maybe Maya should let him move her things from the manager's apartment for her after his workout today. If one of Rishi's friends was still camped out in the lobby, looking for her, he would see her as soon as she tried to access the main-level unit.

He glanced at the directory and headed for the elevator, deciding he would let Maya know about the problem after the marriage ceremony. He went to the county treasurer's office and took care of his parking ticket first, offering an appropriate apology to the cashier, who didn't look like she cared one way or another if he was sorry about his misdeed.

With his receipt in hand, he headed back to the elevator. As he emerged on the sixth floor, he glanced at the sign on the wall that directed him which way to go. When he started down the hallway, he saw Maya.

She sat on a wooden bench halfway down the hall, her body perfectly still. Her head was leaned back against the wall as though she was dozing, but her eyes were still open. He recognized the dress she wore as one his sister had once owned, and Ben suspected that Kari had passed it on to Maya. The waist was tied back to try to hide the fact that the dress was at least a size too big, the hem falling nearly to her ankles since she was several inches shorter than his sister.

Something in him softened a little as he closed the distance between them, taking note of her fragile beauty. "Are you okay?"

She jolted at his voice and winced a little when she straightened. "I'm fine."

Ben offered her his hand and helped her stand. Her hand was small and warm, her grip weak. As soon as she stood beside him, he broke contact and dropped his hand to his side. "Come on. It's this way."

They walked down the empty hallway, Ben finding that he had to slow his pace significantly so she could keep up with him. When he pulled the door open for her, she hesitated before passing through the doorway. Ben saw the questions in her eyes and spoke before she could voice them. "Yes, I'm sure."

"Okay." Maya drew in a breath and let it out in a whoosh. Then she walked past him.

Ben approached the woman sitting behind the desk in front of them. She looked to be in her late fifties, and for once, Ben found himself hoping the person he was about to talk to wasn't interested in baseball. She didn't seem to recognize him or his name and methodically walked them through the relatively simple process of applying for their marriage license.

They had to go down the street to have the actual ceremony performed, and Ben followed his prearranged plan to have the hired driver pick Maya up so she wouldn't have to walk. As they had at the courthouse, they arrived a few minutes apart and then made their way together to the civil celebrant's office, where the actual ceremony would be performed.

Ben sensed Maya's tension. Oddly enough, seeing her nerves helped calm his. As he might have with his sister, he put his hand on her shoulder and gave it a squeeze. "Don't worry. It'll be fine."

Maya nodded, and Ben wondered if she was agreeing with him or trying to convince herself that his words were true. They presented the officiator with the marriage license and stood before him. There wasn't any pomp or circumstance. No words of advice. Ben almost felt cheated by the lack of tradition in the process and then reminded himself yet again that this wasn't real.

A few words from the officiator and two hesitant "I do's" later, Ben was told he could kiss his bride. He saw the flush in Maya's cheeks when he leaned down and pressed his mouth to hers. The kiss was quick and fleeting, but the brief taste of her sent pinpricks of pleasure dancing along his spine.

Surprised by his reaction, he straightened, his eyes staying on Maya. He saw the unspoken questions in her eyes again but found he didn't want to face them. *This is a marriage of convenience*, Ben reminded himself. He repeated the words over again in his mind as he shifted his attention to the officiator and collected the documentation that proved they were husband and wife.

Chapter 19

MAYA STARED OUT AT THE river as she passed back into DC. She felt almost numb, like she was on the fringes of a dream she couldn't quite shake herself out of. The whole marriage process had actually been quite cold, reminding her more of getting a driver's license than of participating in a real wedding. At least it had right up until the moment Ben had kissed her.

She closed her eyes, allowing herself to relive that one brief moment. How could something so simple have caused such a flurry of emotions? The moment his lips had pressed against hers, a pressure had built around her heart, a pressure filled with sweetness and terror. She knew it was natural to react to him, but she had to remind herself this wasn't real.

To her, a real wedding would have included a white dress, Kari standing beside her as her maid of honor, and ultimately, a marriage to a man she loved. Not that she knew what it was like to love a man.

Looking back, she realized that until she saw Ben in the courthouse, she hadn't really thought he was going to go through with this crazy plan. Oddly enough, as soon as they had their marriage certificate in hand, she had walked out of the clerk's office with him, feeling like it had never happened.

Ben had lingered just inside the door of the civil celebrant's office until Maya's driver arrived. It wasn't until she was safely in the backseat and the driver had pulled out onto the street that she saw Ben step outside. As far as she could tell, Ben was going to get his wish that their marriage remain a secret. Except for the person in the clerk's office and the civil celebrant, no one would be aware that Maya knew Ben Evans, much less that she was married to him.

Though he hadn't spoken the words today, when they had talked the day before, he had told her to feel free to move her things back into his apartment after the wedding. Maya thought of her large suitcase and wondered if maybe Ben would be willing to help her bring it up later. Even the prospect of hauling her smaller suitcase upstairs by herself was a bit overwhelming with the way she was feeling right now.

The dull ache in the back of her head intensified, and she glanced down at her watch. She opened her purse to retrieve a pain pill and her water bottle, but when her cell phone rang, she pulled it out instead. "Hello?"

Ben's voice came over the line. "Hey, Maya. I almost forgot. Have the driver drop you off in the parking garage instead of in front of the building."

It was an odd request, but Maya assumed he wanted to make sure she wasn't seen near his building in case someone did happen to see them together at the courthouse. "Okay."

"Also, I'll get your stuff out of the Harrises' apartment after I get home."

"That would be great. Thank you."

"Oh, and, Maya?"

"Yes."

"Do me a favor and don't go into the lobby or anywhere until I get home."

"Why?"

"One of Rishi's friends was hanging out down there today. I don't want you to have to face anyone by yourself."

Maya tensed, and her fingers closed around the pill bottle in her purse. "I appreciate the warning."

"I'll see you later," Ben said.

Maya hung up and put her phone back in her purse, trading it for the water bottle so she could down her pills. Through the window, she saw they were nearing her building. She leaned forward and spoke to the driver. "Excuse me, could you please drop me off by the elevator in the parking garage?"

The driver nodded. "Yes, ma'am."

"Thank you."

Maya was relieved that she didn't see Rishi's limousine out front. She hoped that perhaps he would think she had run away again and give up his search for her, but she followed Ben's advice and went straight to his apartment, quickly unlocking the door and slipping inside.

Unlike the first time she had walked through Ben's door, the apartment definitely looked lived in now. He'd tossed a cotton throw haphazardly over the arm of the couch, and a water glass rested on a coaster on the coffee table next to the remote control. Once again feeling like a trespasser, Maya forced herself to continue forward.

Recognizing that she probably should have eaten something with her pills, she turned toward the kitchen. She was a little surprised to see the counters clear, except for the blender Ben had used. Maya pulled open the cabinet where she had left a box of crackers, relieved to find them still there. She took a few out and leaned against the counter while she ate them. Then she went into the living room and sank back against the plush cushions.

* * *

Ben dropped his bag by the front door with a thud and stripped off his shirt as he strode through the living room. The idea of working out at Nats Park had been a good one, but there had been one minor problem—he had forgotten about the off-season tours, which happened to be going on today, tours that included the locker room, where he normally would have showered.

He heard the gasp of surprise and looked over to see Maya curled up on the couch, a blanket tucked over her legs and a blush rising on her cheeks. He stumbled to a stop and stared. How was it that he had already forgotten she would be here when he got home?

"Hey there. I see you got inside okay."

She nodded, her cheeks continuing to redden.

Ben glanced down at the shirt he held and his well-muscled chest. After dealing with the press coming through the locker rooms after his games, he'd lost all sense of modesty, but obviously, Maya wasn't the type of girl who was used to men walking around half naked in front of her. He noticed the way she stared, and he fought back a grin. After all, a man was entitled to some vanity, especially when an attractive woman took notice of him.

"I'm going to grab a shower, and then I'll go downstairs to get your things so you can get settled in."

She lowered her gaze to the floor and nodded. "Thanks."

"Yeah, sure." Ben continued through the apartment, remembering to close his bedroom door before stripping off the rest of his muddy clothes.

He wadded them up and tossed them into the corner, mentally awarding himself two points when they landed in the hamper.

After he showered and dressed, he headed back into the living room, where Maya was still curled up on the couch. "Do you have the key to Ian's apartment?"

"Yes." She retrieved the key from her purse and handed it over. "Could you do me a favor and also get the food I left down there?"

"Sure." He left the apartment and headed downstairs. He slowed his pace when he approached the lobby area, pleased to see there wasn't any sign of Rishi or his friends.

He let himself into the manager's apartment, immediately struck by the lack of furniture. Maya hadn't even had a place to sit down since Ian and Jessica moved out last week.

Maya's small suitcase was right inside the door, and he noticed an air mattress in the far corner. A larger suitcase had been pushed against the wall and was lying on its side. Ben went into the kitchen and looked through the cabinets, finding them all empty except for a box of saltine crackers. He set that on the counter and opened the refrigerator.

He lifted an eyebrow. A yogurt and two sticks of string cheese. This was what Maya was worried about him bringing up to her? He remembered the yogurt he had found in his refrigerator when he'd first returned home and found himself wondering if maybe this was Maya's favorite food.

Without anything to pack the groceries into, he slid the yogurt and string cheese into the half-empty cracker box. Then he gathered the two suitcases and headed back upstairs to his apartment.

When he entered, Maya was standing in the kitchen, a can of vegetable broth on the counter beside her.

"Here you go." Ben handed her the crackers. "The stuff from the fridge is inside the box."

"Thank you." She motioned to the small saucepan she had set on the stove. "I was going to heat up some broth. Would you like some?"

Ben looked at her skeptically. After his workout, he needed something more substantial for dinner than soup. He hadn't really thought about what he was going to have for dinner, nor had he adjusted his thinking to consider that Maya needed to eat too.

"I have a better idea. Why don't we order out? Do you like Chinese food?"

"You don't have to worry about me. I can eat this."

Ben shook his head. "Whether it was for real or not, we did get married today. I think we can do better than a can of broth for dinner." He opened a drawer in the kitchen and rifled through several take-out menus. "Here. What would you like?"

She looked at him hesitantly. "Actually, I would love some brown rice."

"And . . . ?" Ben prompted.

"Maybe some egg-drop soup?" Maya suggested timidly.

"Don't you want any real food?"

"My stomach still can't handle anything with much seasoning."

"What about some steamed vegetables? From what I've seen, you could use something more in your diet."

Her cheeks flushed a bit. "Fresh vegetables are so expensive. I usually can't afford them."

Ben stared at her, a new layer of reality sinking in. Maya wasn't just too thin because of the cancer; she was hardly eating anything because she couldn't afford to buy food. Not quite sure how to respond, he pulled out his phone and called in their order. Then he lifted the two suitcases. "I'll put these in your room so you can settle in."

"Thank you."

Ben just nodded. He carried the suitcases into what was now Maya's room and found himself wondering exactly what he was supposed to do now that he was living with this stranger he had married.

Chapter 20

MAYA SAT AT THE TABLE, savoring the taste of the steamed vegetables Ben had ordered for her last night. She had forgotten what it was like to eat something besides the few basic staples she had allowed herself over the past few months.

The portion of food in front of her barely covered a third of the small plate she had used to warm it up. After having dealt with nausea during her first two weeks of treatments and then having a limited food supply after that, she knew her stomach wasn't ready to handle a full-sized meal—or even a half-sized one for that matter.

She finished her food, feeling more energy this morning than she had since before her treatments had started. After rinsing off her dish and sliding it into the dishwasher, she picked up her purse and started for the door. She heard Ben's bedroom door open.

"Maya, what are you doing?" Ben asked.

She turned to face him. "I'm going to the hospital. There's a shot I have to get every Tuesday."

Ben cocked his head to one side. "And exactly how were you planning on getting there?"

She gave him a sheepish look. "I was going to walk."

He shook his head and grabbed his wallet and keys off of the coffee table, along with a manila envelope. "Come on. I'll take you."

"Ben, I don't want to be a burden on you."

"I think you spend way too much time worrying about whether you're being a burden on people." He handed her the envelope. "By the way, here is a copy of my insurance policy for you to give to the doctor."

"Do you want me to call the insurance company today so I can get added to your policy?"

"Actually, I was planning on holding off for a few weeks. I'm not quite ready to tell complete strangers that I'm married. I read through the policy, and it says you'll automatically be covered from the date of the marriage. I just have to give them the information within sixty days." He opened the door for her and escorted her into the hall. "How long does your shot normally take?"

"Just a few minutes."

"Great. Then I can wait for you and bring you back home before I head downtown."

She started to thank him but was distracted by his other comment. "Why are you going downtown?"

"I'm meeting a couple of the guys at Nationals Park to get in some batting practice and a workout." Ben led her downstairs to his car and opened the passenger side door for her. Maya slid into the seat and wondered what she might do with her day now that she wouldn't have to spend her morning at the hospital waiting for Henry to walk her home.

As though reading her thoughts, Ben asked, "What are your plans for today?"

"I don't know. I'll probably try to finish unpacking."

"I thought you did that last night."

She didn't want to say she hadn't had the energy to do much more than unpack her toiletries and pajamas. "I'm tackling that project in small doses."

"It occurs to me that this whole living together thing might go a lot smoother if we sit down and go over our schedules. Do you think you'll be up for going out to dinner tonight?"

"I thought you didn't want us to be seen together."

"I didn't want us to be seen walking in and out of the courthouse together," Ben clarified. "It's not like I'm embarrassed to be seen with you or something. I just don't want anyone to realize we're married and living together."

"Oh. In that case, I'd love to go out to dinner. Other than the courthouse yesterday, it's been a long time since I've been anywhere besides the hospital and the apartment."

Ben pulled up in front of the hospital. "I'll let you out here and go park the car."

"Do you want to just wait down here? I should only be about ten minutes."

"Okay. Just text me when you're on your way out, and I'll pull up to get you."

"Thanks." Maya started to push the door open, but Ben reached across her and opened it for her. She wasn't sure if he opened the door because he thought she couldn't do it herself or if he was being a gentleman without taking the time to get out of the car. She liked to think it was the latter.

Already looking forward to the idea of having someone to talk to tonight, she headed for the door.

* * *

Ben saw the sleek black limousine the instant it turned the corner toward the hospital. He pushed out of his car and jogged across the parking lot, already anticipating a confrontation. He reached the curb as Rishi climbed out of the back of the limousine.

The moment he saw Ben, irritation radiated from him.

Ben stepped forward, and the two men sized each other up. Ben closed the distance between them and spoke firmly. "I think it's time you go back to India. Maya doesn't want anything to do with you."

"What she wants is irrelevant. She is my fiancée, and I will have her as my wife."

"That's not going to happen," Ben said firmly.

"You have no business interfering in my affairs."

"I think it would be more accurate to say you have no business interfering in mine."

Rishi dismissed him with a wave of his hand and started toward the door. Ben cut him off before he had taken three steps.

"Let me pass," he demanded.

"There is something you need to understand. The person you are looking for no longer exists."

"Maya's dead?"

The words and the casual way they were spoken hit Ben like a blow. Realistically, he knew there was a very real possibility Maya might not beat the cancer, but hearing the words spoken out loud evoked more emotion than he had thought possible. He didn't have to know her well to be affected by the tragedy it would be for someone so young to die, and he didn't miss that Rishi's response wasn't that of someone who had lost a loved one but rather that of someone who might have had a piece of art stolen from him.

Rishi's eyebrows drew together, and he shook his head. "You are lying to me to make me go away."

"I didn't say she died." The words tasted sour in Ben's mouth. "I'm telling you there isn't a Maya Gupta anymore." Ben straightened his shoulders and forced himself to say the words that would hopefully get rid of this man once and for all. "Maya can't marry you. She is already married. To me."

"Lies!" Rishi's eyes bulged, and he continued to bluster, his words gushing out in a foreign tongue.

The automatic doors slid open behind them, and a calm voice cut through Rishi's words. Ben didn't understand the words Maya spoke, but he turned to see her sitting in a wheelchair with Henry now standing protectively beside her instead of behind her.

"Do I need to go get security?" Henry asked Ben.

"I think that might be a good idea," Ben said, shifting to Maya's side as Henry headed back into the hospital.

Rishi switched to English, his words spewing venom at Maya. "You are making up stories to deceive me."

Her voice was firm, and Ben was pleased to see that she wasn't backing down. "No, I'm not lying to you about anything. Ben and I were married yesterday afternoon."

Fury erupted on his face. "You were promised to me!" He moved forward, and Ben stepped between them.

"That's far enough," Ben said. Then he added a phrase that was foreign to his lips and surprised everyone, especially him. "I want you to stay away from my wife."

"This isn't over," Rishi huffed.

"It is for you," Ben countered.

The doors again slid open behind them, and two uniformed security men approached with Henry. "Is there a problem here?"

Ben kept his eyes on Rishi when he said, "I believe this gentleman was just leaving."

Rishi looked from Ben to the security guards. He muttered something under his breath that Ben couldn't understand and then motioned to his driver. While the rest of them looked on, Rishi climbed back into the limousine, and then the driver took his place behind the wheel and pulled away.

Ben turned to the guards. "I'm going to go pull my car up. Would one of you mind waiting here with Maya for a minute to make sure those guys don't come back?"

"We'll take care of her."

"Thanks for your help," he said and then spoke to Maya. "I'll be right back."

Ben waited for a car to drive by and then jogged out into the parking lot to get his own. He thought of the fury on Rishi's face and was surprised at the sense of satisfaction it gave him to tell this man he no longer had control over Maya. With this problem behind them, maybe now he and Maya could settle into a routine and his life could get back to normal.

Chapter 21

THIS WAS NOT NORMAL. BEN led the way into the restaurant, and three different people greeted him by name. Judging from the friendly banter that ensued, Maya gathered that Ben must come here often. The hostess led them past several empty tables and waited for them to slide into a booth before handing them their leather-bound menus. They were barely seated when someone else approached their table and asked for an autograph.

Maya knew from Kari that Ben had been called up to the majors early last year, but she hadn't realized how well known he already was. It wasn't that she didn't know about baseball. She had grown up watching her older brothers play when she wasn't off somewhere playing tennis, and she had watched it frequently over the years since moving to the United States. Yet never before had she seen firsthand how Americans treated their sports heroes.

After Ben signed the requested autograph and said his good-byes to his fan, he flipped open his menu. Maya followed his lead, looking first at the salads and then zeroing in on the ala carte menu.

"Hey, Ben," their waiter greeted him when he approached.

"Hi, Justin. How's it going?"

"Not too bad." He motioned to Maya. "Is this the new girlfriend?"

"Not exactly." Ben glossed over the question and offered a piece of the truth. "This is my sister's best friend, Maya. Maya, this is Justin. He thinks he's a Red Sox fan, but we tolerate him anyway."

Justin smirked and said, "It's nice to meet you, Maya." He held up his order pad. "Do you already know what you want?"

Both Maya and Ben nodded. Justin turned to Maya first. When she ordered only a small salad without dressing, Ben shook his head. He ordered his meal, including a baked potato as one of his sides. Then he added a second baked potato to his order.

"You're going to have two baked potatoes?" Maya asked after Justin left them alone.

"The second one is for you."

"Ben, the salad will be more than enough. Besides, you're the one who said I needed to eat more vegetables."

"I meant you should have a better balance in your diet. That salad is only going to be about thirty calories. You need something more substantial than that."

"You're starting to sound like the hospital's nutritionist."

"I'm just using common sense," Ben countered. "Even if these treatments are working, you need to keep up your strength for them to take full effect, not to mention for when you have the surgery."

"I know," she agreed ruefully. "It's going to take a little while to get used to eating normally again."

Ben leaned back in the booth and asked, "Do these treatments always make you feel sick?"

"They did at first but not so much now."

"Tell me what your schedule is like. I know Henry was bringing you home every day, but that's really not feasible anymore. The weather is getting too cold."

"How did you know Henry was bringing me home?"

"He told me," Ben said. "Now about your schedule . . ."

Maya spelled out her weekly routine, the infusions on Mondays and Thursdays, the shots on Tuesdays, and blood work on Fridays.

"In that case, I'll probably try to schedule my heavy workout days at Nats Park on the days you don't have your infusions so it'll be easier if my workouts run late."

"Ben, I really feel bad that you're doing all of this for me. Isn't there anything I can do for you?"

"Like what?"

"I don't know. Clean the apartment, maybe."

"Maya, you can barely walk twenty feet." Ben shook his head. "I think it's about time you stop worrying so much about letting people help you."

"I just want to be able to help too."

"I'm not sure you're ready for that quite yet."

"I could cook." She thought about it for a minute and amended her suggestion. "That is, if you wouldn't mind picking up some groceries."

"Why don't you concentrate on getting a little stronger first. I don't think it's a good idea for you to try to stand at a stove for any length of time."

"I can sit down when I need to," Maya protested. "And I am getting stronger."

"I'd hate to know what you looked like when you were weaker."

"Some things are best not to think about," Maya admitted. Their waiter arrived with their food. As soon as he left, she asked, "Do you always eat out?"

"Most of the time. During the season, I didn't usually have time to cook." He seemed to consider for a minute. "Tell you what. You make me a list, and I'll hit the grocery store. That way if you feel up to it and you want to, you can cook. Besides, it would be nice to have something in the house besides juice, soup, and yogurt."

Maya speared a crisp cucumber slice and nodded. "I agree."

* * *

By the time Maya woke up on Wednesday morning, the refrigerator was full and Ben was nowhere to be found. He hadn't mentioned anything the day before about his plans for the day, and she realized that despite having dinner together last night, she shouldn't have expected him to consult with her when he went out. Sure, she was married to the man, but logically, she understood that she was really just a glorified roommate. She had so looked forward to the possibility of having someone here to talk to.

She looked at her watch, seeing that Kari would be heading to class right about now. Wanting some kind of human connection, Maya dialed her number, her heart lifting a bit when Kari's cheerful hello came over the line.

"Hi, Kari. How is everything going?"

"You aren't going to believe what happened," Kari said, her enthusiasm evident in her voice. "Do you remember Austin Mueller from our American history class last spring?"

"I think so. Dark hair, a little taller than you?"

"Yeah, that's him."

"What about him?"

"Well, I've kind of been talking to him for the past few weeks, and he just invited me to go home with him for Thanksgiving."

"That's great," Maya said, not sure how she felt about finding out her best friend had been dating someone for weeks and hadn't even mentioned it to her. "Why didn't you tell me you were going out with someone?"

"I knew you had so many things going on in your own life that it felt weird to talk about the fun I've been having," Kari admitted. "So how are things going with your *husband*?"

Maya noticed the emphasis on the last word and sensed a tension between them she had never before experienced. "Are you mad at me for marrying Ben?"

"I'm not mad. It's just weird. I mean, I love you like a sister, but I never actually expected to be related to you."

"Believe me, I never expected any of this either. If I could have figured out another way, I would have."

"I know," Kari said, sounding more like her normal self again. "Tell me how things are with you and Ben. I really do want to know."

"Everything's okay so far. He seems a little obsessed with making sure I'm eating right . . ."

"Yeah, he's always been a bit of a health freak," Kari told her. "And no offense, but you could use someone to help take care of you for a while."

Maya knew Kari's words were probably true, but even though they were offered in a lighthearted tone, they still stung. Before she could say anything, Kari spoke again. "I'm almost to class, so I've got to go. I'll talk to you later."

"Okay. Bye." Maya hung up and tried not to envy her friend. She thought back to what it was like to be completely independent, to go out with someone because he was interested in her and not because he felt tied to her through pity. Those memories were vague shadows of her past, ones she couldn't quite grasp with any clarity.

With a sigh, she tried to appreciate what she did have. Grateful for a fully stocked pantry, she opened a cabinet and took out the new box of Cheerios. Delighting in the chance to have real food, she poured some cereal and milk into a bowl and sat down at the kitchen table. She thought of her conversation with Ben the night before and decided she should probably use her energy to unpack her bags. Then, if she could convince her body to take a nap, she decided she might go crazy and try to fix a real meal for Ben and her.

* * *

Waiters and waitresses bustled around the busy restaurant, the scent of hush puppies and freshly grilled fish lingering in the air. After a quick trip to the grocery store that morning, Ben had decided to spend the day working out at Nationals Park since Maya didn't need to go to the hospital. Following their workout, he and Gavin had decided to grab some dinner.

Ben pushed back his plate and blew out an appreciative breath. "That was good."

"I told you this place had good food," Gavin nodded. "So are you going to tell me what really happened to bring you back to DC? I assume it had something to do with the girlfriend."

"Ex-girlfriend."

"Ah. Was that your doing or hers?"

"Definitely mine." Ben shook his head when he thought of Heather and the way she had followed him to DC. "She was one of those girls you guys warned me about, the kind who just wants the spotlight and attention but doesn't really care how she gets it. She tried to weasel an invite to Shawn's wedding. From there, things went downhill fast."

"Then it's a good thing you cut her loose before it got too serious," he said with understanding. "What do you have going on tomorrow?"

"The usual. Lift some weights, go for a run. I might hit at the batting cages tomorrow afternoon."

"Do you have any set plans tomorrow morning?"

"Not really. Why?"

"The *Washington Post* is doing a wrap-up piece on our season this year. When the reporter found out you were in town again, he asked if maybe you could come along and be interviewed too."

"Yeah, I guess I can do that."

"Great. I'll swing by and pick you up around nine. We're meeting him at Aquarelle at the Watergate Hotel."

Ben started to agree, then remembered Maya. "Actually, I have a couple things I have to take care of before then. How about I just meet you there?"

Gavin looked at him suspiciously. "You have stuff to take care of before nine o'clock?"

"It's just that I promised to give a friend a ride to a doctor's appointment." Ben went over Maya's schedule in his mind. Thursday was infusion day, so he should have plenty of time to go with Gavin and still make it back before she would be ready to come home. Worst case, he could send a car for her.

"Anyone I know?"

Ben shook his head. He glanced at his watch to see that it was nearly ten o'clock at night. "It's getting late. I guess I'll see you tomorrow morning."

"See you then."

* * *

Maya's whole body ached. She had thought she was doing so well when she'd managed to unpack both of her suitcases. She had even made sure she rested about halfway through. Unfortunately, in the busyness of putting everything away, she had forgotten to take her medicine until the pain had already started pulsing through her head.

She had remembered to eat a couple of crackers while she downed her medicine, then she had climbed back into bed to try to hide from the pain by sleeping.

The idea of cooking dinner had been a good one, one she knew she'd have to postpone for another day.

She had slept away much of the late afternoon and evening and was surprised when she came out of her room to find that Ben hadn't come home yet.

She had debated whether to wait for him before eating dinner. Needing to gather her strength, she had put on a movie and settled down on the couch. When seven o'clock came and went without any sign of him, she decided a handful of almonds was all she had the strength to eat.

The dregs of her headache continued to linger, and when the movie ended, she finally gave up on having anyone to talk to today. Feeling very much alone, she went back to her room in the hope that she could conjure up some good dreams.

Chapter 22

BEN FELT LIKE HE WAS living a dream. When Gavin had invited him to tag along, Ben had expected to have a nice breakfast and maybe answer a few questions. Instead, he arrived to find a whole group of people there, including his manager, two other teammates, the director of public relations for the Nationals, and a photographer. A private chef tended to their table, preparing an incredible brunch as the reporter explained what was actually going to be a series of articles.

A ripple of anticipation mixed with a healthy fear of failure when Ben learned the title of the series: *The Secret to Next Year's Success.*

When the photographer started taking individual photos of each of them, Ben leaned over to Trent Farley, the PR director, and asked, "Am I really supposed to be here? Gavin only asked me yesterday to come."

"Actually, they were going to do a separate piece on you, but I pushed for them to keep it more team oriented. That's why I asked Gavin to invite you along. Jack doesn't like how the pieces on individuals can make players feel too much pressure," Trent said, referring to the team's manager.

"I'm definitely feeling the pressure."

"One of the things the franchise loves about you is that you're so down-to-earth and you haven't let the media dictate your actions. You just keep doing what you're doing, and if the press starts to bother you too much, you let me know. My job is to make sure the media doesn't get in the way of you doing your job."

Ben thought of his secret marriage and said, "I'll definitely keep that in mind."

The photographer called out to him. "Okay, Ben. We're ready for you."

He crossed to where the photographer indicated, going through the routine of having his photo taken, both individually and with his teammates and manager. When the interviews continued and the players shared some of the antics they had pulled on Ben as a rookie, Ben got caught up in the moment.

* * *

Maya looked at her watch, her concern heightening. Admittedly, she didn't know Ben well, but so far, every time he'd said he would be somewhere, he was on time or early. They hadn't really talked much this morning when he'd driven her to the hospital, but he had said he would pick her up between twelve thirty and one. It was now two thirty.

"Hey, Maya. What are you still doing here?" Henry asked when he noticed her sitting on a chair inside the main entrance.

"Still waiting on my ride."

"Ben?"

Maya nodded.

"What time was he supposed to pick you up?"

"Over an hour ago." Maya shook her head. "He's always been on time before. Something must have come up."

"Come on. I'll walk you home."

"Henry, I don't want you to have to do that. It's freezing outside." As if to punctuate her words, the automatic doors opened when a man walked inside and brought with him a frigid gust of air.

"That's why I've got my coat." He pushed his empty wheelchair toward her. "Come on. You need to get home and get some rest."

Maya relented and shifted herself into the chair. "You know, after all of these treatments are over, I'm going to be cooking for you every night for a year to pay you back."

"Now, don't be silly. I think every night for a month will work out just fine."

Maya managed a small smile. "I really do appreciate you."

"Which is why I don't mind helping you out." Henry pushed her toward the door. "Now bundle up. Like you said, it's cold outside."

* * *

Ben was still on cloud nine as he turned the corner toward home. The music was blaring, his stomach was full from the brunch that had lasted into the afternoon, and Trent was thrilled with how everything had gone with the reporter and photographer. Trent's comment about turning problems over to him if the need ever arose gave Ben an extra sense of comfort about the situation with Maya.

His hands tightened on the wheel, and he looked at the clock on the dashboard: 2:52. He let his head fall back, instantly irritated both at himself and this new responsibility. How could he have forgotten that he was supposed to pick up Maya two hours ago? He pulled up to a light, calculating the easiest way to circle back to the hospital, then he saw Henry bundled up in his overcoat, pushing an empty wheelchair.

A ball of lead formed in Ben's stomach. He could only imagine Maya sitting at the hospital waiting for him all this time, and on an infusion day, no less, when she had already been at the hospital half the day. And to have to be escorted home in the cold by a sixty-year-old man. Ben tried to justify to himself with the fact that she was lucky he had offered to give her rides in the first place and that he had gone to the extreme of helping her out by marrying her, but the truth was that he had made a promise and he hadn't kept it.

He parked his car, an apology circling in his head as he made his way upstairs to his apartment. He unlocked the door and walked inside to find the apartment absolutely silent. For a moment, he wondered if perhaps Henry had been helping someone else, but then he noticed Maya's purse on the couch.

He dropped his keys on the coffee table and continued through the living room to her closed bedroom door. He stood there in silence for a minute, listening for any sound coming from her room. When he heard none, he tapped lightly on the door. No response. He knocked a little harder this time. Again, nothing.

He tried to remember if maybe she had left her purse at home that morning, but he was pretty sure it had been hanging over her shoulder when they'd left. Worried that maybe he was wrong and she hadn't made it home after all, he quietly opened the door and spoke in a low voice. "Maya?"

The frail figure on the bed didn't move. Her long hair spilled out onto the pillow, and her face was pale. Her only visible movement was the gentle rise and fall of her shoulder as she breathed.

Based on when Ben had seen Henry walking on the street, he estimated that she couldn't have been home for more than five or ten minutes. How was it that she could be sound asleep so quickly?

Taking a step back, Ben quietly closed the door. Helplessness mixed with a mass of other emotions, and he headed into his own room. After changing into his cold-weather workout clothes, he headed downstairs and outside into the cold. He started down the street at an easy jog, eager to get his body working and his mind clear. He hadn't gone a quarter mile before a gust of wind took his breath away, making his lungs feel like they were filled with shards of glass. Guilt pummeled through him again as he thought of Maya and Henry having to walk through the cold because of him.

How was it, he wondered, that until meeting Maya, he had hardly ever felt guilty about anything, but now that seemed to be a dominant emotion? Sure, he hated it when he struck out in a game or if he fumbled a play at second base. He even felt a little bad about how things had ended with Heather, though that was mostly because he hadn't been more direct when he had first tried to break things off with her. Yet he hadn't felt any real remorse when he'd finally taken a stand and sent her away.

What was it about Maya that made him feel responsible for her? Was it knowing she might be dying or perhaps the way she was so hesitant to ask for help?

The knots in his stomach tightened at that thought. His sister might have been the catalyst in putting Maya in his life, but he had been the one who had offered to take on the responsibility of helping her. As hard as it was to admit it, he had messed up because he wasn't used to thinking about anyone but himself.

He pounded down the sidewalk, his mind rolling these facts over and over in his head, and he put several miles between him and his apartment. By the time he circled back toward home, he was already thinking about how he could apologize to Maya. When he noticed a florist near the hospital, he slowed and decided that flowers were probably a good way to start.

* * *

Maya didn't need a thermometer to know she had a fever. Her skin felt warm and clammy, and chills worked through her body. She wrapped her blanket more tightly around her, hoping to conquer this latest illness with sleep.

She should have known better than to let Henry bring her home today. Ben would have shown up eventually. Unless something really had happened to him.

The thought that he might have gotten in an accident or maybe injured at practice worked its way uncomfortably into her mind. He hadn't told her where he was going today, but she assumed he had gone to the ballpark like he had the last couple of days. She told herself he was probably fine, but her uneasiness prevented her from falling back asleep.

Still dressed in the loose-fitting jeans and long-sleeved shirt she had worn to the hospital, Maya climbed out of bed and pulled on a sweatshirt in an attempt to warm up. The room tilted on her, and she put a hand out on the bed to keep from falling over. The sky was already dark outside of her room, and she didn't bother to look at the bedside clock to see what time it was. All she wanted was to make sure Ben had made it home all right and to get something in her stomach so she could take her evening pills.

It took her a moment to regain her balance, and she kept one hand on the wall as she moved toward the door and then down the hall toward the kitchen. The sound of the television proved that Ben had indeed made it home. She didn't have the energy to worry or care about why he hadn't picked her up today. She simply wanted to get back to her bed as quickly as possible.

She caught the scent of fresh roses but didn't look into the living room, where the smell originated from. She managed to make it to the kitchen before Ben spoke to her from where he was sitting in the living room. "Are you okay?"

Maya didn't answer. Her focus remained on finding the fastest food to put in her stomach so her pain medicine could follow. She glanced at the refrigerator but decided the door would be too heavy to deal with. Instead, she opted for the simplicity of a saltine cracker.

She ate one and started back toward her room to get her pills, but before she could even leave the kitchen, Ben appeared in the doorway, a vase filled with white roses in his hands. "Maya, I'm so sorry about today. I had an interview, and I completely lost track of time."

"It's okay," Maya mumbled, trying to continue past him, even though he was holding the roses out for her.

"I got these for you," Ben offered them again.

Maya looked at the elegant flowers, but all she could think about was the way her legs felt like rubber. When she didn't offer to take the roses, Ben set them down on the counter. "I really am sorry."

She managed a weak nod and took another step forward. Without a wall to hold on to, she stumbled when the room started tilting again. Ben reached out and grabbed her arm, catching her before she lost her balance completely.

"Are you okay?" He seemed to study her more closely and then lifted a hand to her forehead, his fingers cool against her skin. "You're burning up."

"I'll take some Tylenol," Maya managed, wishing he would let her go so she could collapse in her room.

"Do you want me to get some for you?"

"It's with my other pills in my room." Maya took another step down the hall, only to stumble a second time. Then, to her surprise, Ben leaned down and scooped her into his arms. The movement sent her head spinning, and she didn't know what to think of the odd sensation of being cradled in Ben's arms. "What are you doing?"

"You can barely walk." Ben carried her down the hall and into her room.

She wanted to stay right here in his embrace, but the pain wouldn't allow that even if Ben would. "I just need to take my medicine and rest for a while."

He set her down on the bed. "Where are your pills?"

She motioned in the direction of the bedside table, where a framed photo of her grandmother and her was tucked behind a myriad of pill bottles. Ben picked up the pill dispenser that had her pills divided up both by day and morning and night. He handed it to her, along with the water bottle she kept beside it. He then picked up the Tylenol and shook two out of the bottle.

Her hands were still shaky, but she managed to dump her three required medications into her hand. Accepting the Tylenol from Ben, she popped all five pills into her mouth at once, chasing them down with a swallow of water.

Even though she felt awkward having him standing in her room, it was too hard to stay sitting up. She let herself fall back onto the bed and pulled the blanket over her the best she could.

"Can I get you soup or something?"

She shook her head once, her eyes drooping closed. The next thing she remembered was the sensation of a cool washcloth on her face and the soothing tone of Ben's voice.

Chapter 23

BEN SPENT HALF THE NIGHT pacing and worrying. He didn't have a thermometer in the house, but he could tell just by touching Maya's forehead that she was running a fever well over a hundred, and it wasn't breaking. He'd tried putting cool washcloths on her forehead, and he'd awakened her four hours after her first dose of Tylenol in the hopes that a second dose would help her fever break. By eight in the morning, he was on the phone with the cancer center in a panic. His concern heightened when the nurse told him the doctor wanted to see Maya right away.

He got ready to go and went into her room to try to wake her. "Maya, the doctor wants to see you."

"I just need to sleep." She started to roll over, but Ben put a hand on her shoulder to keep her from snuggling back into bed.

"Come on." He pulled the covers back and helped her sit up so he could help her put on her shoes and coat. When she was ready to go, he lifted her gently into his arms and started for the door.

She tried to speak, but it came out in a whisper. "Ben, I can walk."

"Maybe, but let's not take any chances." He carried her out of the apartment and made his way downstairs. It wasn't until he needed to open the car door for her that he finally set her down.

When they reached the hospital, once again, he picked her up and carried her until they reached their destination. He deposited her in a chair in the waiting room and went to the receptionist's desk to sign her in. He had barely scribbled her name on the sign-in sheet when the receptionist said, "She can come right back."

"Thanks."

He started to pick her up again, but Maya said, "I can walk. Really."

Not quite sure if he believed her, he slipped an arm around waist to help support her as he led her out of the waiting room and into the examination room the nurse indicated. He helped Maya onto the table and stood helplessly by as the nurse took Maya's vital signs.

"The doctor will be right with you," the nurse told them and then closed the door.

"This is my fault," Ben said remorsefully. "If I had been on time yesterday, you wouldn't have been out in the cold and never would have gotten sick."

"You can't be sure of that," Maya told him, barely able to sit up straight. "This happens sometimes when people are in treatment."

"Still . . ." Ben trailed off when the door opened and the doctor walked in.

He looked at Ben with curiosity and extended a hand. "I'm Dr. Schuster."

Ben reached out and shook his hand. "Ben Evans."

"And what is your relationship to Maya?"

Ben reminded himself that legally they were more than acquaintances now. "Actually, I'm her husband."

"So you're the lucky guy," Dr. Schuster beamed at him. "Well, let's see what's going on here."

Ben stood off to the side of the room while the doctor looked at Maya's eyes, ears, nose, and throat. It occurred to Ben that he should probably step out of the room to give Maya some privacy, but he couldn't force himself to leave her alone, afraid the doctor might tell Maya something he needed to hear.

As soon as the doctor finished his probing and prodding, he moved to the door and called for the nurse. He issued some instructions quietly, and Ben couldn't make out the words, then he closed the door again and motioned for Ben to sit down. He spoke to both Ben and Maya. "The good news is that it looks like Maya just has a virus."

"So what do I do?" Ben asked.

"She needs a lot of rest, but mostly, we need to keep her hydrated. I'm going to have the nurse give her an IV now, but she has to keep drinking lots of fluids." The doctor shifted his attention to Maya. "How is your appetite?"

"Okay."

Ben shook his head. "She eats like a bird."

"I know it's not always easy, but, Maya, you need to increase your calorie intake. And I'm not talking about milkshakes and candy bars. I mean healthy food that will help your body fight this cancer. Lots of fruits and vegetables, fish and lean meats, whole grains. Keep it basic so your stomach can handle it, but you need to get some weight back on you. And it wouldn't hurt for you to have a slice of apple pie every now and then."

"We've been working on that," Ben told him.

"Good." Dr. Schuster looked over at Ben in a way that made Ben feel like he'd just formed a new alliance. "After the nurse gives Maya the IV, you can take her home, but if the fever doesn't break by tomorrow, I want you to call me."

"I will," Ben agreed. "Thank you, Doctor."

As soon as the doctor left the room, Maya said, "I'm really . . ."

"If you apologize, I'm going to be really ticked off," Ben cut her off. "I'm the only person here who should be apologizing."

Before Maya could respond, the nurse walked in pushing an IV cart. "Okay, let's get you hooked up here, and we'll have you home in no time."

Sitting down in the chair across from Maya, Ben leaned back and prepared to wait to do just what the nurse had said—take Maya home.

* * *

Maya was starting to think Ben was obsessed. After Maya got home from her check-up with the doctor, Ben had insisted that she eat something before she went back to bed. Though all she had wanted to do was dive into sleep, she had managed to eat half of the cup of broth he had fixed for her.

Four hours later, she woke up from a nap to find him standing by her bed with water, Tylenol, and applesauce. Again, he had been insistent that she eat, and again, she had obliged him.

This time when she awoke, she found a fruit basket on her bedside table. Her bedroom door was open, and she could hear movement in the kitchen.

She looked at her clock, trying to remember when she had last taken some Tylenol. She was still trying to put together a timeline of today's events when Ben appeared in her doorway.

"Oh good. You're awake." He held out a glass of water in one hand and two Tylenol in the other. "It's time for you to take your medicine."

Maya tried to shift herself up and found she didn't have the strength. Ben set the water down and knelt beside the bed, putting a hand on her back to help her sit up.

Though she felt odd with Ben kneeling by her bedside, she accepted the pills from him and took a sip of water to wash them down.

When she tried to hand the glass back to him, he shook his head. "You need to drink some more. The doctor said you need to stay hydrated."

Maya lifted the glass again for another sip. With Ben's hand still warm on her back, she let him support her and continued to drink the water until the glass was empty.

She handed it back to him, and he helped ease her down onto the bed.

"Are you feeling any better?"

One shoulder lifted.

He put his hand on her forehead. "You don't feel nearly as warm as you did earlier."

"That's good," Maya managed.

"I've already ordered dinner. It should be here in about twenty minutes. What do you say I help you out into the living room, and we can watch a movie while we eat."

"You don't have to wait on me, you know. I'm sure you have more important things to do than sit around and take care of me."

"Actually, I already worked out downstairs while you were sleeping. I was just planning on vegging in front of the TV tonight."

Maya looked at him. The truth was that though she was still weak, she did feel a lot better. It would be nice to get out of bed and start acting like a human being again instead of a vegetable.

"Come on." Ben stood and leaned down to lift her into his arms, her blanket still wrapped around her.

She started to say she could walk herself, but she wasn't really sure that was true. Instead, she let herself lean into him, noticing the smell of soap on his skin and the strength of his arms around her.

He carried her to the couch and set her down, helping her get comfortable before picking up the remote control to turn on the television. A classic baseball game was playing on MASN, the local sports network that aired most of the Nationals' games. Ben hit the guide button to start scrolling. Maya noticed in the guide description that the game was one of Ben's from last season.

"Do you ever watch the replays of your games?"

"Yeah, a lot, actually." Ben sat on the other couch. "It helps me see what I could have done better and to see how the pitches look when I'm not standing in the box, not to mention how different umps call the strike zone."

"We can watch this if you want."

"I thought you would want to watch a movie or something."

"Actually, I'd kind of like to watch one of your games. The Nationals were hardly ever on television in Tennessee."

"Kari mentioned that." Ben exited the guide so the game filled the whole screen. "That's how she kept finagling airline tickets out of me to come to my games."

"That was really nice of you to do that. It helped give her a break from taking care of me."

"What do you mean?"

Maya looked over at him, surprised. "The reason Kari stayed out at school last summer was that I was going through chemo and radiation."

"I didn't know that." Ben hesitated as though he was debating what to say next. "When did you find out you had cancer?"

"Seven months ago," Maya told him. "Last February, I started having really bad headaches. When they didn't go away, Kari convinced me to go to the doctor. They started running a bunch of tests. April was the first time I heard the *C* word. I started chemo a couple weeks later."

"I gather it's pretty widespread if this treatment is your last resort."

"Actually, the cancer is still contained within the primary tumor. I was extremely lucky we caught it when we did, but the biopsy indicates that it's a pretty aggressive cancer. If the doctors can't remove the tumor, it could kill me within a year. Because of where it's located, they have to get it to shrink to almost half of its original size before they can operate, but even then, the surgery will be risky."

"But this new treatment is working, right?"

"Everything seems to be going well so far." Eager to change the subject, she looked at the TV and saw the image of Ben striding into the batter's box, a stubble of beard on his face, along with a look of determination. "Oh, hey, you're up."

He looked at the image and shook his head. "You don't want to watch this one."

"Why not?"

"Because I'm about to strike out on three pitches."

"Nobody's perfect," Maya said and proceeded to watch Ben foul off a first pitch fastball. He then watched a wicked slider catch the inside corner of the plate. On the third pitch, he swung at another fastball that was high out of the zone. She looked over at him. "What was your game plan?"

"What?" Ben turned his whole body to face her.

"Your game plan. You know, what pitch were you looking for?"

"That's exactly what my hitting coach asked me after I walked into the dugout."

They chatted companionably as one of Ben's teammates struck out, another drew a walk, and then a third popped up to end the inning. "Seems to me that if you can recognize this guy's slider, that would be the pitch to hit. He only throws it to the inside corner," she said.

Now Ben just stared at her.

"What?"

"Do you know my hitting coach?"

Her eyes narrowed. "No. Why?"

"I swear I had this exact same conversation with him. How do you know so much about baseball?"

"My brothers played when I was younger. When I came here to the United States, watching games on television was one of the ways I used to try to improve my English."

"It sounds like you picked up a lot of knowledge along the way."

The doorbell rang, and Ben went to the door to pay for their food. Maya could hear him exchange greetings with the delivery man, and a moment later, he reappeared with a large carryout bag. He set it on the coffee table and pulled it a little closer to the couch. "We can just eat in here."

After collecting plates and eating utensils from the kitchen, Ben sat down beside Maya and put everything on the table. She looked at the dish he placed before her and reminded herself about the conversation Ben had had with the doctor about nutrition. Dr. Schuster would approve of the grilled chicken breast, steamed vegetables, and brown rice.

Then Ben pulled out two slices of apple pie. Yes, Ben was taking her doctor's orders seriously.

Chapter 24

BEN DROPPED HIS DUFFEL BAG on a kitchen chair and lined up the ingredients to make smoothies. Over the weekend, Maya had gotten stronger, nearly as strong as she had been before the virus, but he was still erring on the side of caution. He didn't want to see that sickly pallor on her face again anytime soon.

He dumped strawberries and pineapple into the blender, as well as orange juice and protein powder. He was just pouring it into two large plastic cups when Maya walked in.

"Here. I made this for you." Ben retrieved a straw from a drawer, stuck it in, and handed it to her.

"Thank you."

He then watched her open a cabinet and proceed to put some almonds in a plastic bag. When she slipped the snack into her purse, he asked, "Are you taking those in case you need a snack or because you're afraid I'll forget you again?"

"I just want to be prepared."

"It's not going to happen again. I promise."

Maya fell silent for a moment, and then she said, "I feel bad that you are rearranging your schedule so much because of me. I hate feeling like a burden."

"So you've said before." Ben stuck a straw in his smoothie, but instead of picking it up, he turned his attention fully on Maya. "From listening to my sister talk, it sounds like you were already part of the family before I married you. Even though neither of us planned to have our lives intertwined like this, I think after all we've survived this past weekend, we've proven we can make this arrangement work."

"Okay, but promise me that if you start feeling overwhelmed or you need a break, you'll tell me. I don't want you to start resenting my being here."

"Fair enough." He picked up his drink and hefted his duffel bag. "Let's get this day started."

"Okay." She followed him out into the hall, and he saw her take her first sip of the smoothie. A look of wonder appeared on her face, and she took a second sip. "This is really good."

"Why does that surprise you?"

"I thought the only way you knew how to fix food was by dialing a phone."

He gave her a mysterious grin. "Oh, I'm full of surprises."

She smiled, and her eyes shone a little brighter than usual. "I'm starting to believe that."

* * *

Maya looked at Ben, confused when he parked in the hospital parking lot the next morning instead of dropping her off at the entrance like he normally did. Automatically, she looked around the parking lot to make sure there wasn't any sign of Rishi. Even though they hadn't seen him since telling him she and Ben were married, she wasn't quite able to believe he was out of her life.

She turned to her left and watched Ben climb out of the car and circle to the passenger side to open her door. After he helped her out, she asked, "Why are you coming in with me? I'm just getting a shot today, so it'll only take a few minutes."

"I figured I might as well come in instead of waiting in the car." He took her arm to keep her steady, and they walked the short distance to the entrance.

When they passed through the main entrance, Maya asked, "What are your plans for the day? I assume you're going to the stadium to work out."

"Actually, they have a bunch of tours going on today, so I got up early and went for a run over on the mall. I can hit the weight room later this afternoon."

"What's the mall?"

"You know, the grassy area between the Washington Monument and the Capitol Building."

She shook her head. "I've never been over there."

He looked at her, stunned. "You've been here for over a month, and you haven't seen the sights?"

She shook her head. "We flew in one morning, met with the doctor that afternoon, and I've been in treatment ever since. Besides, I don't have a car, and the doctor prefers that I not take public transportation if I can avoid it."

"Does that include taxis?"

"Taxis are fine. What I'm supposed to avoid is exposure to large groups of people. Taxis are just a bit out of my budget right now."

"We've got to do something about this," Ben told her.

"Something about what?"

He opened the cancer center door. "Your lack of cultural experiences here in Washington."

Maya passed through the door, not exactly sure what he thought could change her DC experience. The nurse called her right back to get her shot, and a minute later, she walked back into the waiting area, surprised to see that Ben wasn't there.

When Maya looked around confused, the receptionist said, "Your husband said he'd be right back. I think he went into the hall to make a phone call."

Maya looked at her wide-eyed. "How did you know he was my husband?"

"He told Dr. Schuster." She gave Maya a warm smile. "Don't worry. Even if I wanted to tell someone who you married, the privacy laws wouldn't allow it. No one knows except for the doctor and me."

Maya let out a relieved sigh. Then the door opened, and Ben walked in. "Are you ready?"

"Yes."

"Let's go, then." Ben raised a hand and said, "See you later, Angela."

Angela grinned at him. "Bye, Ben."

Maya's lips curved up at the way Ben called Angela by name, clearly making her day. "Do you always do that?"

"What?"

"Make it a point of getting to know the names of people you come in contact with."

"What do you mean?"

"Angela, Henry, the people working at the restaurant we went to last week. You call them all by name."

"My dad always told me that if you treat people with respect, you'll never forget that in the big scheme of things, we're all equal," Ben told her.

"Your father is a very smart man."

"He has his moments," Ben agreed and escorted her outside. Instead of heading for his car though, he stopped where a car was parked at the curb. A uniformed driver saw them coming and opened the back door.

"What's this?"

"A little surprise."

Confused, she let him take her hand and help her into the car. He then circled to the other side and climbed in beside her.

"Where are we going?"

"You'll see." He settled back beside her.

Maya watched as the driver pulled onto the road. They passed through the Foggy Bottom area, and then a few minutes later, she saw the ellipse in front of the White House.

"Oh, wow. That's even more beautiful than in the pictures."

"I thought it was about time you saw everything since you live here now."

"How did you arrange this so quickly?" Maya asked in amazement. "You only found out I hadn't seen all of this half an hour ago."

"I can't give away all of my secrets."

She looked up to see the Washington Monument towering over them a short distance away. "This is amazing. Thank you."

Ben gave her a satisfied smile. "You're welcome."

* * *

Ben had called for a car and driver on a whim, but he hadn't expected to enjoy himself so much. Showing Maya the sights and seeing everything as though for the first time helped remind him that he had been new here only seven months ago. In fact, he had been called up to the big leagues about the same time Maya had found out she had cancer. Talk about life changing quickly for both of them.

They drove around the Capitol and then down along Independence Avenue, past the Washington Monument and the World War II Monument again. When they neared the Lincoln Memorial, Ben tapped the driver on the shoulder. "Can you pull up there so I can take her inside the Lincoln?"

"Yes, sir."

Maya looked up at the four flights of steps and said, "Ben, I don't think I can do that many stairs."

"Don't worry. There's an elevator."

Ben climbed out of the car. When he went to help Maya out, he sensed her reluctance. He took her hand and started up the sidewalk, pleased that the crowds weren't too bad today.

They started down the curved sidewalk leading toward the stairs. Ben felt her steps slowing and realized she probably didn't have the strength to make it all the way to the elevator.

He noticed a man a short distance away with his little girl clinging to his back. Deciding that looked like as good a solution as any, he stopped and leaned down. "Here. I'll give you a piggyback ride."

"I'm okay."

Ben cocked an eyebrow and looked at her.

"I'll feel silly."

"So feel silly. Come on. You've got to see inside. It's one of my favorite places in DC."

She shook her head, but she complied, shifting behind him so he could boost her onto his back.

A giggle escaped her when she went a little too high and had to cling to his neck in an effort to keep from flying off of him.

The delightful sound of her laughter surprised him. Ben turned his head so he could see her face and said, "You should do that more often."

"Do what?"

"Laugh."

Maya rolled her eyes. "I feel ridiculous."

"Good." Ben decided in that instant that going upstairs in the elevator was way too simple. Instead, he veered toward the stairs and started up them at an easy jog.

"I thought you said there was an elevator."

"You don't need an elevator. You've got me." Ben slowed to a walk after the first set of steps and steadily made his way to the top. Then he turned so they were facing the other monuments, the reflecting pool in front of them mirroring the Washington Monument, and the piercing blue sky.

"Wow." Maya breathed the word in amazement.

"Pretty cool, huh?" Ben stood there for a moment, enjoying the view. Then he turned and took her inside to meet Honest Abe.

Chapter 25

BEN WALKED OUT OF THE weight room and rubbed a sweat towel over his brow. So far, he was pleased with how his workout schedule had fallen together in the off-season. He finished his first workout of the day before Maya was even ready to go each morning, and he usually headed down for his afternoon workouts when she took her naps after lunch. On Tuesdays and Wednesdays, he still went over to Nationals Park to work out in the mornings, and he had fallen into the habit of hanging out with Maya while she got her infusions on Mondays and Thursdays.

He had to admit that he was surprised he hadn't started feeling trapped with Maya living with him. Her rather in-depth knowledge of baseball had helped open a lot more topics of conversation between them, and he found himself looking forward to hanging out with her each evening.

Of course, he made a point to leave space between them whenever they settled down on the couch together. The memory of that brief kiss the day they got married often haunted him, and he found she was becoming a little too tempting. He didn't want to spoil the easy friendship they were developing.

Ben also had a new sense of admiration for her after seeing her go through her infusions. He could almost see the way the drugs drained her of her energy during the process, but she always tried to stay upbeat, and she never complained.

Tossing his towel around the back of his neck, he headed for the elevator. When his phone rang and he saw that his mother was calling, he changed direction and headed for the stairs. Inevitably, his cell phone dropped calls the minute the elevator doors closed. "Hi, Mom."

"Hey there. I haven't talked to you in a while and wanted to see how things are going. Are you bored with life in DC yet?"

He thought of the cold marriage ceremony, instantly uneasy. He pushed that memory aside and focused on his outing with Maya to the monuments and their subsequent visits over the past two weeks to the various museums within the Smithsonian. "Actually, it's been pretty nice. I've been able to explore more of the city than when I was trying to squeeze everything in in between games."

"That's good that you're getting out and about," she said. "I've been meaning to ask you, when are you flying home for Thanksgiving?"

"Thanksgiving?"

"Yes, you know that holiday that falls on the fourth Thursday in November?"

"Is that next week?"

"Don't tell me you haven't even bought your ticket yet."

Ben thought about his normal routine of going home for the holiday and then wondered what to do about Maya. He had gotten used to being with her. "When's Kari coming home?"

"She isn't. She's going to her boyfriend's house for the holiday, and Danielle is going to her in-laws, so it will just be the three of us."

Ben wondered what Maya would do if he left her home alone, and he found himself uncomfortable with the image. He was equally leery of the idea of taking her home with him when Kari wasn't going to be there. His parents would ask too many questions. "Sorry, Mom, but I don't know if I'll be able to make it home this year."

"What?" Disappointment hung on the single word. "Why not?"

Ben's mind started racing as he searched for a plausible excuse. He didn't want to lie outright to his mother, so he twisted the truth to his advantage. "Actually, I've been going out with someone here. I was planning on spending the holiday with her."

"You didn't tell me you have a new girlfriend."

"Things have been pretty crazy here for the last couple of weeks." He reached his floor and walked down the hall to his apartment.

Apparently resigned to Ben's decision, his mother said, "Well, tell me about the new girl. What's her name? Where did you meet her?"

"She lives in my building," he told her, deliberately not giving her a name. From what he understood, Kari and Maya had been practically inseparable since their senior year of high school. Maya's name was unique enough that his mother might very well put two and two together. Recognizing that his mother's inquisition wouldn't stop at two questions, he walked into his place and said, "I'm sorry, Mom, but I've got a meeting I have to get to. I'll talk to you soon."

Ben said his good-byes and noticed Maya staring at him when he hung up the phone. "What meeting do you have to get to?"

"I'm meeting with you, actually."

"Okaaay . . ." She drew the word out, clearly waiting for an explanation.

"That was my mom. She was starting to ask questions about my new girlfriend that I didn't want to answer."

Maya took a step back, and hurt filled her eyes. "I'm sorry. I didn't know you were dating someone. I shouldn't have been dominating so much of your time lately."

"Maya, I was talking about you. And I didn't say you were my girlfriend to my mom. I just said I'd been going out with someone here."

"Oh." Maya seemed to process what he had told her. "Obviously, your parents don't know what's really going on, then."

"No, I'm not seeing them being really thrilled about our little marriage of convenience."

She was quiet for a moment and then said, "I'm sure you're right."

"My mom did bring up a good point though."

"What's that?"

"Thanksgiving is next week. We should decide where we want to go out to eat and make reservations."

"I thought you would go home for the holiday."

He shook his head. "Neither of my sisters will be there, so I thought I'd stay here with you."

A smile slowly spread across her face. "In that case, have you ever thought of making your own Thanksgiving dinner?"

He gave her a wry look. "I think that's probably beyond my capability."

"The turkey is easy. If you don't mind helping me, we can do dinner here."

Ben weighed the pros and cons of helping in the kitchen with spending the holiday in a restaurant with a bunch of strangers. Then he thought of the football game he wanted to watch that day. "I'd be willing to help cook."

"Great. I bet you'll be surprised at how easy it is."

* * *

Ben opened his apartment door, curious about who could possibly be at his door at two o'clock on a Tuesday afternoon. His jaw dropped when he discovered his answer.

"Surprise!" Jane Evans said, rushing forward to hug her only son. Her blonde hair was pulled back in a messy knot at the base of her neck, and Ben could smell the lingering scent of vanilla from her shampoo.

He automatically embraced his mother and then stepped back to look at his parents, still stunned. "Mom. Dad. What are you doing here?"

"We missed you and decided it was time for a visit." She breezed past him into the apartment, leaving the bags behind her.

Ben watched helplessly, then turned to his father. If it hadn't been for the gray peppering in Steve's dark hair and the laugh lines that came with age, most people would have had trouble telling Ben and him apart. Steve gave Ben a hug and then picked up their bags.

"Here. Let me help with those." Ben took one of the suitcases from his father and followed his mother into the living room.

Then he heard the surprise in his mother's voice when she said, "Oh, hello."

Ben stepped into the living room and saw the look of confusion on his mother's face and the look of panic on Maya's. He bit back a sigh. It looked like his little secret was about to become a lot less secret.

"Mom and Dad, you remember Maya, don't you? She came home with Kari for Christmas last year."

"Of course. We know Maya well. She used to come to our house all the time during Kari's senior year of high school." With confusion still evident on her face, Jane looked from Ben to Maya and said, "I didn't realize you were here in DC. Are you staying for long?"

Maya looked at Ben, clearly at a loss of what to say.

Ben stepped in and hoped to soften the truth. "Actually, Maya is living here in DC now."

"Oh, well, that's nice."

Steve shifted past them and offered to take the suitcase Ben still held. "I can take these into the guest room."

"Actually, why don't you go ahead and put those in my room."

"Why?"

Ben drew in a breath and held it for a moment while he gathered his courage. Then he let it out, and a combination of resignation and apology hung in his voice. "Because the other room is Maya's."

"What?" his parents asked in unison.

"Maybe you should both sit down," Ben suggested, motioning to the couch across from Maya.

"I think I may *need* to sit down for this," his mother said and lowered herself onto the sofa.

"Why didn't you tell us Maya was here?" His father dropped the suitcase where he stood, not moving to sit down until his wife reached for his hand and gently tugged on it so he would take a seat beside her.

Jane put a hand on her husband's arm before she calmly asked, "Why is Maya staying here?"

"It's kind of a long story." Ben sat beside Maya, feeling like he was forming a needed alliance before he started the winding explanation of the events that had brought them to this point.

His parents listened without comment as Ben explained Maya's health issues and the reality that the clinical trial was giving her a new chance at life.

He was trying to gather his nerve to tell them the rest when his mother interrupted. "That's admirable that you want to help, Ben, but that doesn't change the fact that, eventually, someone will find out Maya is here, especially if you're expecting her to stay for the next several months. How are you going to handle it when the story breaks that the man who swore to live by high moral standards is living with a woman he isn't married to?"

"Do you have any idea what the press could do to your reputation if anyone found out Maya is staying here?" Steve asked. "No one is going to believe the separate-bedrooms story."

"If a story breaks, we'll issue a statement telling everyone we're married."

"Ben, you can't just go tell someone you're married. Those reporters can be relentless. They'll check to see if it's true."

"I know." Ben drew a deep breath again and blew it out. "But it *is* true."

Steve shook his head. "What's true?"

"Maya and I are married."

Stunned silence followed for several long seconds. Then both of his parents started talking at once.

"You're *married*?" his mother asked incredulously.

"How could you do this without even talking to us?" his father demanded.

"We didn't really have a choice," Ben started. Then, seeing confusion and accusation in his parents' eyes, he quickly added, "We're only married in the legal sense. We're really just roommates, which is why we have separate bedrooms."

"I'm completely confused." Jane pressed a hand against her right temple. "I thought you said you had a girlfriend."

"No, I said I had started going out with someone here in DC."

"You clearly didn't say you started going out with your wife," his mother countered. "And how could you not have a choice about getting married?"

Maya spoke, her voice quiet and apologetic. "Ben was protecting me."

"Protecting you from what?"

"Maya's family was trying to force her to move back to India to marry someone else."

"So you married her before they had the chance? Ben, there had to be another way. She could have applied for some kind of protected status with immigration."

"Actually, I hadn't really thought about that before, but still, that process can take months. If Maya is forced to drop out of this clinical trial, the doctors don't think she'll have another chance at treatment."

His parents were quiet for a moment, and then Steve said, "Maya, would you mind if we speak to Ben alone for a few minutes?"

"No, of course not." Maya shifted forward and used both hands to push herself up to a stand. Then she slipped into her bedroom.

As soon as the door closed, Steve turned to Ben and said, "I don't understand how you could do something like this. Your whole life we've taught you that marriage is one of the most important decisions you will ever make, and here you've jumped into it on a whim."

Ben stiffened. "It wasn't a whim."

"Do you love her?"

Uncomfortable with his father's question, Ben asked one of his own. "Do you believe that God answers prayers?"

"What does that have to do with any of this?"

"This marriage was the answer to Maya's prayers." Before his parents could respond, he raked his fingers through his hair and added, "We're pretty sure Maya's old fiancé tried to get her visa revoked. Apparently, he's got the money and influence to pull it off. Since he tried to marry Maya when she was thirteen, we already know he thinks laws don't apply to him."

"We appreciate you trying to help her, but what about you? How long do you intend to stay married? From what you've said, I gather this is a temporary situation."

"We haven't really talked about what will happen next," Ben admitted. He ran a hand over his face. "If she survives the cancer . . ."

Jane leaned forward, sympathy in her voice. "Ben, I understand that you want to help Maya, but are you really willing to tie yourself to someone you don't love?"

"And what about dating? Even if this is just a marriage of convenience, you certainly can't start dating someone else in good conscience while you're married."

Ben thought briefly of Heather and his newfound challenges of dating as a professional athlete. Oddly enough, instead of feeling trapped by his current situation, he found comfort in having a reason to avoid the dating scene. He couldn't think of another woman he'd rather spend time with than Maya. "I'm sure you can give me hundreds of reasons why I shouldn't have made this decision, but for whatever reason, I know this was the right thing to do."

"I have to tell you, I'm having a hard time with this, and I still can't believe that you didn't tell us," Jane said. "I know Maya is a wonderful girl, but—"

"Mom, I'm sorry I didn't tell you. I was afraid you wouldn't understand," Ben interrupted. "I guess right now, all I can say is that I hope you'll support my decision."

Steve looked at him. "You still haven't answered my question. How long are you planning to be married to Maya? Is this temporary, or do you plan on this lasting forever?"

"I don't know. Honestly, I'm worried that the reason I got the idea to marry Maya is that her forever isn't going to last very long."

Both of his parents fell silent at that. Apparently not wanting to face the unpleasant possibilities that Ben had laid out, Jane turned to Steve. "Maybe we should get a hotel room."

"You can take my room," Ben told her. "I don't mind sleeping on the couch."

"I think it would be best if we all have our own space," Steve said.

"Dad, it's really okay. Besides, you're going to be here all the time anyway."

Jane looked from her husband to Ben. "You're father's right. We'll be more comfortable in a hotel, and I'm sure we'll all appreciate a little privacy."

"If that's what you want, I'll get a room for you," Ben insisted.

"You've given us a lot to think about," his father said, picking up the suitcases once more. "Would you mind giving us a lift to the hotel?"

"No problem. Let me go tell Maya where I'm going."

His mother's eyebrows lifted, but she simply nodded.

Ben knocked on Maya's door, and when she opened it, he saw the apprehension on her face. "Everything's okay," he said reassuringly. "I'm going to go take my parents over to a hotel so they can settle in."

"I'm so sorry, Ben."

"It's fine. Don't start anything for dinner. I'll see if I can convince them to let us take them out, and then we can have them join us for Thanksgiving dinner."

"Are you sure?"

"Yeah. Can you do me a favor and call the Westend Bistro at the Ritz-Carlton to see if you can get a reservation for six or six thirty? Use my name if you have to."

"I'll take care of it."

Ben reached for her hand and squeezed it. "Stop worrying. Everything is fine. I promise."

He watched her give him a little nod, and then he turned back to his parents and hoped his words were true.

Chapter 26

MAYA PUT ON A SIMPLE blue dress and belted it at her waist, Ben's words playing through her mind. He thought she hadn't heard him talking to his parents, but she had stayed beside her bedroom door listening to their voices as they carried through the apartment to her. She knew Ben was expressing the same concern she had—the possibility that Ben had felt inspired to marry her because she wasn't going to live long anyway—but hearing the words spoken out loud made them seem more real, imminent even.

She thought of her family, regret flooding her as she considered that she might never have the opportunity to see them again. Despite the way she had left India, she always hoped that someday she would be able to go back, that she would find forgiveness and acceptance from the people she loved.

She wasn't surprised to hear Ben avoid the question of whether he loved her. She didn't expect him to, of course, but his comment reinforced the fact that their marriage wasn't real.

She tugged at her belt in an effort to hide the fact that, despite Ben's efforts to help her eat better, her dress was still a size too big. After sliding on her shoes, she put on the hand-me-down jacket she had inherited from Kari. Then she pressed a hand to her stomach, where her nerves were fluttering wildly. Her heart continued to knock hard against her ribs, and she wondered if perhaps she should use her cancer as an excuse to stay home tonight.

Ben had assured her that his parents weren't going to hold a grudge because of the situation, but Maya wasn't sure she believed him.

Ben knocked on her door, and before she could answer it, he called out, "Maya, are you ready? It's time to go." When she didn't answer right away, he added, "Don't even think about making me go through this alone."

She opened the door now and looked at him doubtfully. "I don't know if I can do this."

"Come on. My parents couldn't stop raving about you when you came home with Kari last Christmas."

"At that point in time, I wasn't their newfound daughter-in-law."

"True," he conceded. He reached out and took her hand. "Come on. Once the shock wears off, they'll be fine."

Her hand felt warm in his, but her voice was wary. "Are you sure?"

"Not really, but it sounded good."

Maya rolled her eyes. "Thanks a lot."

"I can lie if you want me to, but I'm not very good at it." Ben tugged on her hand to lead her toward the door.

"Are we picking your parents up at their hotel?"

"No. I got them a room at the Ritz, so they just have to walk downstairs to the restaurant. I told them we would meet them there."

When she and Ben stepped out of the elevator, Maya shuddered against the chill in the underground garage. Ben looked down at her, his eyebrows drawing together in a look of concern. "Are you going to be warm enough in that jacket?"

Maya didn't want to admit it was the only one she owned. "I'll be okay."

Ben looked unsure, but he continued leading her to the car, her hand still gripped in his.

As soon as he let go to open the door, as soon as that gesture of comfort was taken away, Maya's doubts crashed over her again. "Are you sure you really want me there tonight? Your parents came to see you, not me." She heard the slight waver in her voice and took a tentative step back.

"Hey, come here." As though he could sense the whirl of emotions she was battling, he stepped closer and pulled her against him. "You're borrowing trouble. We're both adults, and there's nothing my parents can do to change the fact that we're married."

Her arms came up to encircle his waist, and she wondered if he knew how desperately she had needed this simple human contact. Warmth flowed through her, and she wished she could stay in his embrace indefinitely. She rested her cheek against his chest and spoke in a low voice. "It's just that they've always been so kind to me, and I don't want to cause any hard feelings between you."

"Which is why you need to come with me tonight. They need to remember why they were so enamored with you when you were just Kari's friend. Besides, I don't want them to try to divide and conquer."

She pulled back so she could look up at him. "What do you mean?"

"You know, when you're not around, they'll tell me all of the reasons this is a bad idea, and then they'll get you alone and tell you about all of my bad habits." Ben stepped back and motioned at the passenger seat. "Let's go, and we'll get through this together."

With her heart still pounding rapidly, she nodded and slid in. She felt like her whole body was shaking by the time Ben turned his keys over to the valet and escorted her into the Ritz-Carlton to the restaurant entrance, where his parents were waiting. She slowed as they approached, and Ben put his hand on her back to guide her gently forward.

Maya didn't miss the difference in how the Evans looked at her now compared to when she had come home with Kari. They had been so warm and welcoming last December, and now they were stiff and formal.

After they were seated, Jane said, "It occurred to me while we were settling into our room that Kari may have had some involvement in everything that has happened between you two."

Maya tensed when she noticed a waiter hovering nearby. Ben was being so careful about not talking about their marriage in front of anyone, and here his mother was trying to bring it up in public.

Ben must have been thinking the same thing. "Mom, I'd rather not talk about that here. Tell me how everyone is back home. How's the grandbaby?"

Jane relaxed enough to tout the latest exploits of Ben's older sister's little girl, who was now nearly two years old. Maya listened to the story of exactly how far a gallon of milk could go when spilled on a kitchen floor, a little pang of envy running through her. If she was cured of her cancer, her doctors said she could have a normal life, possibly one that included children, but right now, she still couldn't get past that little two-letter word: *if*.

She tried to force her unspoken dreams aside and read through the menu. She was debating between a salad and the salmon when Ben asked, "Do you know what you want?"

"Not really."

"You should get the salmon. Then you can take the leftovers home and put it on a salad tomorrow."

"That's a good idea," Maya agreed, already knowing he would get a steak and then eat some of her meal.

After the waitress took their orders, Ben's mother turned to Maya. "Maya, have you spoken with Kari lately?"

"Yes, I called her a few days ago."

"Then I gather you know about the new boyfriend."

Maya managed a small smile. "She mentioned she was going home with him for Thanksgiving."

They chatted for a few minutes about Kari's love life, and Maya was grateful the earlier tension seemed to have eased somewhat. When their meal was served, Maya automatically cut her salmon fillet in thirds, one to eat, one to take home, and one to give to Ben.

Before taking a bite, she slid her plate toward Ben's, and he scooped off the offering. Then she pulled her plate closer once more and started eating her dinner.

Conversation over dinner flowed easily between Ben and his parents, and they seemed to take Ben's earlier hint that he didn't want to discuss personal matters in public. Maya sat quietly, rarely commenting, except when someone asked her a question.

When they finished dinner, Ben's mom said, "I hope it's okay if I make a turkey dinner for all of us on Thanksgiving. I should be able to go shopping tomorrow."

"Actually, we already bought a turkey," Ben told her. "Maya wanted to make dinner at home instead of going out to eat for Thanksgiving."

"Oh."

Realizing that Ben's mother might think she wasn't wanted or needed, Maya said, "Is there any way you might be willing to come over tomorrow and help us get ready for the dinner? I was going to have Ben help me make a pumpkin pie, but if you wouldn't mind doing some cooking . . ."

Ben picked up where Maya left off. "Yeah, Mom. It would be so great if you could help us. Maya isn't strong enough to stand for long, and we both know how I am in the kitchen."

His mother chuckled. "I still keep a fire extinguisher in the kitchen even though you haven't lived at home for years."

"Then you'll help?"

"I'd be happy to. Why don't you pick us up tomorrow around ten."

"I can do that," Ben agreed. He signed the credit card slip and pushed back from the table. Then he eased Maya's chair back and put a hand under her elbow to help her up. "We'll see you tomorrow."

Ben noticed the speculation on his parents' faces when they all said good-bye, but he didn't understand the cause. A little uneasy, he led Maya toward the exit and leaned down to whisper in her ear, "See. You survived."

"Yeah. I survived."

* * *

Ben held the door open and waited for his parents to walk inside. They both took a good look around, and then his mother turned back to Ben. "Where's Maya?"

"She's at the hospital. The doctor adjusted her treatment schedule so she wouldn't have to go in on Thanksgiving."

"Should I wait for her to get back before I get started?"

"Mom, Maya will be thrilled with anything you do. She didn't say so, but I can tell she's been stressing over whether we could really cook a whole Thanksgiving dinner by ourselves or if we should pick up some things premade from the store."

"Well, I am not eating store-bought pumpkin pie for Thanksgiving," Jane said with a combination of pride, stubbornness, and humor.

"Of course not." Ben chuckled. He leaned down and kissed her cheek. "You know, I'm really glad you're here."

Simple satisfaction gave her cheeks a warm glow. His father headed for the living room while his mother walked into the kitchen and retrieved an apron from the bottom drawer. She opened one cabinet after another, taking stock of their contents, apparently pleased to find everything was arranged the same as when she had visited last. "Ben, go ahead and keep you father company. I'll be fine in here."

"Okay. If you need anything, let me know. Maya gave me a grocery list a couple of days ago, but if we missed something, I can run by the store on my way to pick up Maya at the hospital."

He watched her open the refrigerator and riffle through a few items on the second shelf. She muttered to herself. "Sour cream, more butter, celery . . ." She glanced at Ben. "I'll make you a list."

"Sounds good." He went into the living room to join his dad. He dropped down on the couch beside him and looked at the television screen, where his father was scrolling through the guide in search of something worth watching.

"Keep scrolling down if you want sports or up if you want one of your Westerns."

He scrolled up.

He was still deciding between John Wayne and Clint Eastwood when Jane walked into the living room holding a narrow piece of paper. She handed it to Ben. "Here you go."

Ben glanced at the rather extensive list of spices and other ingredients. Knowing it might take him some time to find everything, he stood. "I think I'll head to the store now. If you need anything else, call me on my cell."

"Thanks, Ben. While you're doing that, I'm going to start on the pies."

"Pumpkin pie?" Ben asked hopefully.

Jane chuckled. "Yes, pumpkin pie."

Already looking forward to Thanksgiving dinner, Ben left his mother to her baking. He took care of her shopping list, though he had to ask someone to help him find the water chestnuts, and then picked up Maya from the hospital. When they arrived home, Ben carried the groceries upstairs and found his mother pulling the pies out of the oven.

"What can I do to help?" Maya offered.

"Let's see." Jane picked up a worn piece of paper off of the counter that Ben knew to be her outline for her Thanksgiving routine. "You can put those groceries away and then help make the corn bread for the stuffing."

"I'll put away the groceries," Ben told them. Then he pulled out a tall step stool and placed it beside the kitchen counter for Maya.

He noticed his mother's surprise when he leaned over to read the recipe she'd pulled out and gathered the ingredients for Maya. He looked at her curiously. "What?"

"Nothing. It's just nice to see you helping out in the kitchen."

"Putting stuff in and out of cabinets is easy. It's the cooking part that's beyond me." He edged closer to the counter, where two pumpkin pies were cooling. "I'm happy to sample one of the pies though. We don't really need both of those for tomorrow, do we?"

His mother shooed him out of the kitchen. "Yes, they're both for tomorrow night. Go watch TV with your dad. I think Maya and I could use a little girl time."

"Fine." Ben took a few steps. Then he turned back and gave his mother a hopeful look. "Just one piece?"

The shake of her head was instant. "Tomorrow."

Chapter 27

BEN WASN'T SURE WHAT TO think about his mother since her visit at Thanksgiving. He had expected her to spend the better part of the weekend interrogating Maya and him or at least trying to convince them to find another solution to Maya's problems, but to his surprise, except for that first day, his mother had taken Maya's presence in stride.

Now that his parents were gone, Ben was enjoying getting back to normal life again. Or, he supposed he should say, his new normal. Maya's treatments seemed to be going well, at least well enough that she was slowly regaining her strength and her appetite. Her next scans wouldn't occur until January, but the doctor seemed optimistic that she might be able to have her surgery as soon as early spring.

With that eventuality looming, Ben now had to deal with the challenge that he had thus far been putting off. He was going to have to talk to someone in the Nationals' front office about adding Maya to his insurance.

He had given Maya everything she needed to satisfy the doctor right after their wedding, but when he found out the clinical trial was covering her current treatment and that she was automatically covered for the first sixty days, he hadn't felt any sense of urgency. Besides, deep down, he hadn't wanted to talk to anyone about his marriage until his parents knew about it. Now that he had crossed that bridge, he knew he needed to take this next step.

Not quite sure how to go about it privately, he headed for Trent Farley's office. As the director of public relations, Ben hoped Trent could advise him on the best course of action.

Ben rapped on the open door.

"Hey, Ben. Come on in." He waved him in and motioned to a chair. "What can I do for you?"

Ben stepped inside and closed the office door to ensure some privacy. "I have a situation I'm hoping you can help me with."

"Uh-oh. Don't tell me you've done something to ruin that clean-cut image you've got going."

"Not exactly, but I do have something I need to take care of that I would like to keep private." Ben took a seat and leaned forward, resting his elbows on his knees. "I need to add someone to my insurance without it hitting the press."

Trent's eyebrows drew together. "Ben, the only way you can add someone to your insurance is if you get married."

Ben nodded.

"You're getting *married*?" Trent asked incredulously in a near mirror image to his parents.

"I am married. Her name is Maya."

"Why the big secret?"

Ben thought of his initial reasons and the fact that he didn't want to tarnish his positive image by being linked with Heather such a short time before marrying Maya. Now he found that he wasn't as concerned about those things. Instead, he thought of the effect the scrutiny of the press could have on Maya. "My wife has some health problems, and I don't think she's strong enough to deal with the media right now."

"What kind of health problems?"

"Cancer."

"Did you know about this before you married her?"

"I did."

Trent stared for a moment and then shook his head. "Wow. You really are a good guy."

"I don't know about that, but I would appreciate it if you could help me figure out how to put her on my policy without the information leaking."

"I'll take care of it," he told him. "I assume you're heading to work out?"

"Yeah."

"Swing by my office before you leave, and I'll have the paperwork for you. Then you can fill it out and get it back to me on Monday. I'll send it in for you so no one will have to know."

"Thanks, Trent. I appreciate it."

"I should be thanking you. If this is as bad as your secrets get, you're going to make my job a dream." He stood and took Ben's outstretched hand. "By the way, are you going to make it to Liam's wedding on Saturday?"

Ben tried to visualize what it would be like to take Maya, but he wasn't sure either of them was ready for the speculation they would endure from his teammates. But when he thought of being with all of his friends without Maya, he couldn't quite picture it. Not ready to commit one way or the other, he said simply, "I'll be at the wedding. As for the reception, I'll do what I can."

* * *

Ben jogged up the stairs from the parking garage and stopped in the lobby to retrieve his mail. He unlocked the box to find it stuffed full. When he pulled it all free, a thick manila envelope ripped open and several legal-sized envelopes fell onto the floor. He scooped them up and headed for the elevator. On the ride upstairs, he ripped open the top envelope to see that he had been invited to another movie premiere party in Los Angeles.

He was just thinking that Maya wouldn't react the same way Heather had if she saw an invitation like this when he noticed the red "Past Due" stamp on the next envelope. Certain he didn't have any bills he hadn't paid, he shifted the invitation to the back of the pile and ripped open what was clearly a credit card bill. His eyes widened when he saw the balance: $15,014.72. He scanned through the charges to see that except for the interest and past due fees, the entire balance was carried forward from the previous month.

Afraid that maybe someone might have succeeded in stealing his identity, he shuffled through the rest of his mail to see two more envelopes that appeared to be unfamiliar bills. He opened the second, this one with a balance of nearly ten thousand dollars. Like the other, most of the balance had been carried forward from the previous month. Only one new charge was listed, and that was at a pharmacy down the street.

Ben couldn't remember going there since returning home, except to pick up something for Maya, but he distinctly remembered paying cash.

Maya. He looked up at the top of the statement for the first time to see that her name was on the top, not his. He also noted that the address wasn't his here in DC but was his sister's in Tennessee.

He turned the manila envelope over to see that it was addressed to Maya, and the return address was Kari's. Realizing his sister must have been forwarding the mail to Maya, he carried it all into his apartment and dropped it on the coffee table.

"How was your workout?" Maya called out from the kitchen.

Ben didn't answer. He was still trying to wrap his mind around the credit card debt she was carrying and the sudden realization that he hadn't seen her buy a single thing since she had moved in with him.

Had she been using him for his money this whole time? He hadn't really thought about the fact that he always paid for dinner, aware that her means were limited, but now he found himself needing to know exactly how bad her financial situation was. Had she married him so she could continue her treatments, or was it because she was destitute?

"Ben?" Maya called out, concern in her voice. "Are you okay?"

"Actually, can you come here for a minute?"

"Yeah, sure." Maya walked into the living room and sat beside him. "Is something wrong?"

"It looks like Kari forwarded some of your bills to you." Ben held out the manila envelope, only part of the contents still inside.

"Did some of it get lost along the way?"

"The other bills are right here." Ben held them up and recognized the moment she saw that they were open. "I thought they were mine, so I opened these. Why didn't you tell me you had so much debt?"

"It didn't matter."

"Maya, we're married. Of course it matters. This could come back and hit me."

She snatched the bills from his hand. "These aren't your responsibility. They're mine."

"Right now, you're my responsibility," Ben insisted. "How did you get so far into debt anyway? And credit card debt, no less. That's the worst."

Maya stared at him with hurt in her eyes. "It's amazing what someone will do when they're fighting for their life."

"I guess I already knew that," Ben agreed with anger in his voice. "After all, you married a complete stranger to get what you wanted." He froze the moment the words were out of his mouth, wanting to take them back but knowing he couldn't.

Maya stood. "This was your idea. If you want me to leave, just say so."

"Where would you go?" Ben shot back. "Like it or not, we're stuck with each other, at least until your treatments are over."

The flush of anger in her cheeks drained. She took several steps toward the bedrooms before turning back to face him, tears shimmering in her eyes. "I never meant for you to be *stuck* with me."

His own anger faded, softened by her tears. "Maya . . ."

Her only response was to continue into her room and close the door. Through the silence, he could hear the quiet click of the lock.

* * *

Maya held the phone to her ear, Kari's voice carrying through it. "Okay, so what happened?"

"Nothing happened."

"Nice try. This is me, remember?" Kari countered. "I haven't been able to get two words out of Ben all weekend, and you aren't much better. Did the two of you have a fight?"

Maya crossed her bedroom and looked out through the glass door that led to the balcony. She was going stir crazy staying locked up in here, but it was better than having to face Ben. She had nearly thrown her things into a suitcase and followed through on her implication that she would leave, but the truth was that she didn't have anywhere else to go, and Ben knew it.

"Come on, Maya. Spill it," Kari pressed.

"He saw my credit card bills, and he freaked out. I think he's scared he's going to get stuck with all of my medical bills or something."

"He should know you well enough by now to know you would never do that."

Maya's voice grew quiet. "Not intentionally."

"What's that supposed to mean?"

"If something happens to me while we're still married, my creditors could try to get him to pay. His name isn't on any of my cards, so he should be protected from my debt, but that doesn't change the fact that he's legally my husband."

"I never thought about that," Kari admitted.

"Well, he's thinking about it now." Maya turned from the window and flopped down on her bed. "What was I thinking getting myself into this?"

"You were thinking that you want to live to see your twenty-first birthday, remember?"

Tears shimmered in Maya's eyes. Her birthday wouldn't come until July, but if she and Ben were right, she very well might not make it that long. She tried to swallow the tears so Kari wouldn't hear them in her voice. "Twenty-one is starting to sound overrated."

"Yeah, right," Kari said sarcastically. "Just talk to him. You've already been living together for over a month. I'm surprised you weren't ready to kill each other after the first week. *And* you survived my parents' surprise visit."

"I'm sure they'll be glad when this is all over and Ben is free of me."

"What are you talking about?"

"Never mind."

Kari was silent for a moment before she pressed forward. "Don't worry about my parents. I'm sure they'll be fine with everything once they get used to it," Kari assured her. "By the way, are you and Ben coming home for Christmas?"

"I assume when you say *home*, you mean your parents' home in Cincinnati."

"Yeah, that home."

"I don't know what Ben's planning. Dr. Schuster said he's going to suspend my treatments during the week of Christmas, but he doesn't want me to fly because there is too great a chance I'll get sick."

"You could drive," Kari suggested.

"I don't think I could make a trip that far yet. It's almost nine hours by car," Maya said. "If you get a chance, you should talk to your brother. I don't want him to feel like he has to stay home and babysit me."

"I'll talk to him, but I really wish there was a way you could come too."

"Me too, but everything doesn't always work out the way we plan."

"No, but sometimes it can work out better."

Maya sighed. "I hope you're right."

Chapter 28

Two days was all it took for Ben to decide he didn't like the silent treatment. Since his argument with Maya, the only time he had seen her was when he'd taken her to the hospital for her blood work on Friday. The whole way there she hadn't said a word, and as soon as they'd returned, she had gone back into her room and stayed there.

That entire day, he had reminded himself that everything he had said was justified. She should have told him how bad her credit card debt was before they had gotten married.

Then, as time went on, he realized how clueless he had been, not to mention how spoiled and pampered his life had been compared to hers.

Even though he hadn't wanted to think about it, he knew how desperate her situation was. He had already seen for himself that she wasn't working and couldn't afford an apartment. In a roundabout sort of way, she had admitted that she chose her food based on how much it cost. He also knew that if she hadn't been denied, she would have used her new credit card to finance her living expenses while going through treatments.

By the second day, he had started to worry that she wasn't eating, but then he had seen the empty yogurt cups in the trash. Now he just worried that she wasn't eating well.

His cell phone rang, and he saw Kari's name on his screen. Again. This was the third time today that she had called, and he had lost track of the number of text messages she had sent. Even though he didn't want to deal with her interference between Maya and him, he finally answered the call.

Kari didn't bother with a greeting. "I have a plan."

"Dare I ask for what?" Ben asked.

"For how you're going to make up with Maya."

"Kari, stay out of this. Maya and I can handle our own problems."

"Then handle them," she demanded. "I talk to Maya, and she sounds miserable. Then I talk to you—when you'll answer your phone—and you're downright grumpy. Go talk to her."

"I tried that already."

"Try harder," she suggested firmly. Then her voice softened, and she added, "Do you even know what's bothering her?"

"Yeah. She's annoyed at me because I called her out about her credit card debt."

"All of which is a result of her medical expenses," Kari told him. "But that isn't why she's upset."

"That's what it looks like to me."

"She's worried she'll die before she can pay off her bills and that you really will get stuck with her debts," Kari told him with a hitch in her voice. "She doesn't want you to have to deal with any of that if she doesn't make it."

Ben felt that same hollow feeling he had when he first found out about Maya's illness. Whether Maya had months to live or years, it was about time she stopped waiting to see if she was going to live and start actually *living*. Remembering Trent's comment about Liam's wedding, he decided it was time to show Maya what life could be like. "Do you know what size dress Maya wears?"

"Yeah. Why?"

"Because I think I need your help. How would you like to go shopping with me?"

"Ben, I'm in Tennessee."

"We both have cell phones, and we know how to Skype."

"True," Kari agreed with a smile in her voice. "Very true."

* * *

Maya sat on her bed and stared out her window. The sky was overcast, but the temperature still wasn't quite cold enough for snow, even though it was already December. It had only been two days since her argument with Ben, and she was annoyed to find that she already missed him.

She would have liked going to that new art exhibit at the Smithsonian today or maybe hanging out and watching a movie. They could have gone for a walk before the rain started and talked about their plans for the week. She hated to admit that talking to him was what she missed the most.

Her breath caught, and reality struck. She was falling for him. Ben Evans was no longer Kari's older brother. Maya didn't think of him as a professional athlete with his star on the rise. He was just Ben. The man she had married—and now knew well enough to love.

Startled by this new reality, she jolted when a knock sounded on her bedroom door.

"Maya. I have something for you."

She closed her eyes. How could she face him now? What would he think if he knew she had fallen for him?

"Come on, Maya. This is getting ridiculous. We need to talk."

He was right. Drawing a deep breath, Maya pushed herself off her bed and crossed to the door. She pulled it open, surprised to see that he was dressed in a tuxedo and holding a garment bag.

"Kari helped me pick it out. Hopefully, it will fit okay."

She kept her hands by her side. "What's this for?"

"One of the guys on my team got married this afternoon. The reception is tonight. I'd really like it if you would come with me."

She didn't speak, not quite ready to forgive him and not quite sure how to deal with her newly recognized feelings.

He sighed. "I'm sorry I jumped on you about your credit card balances. It's been a long time since I've had to worry about money. I should have known everything on there was medical."

She blinked in confusion. "It is, but how did you know that?"

"Kari told me, but she shouldn't have had to. I should have known better."

As far as apologies went, it was a good one. Maya could also admit to herself that she yearned to go out with Ben, go out where she could pretend they were a real couple. Maybe if she pretended often enough, Ben would get used to her. Maybe someday their marriage would feel real.

When Maya didn't say anything, Ben took a step back and motioned to her room. "Go on. Go try on your dress."

A touch of regret made it into her voice when she spoke. "I thought you didn't want your friends to know about me."

"We don't have to tell them you're my wife. We can say you're my date."

Her heart fluttered, and she lowered her gaze for a moment before she asked, "Are you sure?"

"Yeah, I'm sure." He handed the garment bag to her. "Here. Go try this on."

"Okay." Recognizing the gesture as a peace offering, she nodded and closed the door between them. She opened the bag to reveal an elegant, teal-colored dress. She took it out, running a hand along the silky fabric.

Then she noticed a second article of clothing, a long coat in basic black. At the bottom of the bag was a shoe box. She lifted the lid to reveal a pair of pumps the same color as her dress.

She tried it on, instantly wishing she had a full-length mirror so she could see how it looked. She couldn't remember the last time she had something new, much less something her own size. The dress fell to her knees, and when she slipped on the shoes, she found that they fit too.

She opened the door so she could see herself in the bathroom mirror and found Ben still standing right outside her door.

He turned to face her, his eyebrows lifted, and he let out a low whistle. "Wow. You look amazing."

She could feel the blush rising in her cheeks. She looked down at the dress and shoes. "How did you know my sizes?"

"Kari helped me."

"This is really sweet of you. Thank you."

"You're welcome." Ben glanced at his watch. "Are you ready to go? We need to leave in about ten minutes."

"Just give me a few minutes to fix my makeup and hair. It won't take me long."

"Hey, Maya."

She turned back to look at him. "Yes?"

"Do me a favor and leave your hair down. I like it that way."

Her blush deepened. She disappeared into the bathroom, hoping a little makeup would help hide any evidence that might indicate she was a cancer victim. Maybe for one night she could play Cinderella and feel like her future was limitless. And maybe she could even pretend that her Prince Charming loved her too.

* * *

Ben took Maya's arm and escorted her into the ballroom where the reception was being held.

"Hey, Ben." Gavin called out to him and crossed to greet him.

"Hey, Gavin. How's it going?" Ben shook Gavin's outstretched hand and proceeded to introduce him to Maya.

"It's good to meet you, Maya. Do you live here in DC?"

"Yes, I do now."

Before the small talk continued, Shawn and his wife, Celeste, approached. They made more introductions, and Ben didn't miss the speculation in his teammates' expressions.

When the conversation turned to baseball, Celeste put a hand on Maya's arm. "Come on, Maya. Let's go find a place to sit down. I get exhausted just listening to them talk shop."

Maya gave her a smile and nodded. As she stepped away from Ben, he called after her, "Save me a seat."

"I will."

Ben listened to Celeste ask the inevitable question as she led Maya away. "So how long have you known Ben?"

"It works every time," Shawn said with a chuckle.

"What?" Ben asked.

"Start talking about baseball, and the girls bail."

"Not Maya. I swear, the first time we watched a game together, she sounded just like a hitting coach," Ben told them. "We were watching the game when Dobkins struck me out in three pitches."

"I remember that. It wasn't pretty."

"Yeah, I know," Ben muttered. "Anyway, Maya asked me what my game plan was."

"That's what our batting coach always says."

Ben nodded. "And then she proceeded to tell me that she thought I should sit on a slider because he always throws it to the inside corner."

"She's right. That's how I got my last home run off of Dobkins," Gavin commented, glancing over at where Maya and Celeste had settled at a table. "She's pretty and knows baseball. She might be a keeper."

Before Ben could respond, Shawn asked, "Where's she from?"

"Ohio."

"You're from Ohio, and your accent isn't like hers."

"She's originally from India."

Gavin put a hand on Ben's shoulder and nodded at where Maya was now sitting with Celeste. "So what's the deal?"

"There's no deal," Ben shrugged off the question.

Humor flashed on Shawn's face. "That's what I said two years ago, and now I've got a ring on my finger."

"What do you think, Ben?" Gavin asked. "Is Maya the ring-on-the-finger type?"

"You guys are impossible," Ben said, not prepared to give his friends an answer. "Come on. Let's go get something to eat."

They had hardly sat down with Maya and Celeste when Shawn addressed Maya. "Ben tells me you like baseball."

"I do."

"Who's your favorite team?"

"In this crowd, I think the safest answer would be the Nationals," Maya said, a touch of humor in her voice.

"Smart girl," Gavin agreed.

Ben reached out and rested his arm across the back of Maya's seat, his fingers toying with the ends of her hair. He had worried that Maya's strength might falter in a social setting like this, but so far, she seemed to be doing okay. Unlike Heather, Maya didn't constantly try to insert her opinions and dominate the flow of topics. Rather, she simply seemed to enjoy everyone's company, acting the same now as she did when they were alone.

Over dinner, conversation was surprisingly easy, and Ben was a little surprised at how well Maya could hold her own in a group of dominant personalities.

When the dancing started, Ben looked out at the bride and groom sharing their first dance and wondered what it would be like to be so blissfully happy. When the traditional dances concluded and the dance floor opened for everyone, Ben stood and extended his hand to Maya. "Would you like to dance?"

"Sure." Maya placed her hand in his, and Ben led her to a corner of the dance floor.

Ben pulled her into his arms, aware of how frail she still was. Yet holding her close, he quickly forgot to think of her as the girl fighting cancer. This whole night had been so delightfully normal, the frustrations of the past few days hopefully behind them.

"I think my friends like you," Ben whispered when Shawn gave him a thumbs-up from where he was dancing with his wife.

"Really?" She tipped her head to look up at him.

"What's not to like? I enjoy spending every minute with you, you're beautiful, *and* you know baseball. That's quite a combination."

Surprise flickered on her face, but she kept her eyes on his. "That's sweet of you to say."

"It's true." Ben nodded toward Shawn. "What do you think of my friends? Would you mind hanging out with them again?"

"Not at all. They all seem really nice."

Ben gave her a wicked smile. "They're nice now. Just wait until baseball season starts. Then things can get a little crazy."

She stared at him, an odd look on her face. "I probably won't be around to see that."

"What do you mean? Where would you be?"

"If my scans are good enough in January, I could have my surgery as early as March."

"And . . ."

She lowered her voice, apparently concerned that someone might overhear her words. "Ben, we both know my chances aren't that good, and I think we both know our relationship probably happened the way it did because I don't have much time left."

His chest tightened for an instant, a bolt of terror ripping through him at the potential meaning of her statement. By opening day, she would have had her surgery. If things didn't go as they hoped, he could be a widower before his sophomore season even began. He shook his head against the image of that permanent kind of gone and said, "I think we should plan for the positive outcomes. There's no point in wasting time expecting the worst."

"What do you envision will happen if I do survive my surgery? I imagine you'll be ready to get rid of me by then. You know the media will pay a lot more attention to you once the season starts."

"That's true, but I don't think we should start making any plans quite yet." He didn't want to think about what life would be like without Maya, especially right now while he was holding her in his arms. "Let's get you better first. Then we can talk."

Maya looked up at him, her eyes dark and somehow more mysterious under the dim lights and the disco ball. His gaze lowered to her lips, and for a second, he found himself leaning toward her. Her eyes widened slightly as though expecting the kiss. Then someone bumped into him, and it was as though a bubble burst.

He continued to stare at her, now noticing how pale her face looked. "Are you okay?"

"Just a little light-headed."

"Do we need to go?"

She gave him an apologetic look. "I'm sorry, but we probably should."

"Come on." Ben took her hand and led her back to their table so they could say their good-byes to the few people still sitting there. They were nearly to the door when Trent caught up with them.

"Hey, Ben. Is this the one you were telling me about?"

"Yes, this is Maya. Maya, this is Trent Farley. He's in charge of public relations for the team." Ben lowered his voice and added, "He helped me figure out the insurance stuff."

"Thank you for that," Maya said, shaking the hand Trent offered.

"It's my pleasure." He turned his attention back to Ben. "By the way, I wanted to find out when you're heading home for Christmas. I was hoping you might be able to take some time to visit a children's hospital later this month."

"Maya really isn't supposed to fly commercial, so we may end up staying here for the holidays. It's too far for her to drive."

"Why can't you fly?"

"My doctor is afraid I would get sick. This time of year, it's pretty typical for people to fly with a cold or the flu."

"With the treatments she's on, she can't afford to get sick."

"I guess that makes sense," Trent said. He reached out and put a hand on Ben's shoulder. "I'll give you a call when I get those dates locked in, but it will be sometime the week before Christmas."

Though Ben normally tried to bow out of events at hospitals, he found himself agreeing. "All right. I'll see you later."

Ben escorted Maya out of the ballroom, and they collected their coats. As soon as they were in his car, Maya turned to him. "You aren't really going to stay here for Christmas, are you?"

"I was thinking about it."

"You don't have to do that. Your parents will be crushed if you don't come home."

"I don't want to leave you here alone though."

"Believe it or not, I actually am capable of taking care of myself."

"It's not a matter of being able to. I just hate the idea of anyone being alone for Christmas."

"I appreciate the gesture, but I think you need to put your family before me for this one."

Ben pulled up to a stoplight and glanced sideways. "Right now, you are my family."

Maya looked at him, the glimmer of a tear in her eye. "That's really sweet, but I don't think your parents will want to hear you say that."

"It's true," Ben told her, a little surprised by how the simple statement could make him feel like his world was tilting dangerously toward something unknown. His eyes met hers, and once again, he saw her only as a woman. "Did I mention that you look beautiful tonight?"

She smiled. "I believe you did."

"Just checking."

Chapter 29

BEN WASN'T BUDGING. SEVERAL TIMES over the past three weeks, Maya had encouraged him to get a plane ticket to go home or at least make plans to drive home. His answer remained the same. He refused to go unless she could go with him. He also refused to talk about the future.

Now that a full month had passed since they had last seen Rishi, and the main reason for their marriage had faded, Maya wondered what would come next. Several times since Ben's teammate's wedding, Maya had tried to pose the question of what Ben wanted for his future if she did survive this cancer. Every time, he pushed the conversation off, insisting that they could talk about it after she got better.

Already edgy about the possibility of not surviving, she found herself eager to plan for a future that included turning twenty-one and living beyond the next few months. She also ached to know if Ben saw a future for them together, if there was any chance he might return her feelings. Unfortunately, Ben didn't want to discuss it. Any of it.

Aware that he wasn't going to help her find the peace she was looking for, she now found herself focused on making sure she didn't get in the way of him being with his family for the holidays. She had even asked the doctor about the various possibilities—plane, train, automobile, or even bus. Dr. Schuster's opinion remained the same.

Driving would be nearly impossible with her needing to stop every thirty minutes to get out and stretch. He also didn't want her in the car for more than two hours a day. At that rate, it would take them more than four days to get there and the same to get back. With only seven days off of treatment, traveling that far wouldn't work. Well, actually she would have eight days off since the doctor said she wouldn't have to come in for blood work tomorrow. Still, if she went all the way to Ohio, she understandably wanted to have at least a day or two to spend there.

With a particularly nasty strain of flu currently going around, the doctor was adamant that she not use public transportation of any kind.

She walked out into the waiting area of the cancer center after her infusion to find Henry waiting for her. "Hi, Henry. How are you doing?"

"I think I'm about ready to get these holidays started."

Maya didn't comment, wishing she felt the same way. Instead, she motioned to the wheelchair between them. "You know, I really think I'm strong enough to walk downstairs on my own now."

"Strong enough or not, you can't take away my excuse to spend time with you." He took her arm and helped her into the chair. "Humor me. It's better to play it safe when it comes to your health."

"You're as bad as Ben. He's always afraid I'll overdo it too."

"How are things going with Ben?"

"What do you mean?"

"Well, you've been together for a couple of months now," he said. "Things look like they're starting to get serious."

Maya felt her cheeks flush, but her voice was steady when she said, "It's not like that."

The elevator doors slid open, and Maya could see Ben standing beside his car at the curb. He saw her coming, and his eyes met hers and held.

"Honey, when a man looks at a woman the way he looks at you, things are definitely getting serious."

Nerves jumped in her stomach. Dare she hope he might have feelings for her? She didn't respond to Henry. What could she say? That she hoped Ben cared for her as much as she cared for him? That as much as she looked forward to beating this cancer once and for all, she also dreaded that day because she was afraid Ben would no longer have a reason to be in her life?

Henry pushed her outside, and Maya felt her cheeks flush once more.

"Hey, Henry. How's it going?" Ben stretched his hand out in greeting.

Henry shook his hand and gave him a friendly smile. "I'm good. How about yourself?"

"Good. I have to admit, though, that I'm looking forward to having a week off from coming here," Ben told him. He pulled a card out of his jacket pocket and handed it to Henry. "I know Maya has been promising to make you Indian food when she's stronger. Since that's still going to be a while, I thought you and your wife might enjoy this."

"What is it?"

"Open it."

Henry tore open the envelope to find a gift certificate to a local Indian restaurant. "Thank you, but you didn't have to do that."

"We were happy to do it," Ben countered. "You've been a good friend, and I just wanted to say thank you."

"Well, I appreciate that."

"You have a good holiday. We'll see you after Christmas."

Ben reached for Maya's hand and helped her into the car.

"That was really thoughtful of you," Maya said as soon as they were alone.

"It wasn't a big deal."

"Are you kidding?" Maya looked at him. "One of his favorite baseball players ever thought enough of him to give him a Christmas gift. He'll remember that forever."

Ben shrugged. "I didn't think of it that way."

"Which is why it was so sweet," Maya told him. "Thank you."

"You're welcome."

* * *

On the Friday before Christmas, the first day of Maya's break from treatment, Ben answered his cell phone, surprised to find Trent on the line. He had already fulfilled his obligation to visit the children's hospital and assumed the corporate offices for the Nationals would already be closed for the holidays.

"Trent, what can I do for you?"

"Actually, it's what I can do for you."

"What are you talking about?"

"Remember how you were telling me a couple of weeks ago how you couldn't go home because of Maya's health problems?"

"Yeah."

"Well, you can now," he said cheerfully. "I mentioned your problem to the team's owner, and he offered to help you with your transportation issues."

Before Trent could continue, Ben asked, "Did you tell him I'm married?"

"Actually, I had to tell him back when we put Maya on your insurance," he said. Then he went on to explain that the team's owner had offered to let Ben and Maya use his private jet to fly to Cincinnati. Ben listened to the offer and found himself practically speechless.

"I can't believe he's willing to do that."

"He was happy to do it," Trent said. "The plane is going to be ready for you in two hours, so I suggest you get packed."

"Thank you, Trent. Thank you so much!"

"Merry Christmas."

"Merry Christmas," Ben agreed. He walked out of his room and into the living room, where Maya was curled up with a book. He was almost giddy when he said, "Hey, Maya, it's time to pack."

Her eyebrows drew together. "Pack for what?"

He grinned at her. "We're getting out of here for the week. It's time for a change of scenery."

"Ben, you know I can't travel. And you're welcome to go somewhere. I already told you I don't need a babysitter."

"Humor me. Go pack your things. We'll be gone for the week." Ben led the way into her bedroom. "Where's your suitcase?"

Maya followed him. "It's in the closet. Where are you planning on us going?"

"It's a surprise." Ben opened the closet and pulled the suitcase out of the corner, where he had stashed it for her weeks ago. Then he set it on her bed and opened it. "Let me know if you need any help. I'm going to get my things together."

He looked back over his shoulder to see Maya open a drawer despite her obvious confusion. Satisfied that she would do as he asked, he went into his room and gathered the few things he would need. Now it was beginning to feel a lot like Christmas.

* * *

Maya's jaw dropped open, and she stared at the sleek private jet in front of them. The hired car hadn't surprised her that much. Ben occasionally hired a car and driver when they went places in the city so she wouldn't have to walk too far, but hiring a jet was over the top, even for him. "You hired a private *plane*?"

"Actually, it belongs to the Nationals owner. He found out about our transportation problem and offered to solve it for us." Ben slid out of the car and offered his hand. "Let's go."

Maya let him lead her to the plane, noticing the driver tending to their bags. The pilot greeted them as they came aboard, and Maya looked around the interior, thinking it looked more like a living room than a mode of transportation. Leather reclining seats, a table for work or to eat a meal on. Ben showed her to one of the wide chairs and sat in the one beside her.

He leaned back and nodded. "I think I could get used to this."

"This is incredible," Maya said.

"I definitely got drafted by the right team."

"Mr. and Mrs. Evans, we'll be leaving shortly. Please buckle your seat belts."

"Thank you," Ben said, looking nearly as surprised as Maya was to hear her addressed as Mrs. Evans.

"How many people on your team know we're married?"

Ben buckled his seat belt before looking over at her. "I thought it was just Trent and the owner, but I guess our pilot is in that inner circle too."

Concern crept into her voice. "What if he says something?"

"If someone from the team confided in him, I'm sure he can be trusted."

"I hope you're right."

His eyebrows lifted. "Are you getting worried that you'll be linked to me?"

"It's not me I'm worried about. You're the one who doesn't want any of this in the press." She gripped her hands on the armrests as the plane started forward.

"You're not afraid of flying, are you?"

"Not really. I just get a little nervous during takeoff," Maya admitted. "It's silly, I know."

"It'll be fine." Ben put his hand over hers. Maya turned her hand over and linked her fingers with his as the plane continued toward the runway. Her stomach lurched as the airplane picked up speed and she felt its nose tilt up.

Ben gave her hand a squeeze, and as soon as they leveled off, Maya's body slowly relaxed.

"Are you ready for a snack?" Ben asked.

Maya couldn't help but smile. "I think you are obsessed with feeding me."

"You have to admit that you seem to be a lot stronger now than when you first moved in with me."

"That's true." Maya thought of her conversation that morning with Henry. "I was just talking to Henry about how I can walk myself from the cancer center to the front doors of the hospital."

"You can't change Henry's routine. He'd miss you too much."

"I'd miss him too. It'll be strange once my treatments are over."

Ben cocked his head to one side. "I don't think I ever asked you what you were studying in college."

"Social work," she said without hesitation.

"What made you decide on that?"

"I had hoped to work in the foster-care system. After living with a family that didn't want me, I thought maybe I could help other kids avoid those kinds of problems."

"You were a foster kid? I didn't know that."

She hadn't ever told anyone about her foster-care experience, and she couldn't say why she was prompted to do so now. "My grandmother died the summer after my junior year in high school, so I was dumped into the foster system."

"You said your foster family didn't want you?"

"They wanted the monthly check that came with me, but no, they didn't want anything to do with me. I got a bed to sleep in and free lunches at school. Other than that, I was pretty much on my own."

"But they at least fed you?" He phrased it as a question, and Maya could see the disbelief in his eyes.

"Sometimes, but grocery shopping and family meals weren't really their thing," Maya remembered too well the way the refrigerator always seemed to be empty and the accusations her foster mother spewed at her every time she made herself something without asking. Of course, when she asked, she was rarely told she could eat anything beyond a piece of toast.

"How did you survive living like that?"

"I'd buy food and hide it in my room. When they went out to eat, which was almost every night, I'd fix myself something, or I'd walk down to the corner deli," she admitted. "I always wondered if Kari knew what was going on because your family used to invite me over for dinner a lot."

"Where did you get the money to buy your own food? I can't imagine they were giving you any if they weren't even making sure you were eating right."

Her voice was soft, wistful. "I sold my grandmother's ring. It was a beautiful square-cut emerald that she brought here from India." She shook her head, trying to free herself of the past. Then she changed the subject. "What is your plan for this week? Do your parents even know we're coming?"

Ben didn't smile the way she had expected. As though he understood her need to leave the past behind her, he seemed to force himself to lighten his mood and say, "They don't have a clue."

Chapter 30

BEN PUSHED OPEN HIS PARENTS' front door, a sense of both excitement and anxiety bubbling up inside him. Maya hadn't been the only person he planned on surprising today. When Trent told him about the offer to use the private jet, Ben considered letting his parents know he and Maya were coming but then decided that surprises were too much fun.

The scent of spaghetti sauce and fresh bread told him his family was home, and he could hear the television droning on in the background. Maya held back, and he recognized her reservations.

He lowered his voice and whispered, "Come on."

When she stayed frozen in the doorway, he set down their bags, took her hand, and tugged her inside. Then he called out, "Anybody home?"

"Ben?" his mother's voice carried through the house. Then she rounded the corner from the kitchen into the hallway. "You made it!"

"Merry Christmas."

"Oh, I'm so glad you're here." She hurried toward him and gave him a big hug.

"Me too." Ben stepped back, not quite sure what his mother would think about Maya's presence. To his surprise, she stepped out of his arms and headed straight for Maya, giving her a welcoming hug too.

"Maya, it's so good to see you. Come on inside and sit down. Ben can take your bags upstairs."

Ben managed to keep his jaw from dropping open. He didn't know what to think about his mother's warm greeting.

Jane looked up at Ben. "Kari is upstairs. Why don't you go say hello and tell her Maya is here."

Maya looked over at him, reminding him of a deer in the headlights. Ben put a hand on her shoulder. "I'll be back in a minute."

Ben grabbed their suitcases and hauled them upstairs, setting his in his childhood bedroom and carrying Maya's bag to Kari's room.

He poked his head inside the open door and saw his sister stretched out on her bed, a magazine in front of her. "Hey there. Are you up for a roommate?"

"Ben!" Kari scrambled off of her bed and launched herself at him. "You're home!"

"Maya really didn't want me to miss Christmas with the family."

"You left her in DC alone?"

Ben shook his head and held up her suitcase. "She's downstairs."

Her eyes lit up. "Really?"

By the time Ben set Maya's suitcase inside the bedroom door, Kari was already halfway down the hall. He wasn't sure how he felt about his family being more excited to see Maya than they were to see him.

He headed back downstairs and followed the voices into the kitchen, where his mother was stirring spaghetti sauce in a pot and Kari and Maya were now sitting at the kitchen counter visiting.

His heart warmed as he stood at the edge of the hallway and watched the three women talk. He couldn't hear the words at first, but the laughter that followed something Kari said was warm and friendly.

Maya noticed him first and held his stare until he crossed to her.

Ben put a hand on the back of her chair and said, "You already know you aren't supposed to believe anything they say, right?"

"Only the good stuff," Maya told him with a smile.

"Glad to see we're on the same page." Ben turned to his mother. "Where's Dad?"

"He should be home from work any minute. I have a feeling he might have stopped off at the store to do some Christmas shopping."

"There are still five days until Christmas."

"Yeah, he's starting early this year," Jane said. "Ben, why don't you and Kari set the table? Maya can help with the garlic toast."

Ben nodded and went to retrieve the plates from the cabinet. Then he headed for the table, and a startling thought struck him. What was he going to get Maya for Christmas?

* * *

"What can I possibly get Ben for Christmas?" Maya asked Kari as they lay in Kari's room that night. "He has given me so much, and I feel like nothing I can do will ever show my gratitude."

"It's Christmas, Maya. Your gift doesn't have to be a thank you present," Kari told her. "Besides, he knows you don't have money to go shopping."

"That's another problem."

"You know I can spot you some cash if you need me to."

"I appreciate the offer, but I don't want you to do that." Maya shook her head. "I'll think of something."

"You know, you could write him a poem. You used to write all the time when we were in high school."

"I haven't done that in forever."

"It was two years ago."

"It was a lifetime ago," Maya corrected.

"Think about it," Kari suggested. She shifted the pillow behind her back and asked, "How are things going between you and Ben?"

"Fine."

Kari cocked a brow. "You've been living with my brother for six weeks, and all I get is 'fine'?"

"There's not much to tell. He takes me to the hospital for my various appointments and works out a couple times a day. I usually don't have enough energy to do much more than read, sleep, and watch TV."

"Ben sent me pictures of you guys in front of the Lincoln Memorial."

"Well, yeah. We try to go out and see stuff when the weather's nice."

"I'm jealous. I haven't had time to see more than the basics in DC. Every time I've gone there, it's been to see Ben play."

"This summer you won't have to worry about taking care of me, and you'll be able to stay longer when you visit him."

"I didn't mind helping you out last year."

"I know, and I appreciate everything you did for me. I don't know how I would have gotten through chemo and radiation without you."

"Is Ben taking good care of you?"

"Yeah, he seems to think that's his full-time job." Maya cocked her head to the side. "Is that a character trait with your family? This incessant need to take care of people?"

"Apparently so," Kari said.

Maya couldn't help but laugh at Kari's nonchalant answer. She picked up a pillow and tossed it at her.

Kari giggled right along with her. "I'm really glad you're here."

"Me too."

* * *

Ben sat at the kitchen counter across from his mom, his confusion continuing to grow. He had expected Kari to be thrilled to see Maya, but the best he had hoped for from his parents was cool politeness. Instead, they had both been warm, welcoming, and downright cheerful.

"I still can't believe you and Maya were able to make it. I was heartbroken to think this would be the first Christmas I wouldn't have you here," Jane said as she retrieved a bowl from a cabinet and started mixing ingredients together. Ben recognized the line-up as a future pumpkin pie.

"Forgive me for being confused, but four weeks ago, you and Dad were both livid that I had married Maya, and now you're treating her like she really is my wife."

"Ben, Maya *is* your wife."

Ben ignored the humor in his mother's voice. "You know what I mean. Why are you and Dad suddenly so cool with all of this?"

"For one thing, we've had a little time to get over the shock of not being at your wedding."

"And?" Ben prompted. There was no way a few weeks could have changed their attitudes so completely without another reason.

"And we realized this isn't just a marriage of convenience."

"What do you mean? Of course it is."

His mother dumped sugar into the bowl and shook her head. "Then you put on a good show because it sure looks like the two of you love each other for real."

"It's not like that. I've never even really kissed her," Ben insisted, though the images of their brief kiss at the courthouse and of them dancing together popped into his mind. He wasn't about to admit that he'd been wondering for weeks what a real kiss would be like.

"That surprises me, but it also has nothing to do with whether you really love her," Jane countered. She set the bowl of pie filling aside. "Loving someone is caring enough to change your world to make theirs better. That's what you do for Maya. And as much as she can, that's what Maya does for you."

"I think you're both losing it." Ben shook his head.

"No, but you might want to put some thought into this before *you* end up losing the most important thing in your life. Don't let Maya think she's the only one in love."

His heart jumped in his chest at his mother's words. Could Maya have really fallen for him, or were his parents just mistaking her gratitude for something more? "What makes you think she loves me?"

"It's written all over her face. The sun rises and sets on you as far as she's concerned," she told him. "And as for you, I've never seen you so considerate before. You anticipate Maya's needs almost before she knows what they are, and she appreciates it every time. It's the kind of marriage I've always wanted for all of you kids."

Ben fell silent, lost in his thoughts. He'd always been pretty good about opening doors and stuff like that for girls. His mother had trained him well in old-fashioned courtesies. Now that she pointed it out though, he couldn't remember a time he had gone out of his way for a girl. He knew he had led Heather to believe he decided to move to California to be closer to her, but he could admit that Heather had really just been an easy excuse to spread his wings and keep from moving home during the off-season.

He supposed he had rearranged his schedule a bit for Cassie, but when she had started hinting about marriage last Christmas, he had known it was time to move on. After being so panicked about the idea of getting married only a year ago, he never would have imagined he'd end up married so soon—to someone he'd never even dated.

Memories of his time with Maya last Christmas came to mind. They had both been heading out for a run the day after she and Kari had gotten home from college and had fallen into the routine of running together over her college break. He remembered now how much he had looked forward to that part of his day.

His eyebrows drew together. Could he have been falling for Maya back when he'd first met her? He had been so eager to get out of his relationship with Cassie that he hadn't considered entering into a new one, and certainly not with his sister's best friend, but could that have been a subconscious thought at the time?

His mother interrupted his thoughts. "By the way, your grandparents are arriving tomorrow. They're looking forward to meeting Maya."

"Did you tell them we're married?"

Jane shook her head. "No. I thought I would let you do that when you were ready."

"Thanks. I appreciate that." He thought once more about what he might give to Maya for Christmas, and a burst of inspiration flashed into his mind. "What time does the mall close tonight?"

"I think it's open until ten."

Ben looked down at his watch to see that it was already 8:45. "Can I borrow your car? I have to run out for a bit."

"Sure. The spare key is on the hook over there." She gestured at a key rack near the back door.

"Thanks. I'll be back in a little while."

He snatched the keys and darted out the door.

Chapter 31

BEN CARRIED THE SMALL BAG through the mall, ecstatic to have found exactly what he was looking for and in the first store he had tried. Now he headed for the mall exit, feeling like he'd just won the World Series. At least, he thought this was what it might feel like to win a World Series.

He was passing by one of the restaurants near the mall entrance when he heard someone call his name. Recognizing the voice, he turned to see his old girlfriend, Cassie, hurrying toward him. "Ben! I didn't know you were in town."

"I'm just home for a few days. How are you doing? How's your family?"

"Everyone's doing fine. I just graduated from Iowa State in the spring. Now I'm teaching at our old high school."

"Good for you."

"I can't believe how your year went. I'm sorry you didn't get rookie of the year. You deserved it."

"Thanks, but there were a lot of good candidates," Ben said, reciting his standard line.

"Where are you heading now? Do you have time to grab a late bite to eat or something?"

"Actually, I really need to get home."

"Some other time, then." She stepped forward and gave him a hug.

Automatically, his hand lifted to her waist, despite the package he held in it. Feeling awkward hugging a woman he was no longer involved with, he pulled back, but not before she brushed a kiss across his cheek.

Before he managed to step away, she put a hand on the package he carried and raised her eyebrows expectantly. "I gather there's someone special in your life these days."

Ben started to deny it but found no reason to lie. "Yeah. I guess you could say that." With a step back, he lifted a hand to wave good-bye. "I'll see you later."

"I hope so," she said in a tone that left little doubt that she would be more than willing to jump back into a relationship with him again. She certainly hadn't been this friendly when he had broken things off eleven months ago.

Anxious to get away from a potentially awkward situation with the ex, Ben hurried to the mall entrance and pushed the door open, glancing back to see Cassie still watching him; only now there was another girl standing beside her.

Ben stuffed Maya's present into his coat pocket, put on his gloves, and stepped outside. A gust of wind prompted him to dig his scarf out of his pocket as he made his way to the car. By the time he arrived home twenty minutes later, he'd all but pushed his run-in with Cassie out of his mind, and instead, he focused on what Maya would think of her present.

* * *

Maya hadn't followed Facebook or Twitter for months, so when she walked by Kari and saw an image of Ben with his ex-girlfriend on the computer screen, she assumed it was an old photo. Then Kari turned to face her, a look of alarm and concern on her face.

"I'm sure there must be a logical explanation."

"For what?"

"For this." Kari pointed at the screen.

Maya looked a little closer, noting the way Ben and Cassie were embracing, the attractive blonde's face tilted up as though about to kiss him, Ben's hand planted firmly around her waist. His face was turned slightly away from the camera, so his expression was hard to make out, but Maya didn't have any trouble filling in the blanks. The spurt of jealousy surprised her, and she had to struggle to keep her voice causal. "I don't understand why Ben would have to explain an old picture of him and a girlfriend."

"Because this picture was supposedly taken last night, and Cassie is saying she and Ben are back together."

Maya looked closer at the photo and noticed the Christmas decorations visible in a storefront behind them. It definitely could have been taken recently. Maya had met Cassie several times last Christmas, but she remembered her hair being much shorter then. Her stomach tightened when she noticed Ben's overcoat, the same one she remembered him purchasing only a few weeks earlier.

Doubts rushed through her. He hadn't been home when she'd gone to bed last night, nor had he told her where he was going when he left.

In fact, his mother had been oddly quiet about where Ben had run off to after dinner.

Maya's heart squeezed in her chest. She remembered all too well how wrapped up in each other Ben and Cassie had been last Christmas. According to Kari, they had broken up a week or two later, but Kari hadn't been sure what had prompted the breakup, which surprised her since they'd been together for several years. "Do you think it's true?"

"Of course not. Stories like these get blown out of proportion all the time. It's probably just an old photo that someone put up." Kari pushed back from her desk. "I'd better go tell Ben about it."

Kari was all the way to her bedroom door when Maya called out to stop her. "Kari, wait. It's Christmas Eve. Ben doesn't need to deal with this right now. If you think he needs to know about it, why not wait until after Christmas? Maybe it will have blown over by then."

"I guess you're right. It just makes me so mad when people do things like this." Kari stepped into the hall and said, "Let's go get some breakfast and forget about it."

"Sounds good." Maya headed for the door but couldn't stop herself from looking back at the photo one last time and seeing the one thing Kari hadn't: a small shopping bag with a jewelry store logo gripped in Ben's hand.

Her heart beat painfully, her stomach hollow. Ben himself had admitted that he had gotten stuck with her, and yet it was no secret that all of the girls who had come before her were ones he had chosen.

As much as she wanted to forget about the image Kari had shown her, she found herself wondering if Ben was unwilling to discuss the future because he didn't know how to tell her he didn't plan on them spending their futures together.

* * *

Ben lowered himself onto the couch beside Maya while the rest of the family lingered in the kitchen. After dinner, she had moved away from the noise and commotion, probably his two-year-old niece in particular, and curled up on the sofa. Concerned by how quiet she had been at dinner, Ben had gone in search of her. "Is everything okay?"

"I'm fine." Maya smiled at him, but it didn't reach her eyes.

"You don't seem like yourself. What's going on?"

She didn't look at him, staring instead at the Christmas tree across the room, the white lights illuminating the otherwise dark corner. "I was just thinking how nice it's been to have a real Christmas this year, to have a family to share it with."

He caught her wistfulness and the melancholy. "You were here with my family last year. It isn't any different."

"It could be."

"What do you mean?"

She fell silent for a moment, and he could hear her emotions choking at her words when she managed to say, "This could be my last."

"I don't like it when you talk like that."

"You have to be thinking the same thing." She continued to stare at the lights on the tree. "You knew when you married me that it would probably only be for a few months."

"That's not true."

"It is." She shifted now to face him. She looked so serious, so sad. "I heard you talking to your parents Thanksgiving weekend. I know you think you were inspired to marry me so I wouldn't be alone when I die. It's just hard facing the end when I thought I would have so many more years than this."

"Maya, neither one of us will know why things happened this way until we're on the other side of it. In a few months, you could be cancer free and complaining about how I'm too loud when I get home after my games or how my road trips are too long."

Her elegant eyebrows lifted slightly, a small glimmer of hope crossing her face. "You know, that's the first time you've talked about what life could be like after my surgery."

"What do you mean?"

"I've been trying to find out what you expect from me, what you envision for us if I survive. You never want to talk about it. It makes me think you don't expect me to be around for the future."

Ben stared at her, stunned. Had he really made her think he didn't want her around? Or even worse, that he didn't want her to survive? He reached for her hand, his eyes intense and focused when he spoke. "Maya, I am so sorry. I never meant to make you feel that way. I guess I've just been afraid to plan for something that has so many unknowns. I hate knowing that you'll be having your surgery right when I have to leave for spring training. I want to be here for you, and talking about it makes me feel like I'm letting you down."

Tears swam in her eyes. "You could never let me down. Besides Kari, no one has ever done so much for me. Not even my own family."

"You miss them."

"I miss who we were before my father promised me to Rishi."

"You know, we could go to India," Ben suggested. "Maybe next off-season, after you've recovered, we can visit them. Assuming they'll let us."

"I don't know if my father will ever forgive me for disobeying him. He feels I've shamed him, that I've shamed the family."

"Supposedly, time heals all wounds."

"Sometimes time makes them deeper," Maya said softly. "I'm just glad Rishi seems to have finally given up on me."

"I guess we should be thankful for the miracles we do have this Christmas."

Maya nodded. "I suppose you're right."

Chapter 32

MAYA LOOKED AT THE MOUNTAIN of presents beneath the Christmas tree, already nervous about whether Ben would like her gift for him or not. She had been creative in coming up with this one.

Unlike last year when she had sat next to Kari on Christmas morning, this year it was Ben who sat on the loveseat beside her. Now that she had already experienced one year of an Evans family Christmas, she had a better idea of what to expect. Ben's older sister, Danielle, lived nearby and had arrived with her husband and two-year-old daughter a little before eight in the morning. Once little Ava was there and saw the presents, the house woke up quickly.

Kari took on the role of Santa's helper, passing gifts around to everyone, occasionally sitting down long enough to open something for herself. Choosing a gift for Kari had been nearly as difficult as buying one for Ben, but Ben had saved her on that one by helping her put together a fun sightseeing package for Washington, DC, along with plane tickets for her to come visit that summer.

They had done something similar for his parents, only for them, the vacation was for Jamaica, a place his mother had mentioned always wanting to visit when she was in DC at Thanksgiving.

By the time Kari handed Ben the present from Maya, he already had quite a stack of various clothing and assorted gifts beside him. He read the card and turned to Maya. He lowered his voice and whispered, "You didn't have to get me anything."

"It isn't much," Maya told him, gripping her hands together.

Ben kept his eyes on hers as he slid a finger beneath the tape and started opening the gift. Then he shifted his attention to the contents beneath the shiny silver paper.

The nerves in Maya's stomach loosened when Ben looked down at the binder she had decorated and laughed. On the front, she had stenciled the words *Game Plan* in large letters. Inside, she had typed her personalized résumés on the various pitchers he had faced during his first season.

"Maya, this is great!"

"Do you really like it?"

"Are you kidding? I'm going to have to hide this from my teammates. They'll all try to steal it."

Relief flowed through her, and she smiled at him. "I couldn't think of anything else to get for you. Usually, if you want something, you just go out and buy it."

"That's true." Ben motioned to his sister. "Hey, Kari. Can you get the present from me to Maya? It should be over there on the left."

Kari shifted a couple of larger gifts aside, picked up a much smaller one, and handed it to Maya. "Here you go."

Maya curled her fingers around the small box. "I think everything you've done for me the past couple of months is more than enough."

"I wanted you to have something to remember this holiday by." Ben motioned to the present impatiently. "Go ahead. Open it."

Maya carefully peeled away the wrapping to reveal a ring box. She looked over at him, confused. If they had really been dating, she would have thought he was giving her an engagement ring. Since they weren't really involved and were already married, she didn't know what to think. The image of him hugging his old girlfriend earlier in the week confused her even further.

"Go on." Ben prodded again.

She lifted the lid, and her breath caught. The ring inside featured a square-cut emerald, not unlike the one her grandmother had given her. This one was slightly larger than her grandmother's, probably five carats, and had two square-cut diamonds flanking the emerald, the platinum band simple and elegant. She also knew from her experience selling her grandmother's ring that it must have cost tens of thousands of dollars.

"Ben, this is beautiful." She lifted her eyes to meet his and shook her head. "But I can't accept this. It's too much."

"No, it's not." Ben took the ring box from her and removed the ring from it himself. "Here. Try it on."

She tried not to notice that he reached for her left hand rather than her right. Then he slipped the ring on her finger and gave her a satisfied smile when it fit. "See, it's like it was made for you."

She looked down at her hand still resting in his, the gem gleaming in the sunlight streaming through the window. Her heart fluttered, and she let herself revel in the joy of wearing the ring Ben had chosen for her. She knew she shouldn't accept it, but she couldn't bring herself to refuse a second time. She looked up at him, certain her love for him reflected in her eyes. "It really is beautiful."

He gave her hand a squeeze, brushed a kiss across her cheek, and said quietly, "So are you."

* * *

"Are you going to tell me what's really going on with you and my brother?" Kari asked.

Maya looked up with a blank expression on her face. "What do you mean?"

"Maya, you're wearing his ring."

Her eyes lowered to the brilliant emerald. "You were there when he gave it to me. It was a Christmas gift. That's all."

"Men don't give jewelry that goes on your ring finger as gifts unless there's something going on," Kari insisted. "So what's going on?"

"Nothing."

Kari studied her friend's face. Either Maya was a better actor than Kari thought, or she truly didn't recognize the sparks snapping between Ben and her. "It's a beautiful ring."

Maya's cheeks flushed slightly when she nodded. "It really is."

* * *

The day had been a dream. She couldn't have ever imagined experiencing a Christmas like this one, everyone happy and welcoming, the love of the Evans family making everything feel like a fairy tale.

The ring Ben had given her remained on her finger. She supposed it was silly, but she felt like if she took it off, the fairy tale might end.

They had all stayed up much later than she normally allowed herself, and even now, Ben and Kari were still visiting with some cousins who had come over for Christmas dinner.

She had wanted to stay up and share in the fun, but exhaustion had finally taken over, enough so that even Ben had suggested she go to bed.

She had expended what little energy she had changing into her pajamas and then had let herself collapse onto the twin bed she had claimed as her own in Kari's room, too tired to follow the rest of her bedtime routine.

The thought that she should at least go brush her teeth registered in her brain, but instead of following through, she slipped beneath the covers and quickly fell asleep.

* * *

Ben awoke from a deep sleep and prepared to kill whoever was pounding on his door at this ridiculously early hour. It had to be an early hour because he hadn't gone to bed until nearly three o'clock this morning, and it was still dark outside.

He squinted against the red lights illuminating the time on his bedside alarm clock: 4:29 a.m.

The pounding continued.

"What?" Ben yelled out grumpily.

"Ben, wake up," Kari called urgently through his locked door. "Something's wrong with Maya."

His mood changed instantly, and he forced his body to sit up. "What?"

"I think she needs to go to the hospital," Kari added, and Ben could hear the worry in her voice.

Throwing the covers back, Ben quickly got up and pulled on the jeans he had discarded on the floor the night before. He grabbed his wallet and keys off his dresser, putting both in his pocket, and then yanked open a drawer to retrieve a sweatshirt. Kari was lifting her hand to knock again when he pulled the door open.

"What's wrong?" Ben asked, already heading for Kari's room.

"I don't know. She rolled over, and I heard her cry out in pain. When I asked her what was wrong, she didn't answer. I got up to check on her, and her face was all pale."

The light was already on in Kari's room, and Maya was curled up in a ball. He could see the perspiration on her face, not unlike when she had caught that virus after he had forgotten to pick her up. He put a hand on her forehead. She wasn't running a fever, but she winced in pain when he touched her.

Ben turned to Kari. "Do me a favor and go find her pain pills."

Kari looked at him, confused, but she stood and headed for the bathroom. "Maya? Can you hear me?"

"Mmmm." Her eyes fluttered slightly, but she didn't open them.

Ben fought back the sense of panic that tried to surface, and he took her hand in his. "Maya, you need to wake up."

Her eyes fluttered again, this time opening enough that she could peer at him beneath her lashes.

"Did you take your pills last night?"

Her eyebrow furrowed in the way they did when she was concentrating. "Don't remember."

Kari rushed back in with Maya's pill organizer in her hand. "Is this what you wanted?"

"Yeah." Ben shifted and took it from her, flipping the compartment open from last night to reveal all of Maya's pills still inside. "I think we found the problem."

He started to hand it back to her and then noticed that the two previous compartments were also still full.

"What is it?" Kari asked.

"It looks like she hasn't been taking her medicine."

"I saw her take her pain medicine with dinner last night."

Ben shook his head. "The pain medicine is the only one she doesn't take with the others." He dug his keys out of his pocket. "Go pull Mom's car around. I'm going to take her to the ER."

Kari grabbed the keys from him and headed downstairs. As soon as she left, Ben stuffed the medicine dispenser in his hoodie pocket and pulled back Maya's covers. Then he leaned down and picked her up, grabbing the top blanket to wrap her in. By the time he made his way down the stairs and out the front door, Kari had already pulled into the driveway and was waiting with the passenger side door open.

"Thanks," Ben told her, helping Maya into the car and buckling her in himself. He closed the door and circled to the driver's side. "I'll call you as soon as I know anything."

"I can take her. You hate hospitals."

"I've got this. Besides, someone needs to tell Mom and Dad what's going on."

Kari looked at Maya helplessly and then back at Ben. "Okay, but promise you'll call me."

"I promise." Ben got in and pulled out of the driveway. He glanced over at Maya, and again, a sense of panic crept through him. Her eyes were closed, and her color was too pale. Fighting against feelings of helplessness, he sped out of his neighborhood. When he reached the hospital, he pulled alongside the curb in front of the ER instead of parking. Then he hurried around to lift her out of the car, his concern heightening when she fell limply against him.

He kicked the car door closed and rushed through the sliding glass doors, making a beeline for the check-in counter. Urgency and panic filled his voice. "I need a doctor."

The nurse took one look at Maya and immediately picked up the phone, asking Ben questions as she did so. When the nurse asked Ben if Maya had taken any drugs, he nodded. "She's a cancer patient. She takes a lot of pills."

"I'll need a list of what she's on. And I'll need her insurance information."

"I think the problem is that she forgot to take her meds. I have most of her pills with me, but as soon as you get her into a room, I can call my sister and have her read me the prescription bottles."

The automatic door beside the reception desk opened, and another nurse appeared and motioned to Ben. "Bring her back here."

Ben followed and laid Maya on the bed in a curtained examination room. She moaned as though in pain, and her eyes fluttered open for a brief moment. The nurse nudged Ben aside and started taking Maya's vital signs. The woman from the reception desk entered and handed him a clipboard and pen.

"The doctor is going to be right here, but please make sure you list the medications she's on. He'll need that."

"Okay." Ben called Kari and had her read the names and doses of all of Maya's prescriptions to him. Once he was off the phone, he started filling out the other required forms, reminding himself to write Maya's last name as Evans since that's how it was listed on the insurance.

As he continued to write, the nurse started firing off more questions. "How long has she been like this? When did she last eat? Does she have any preexisting medical conditions?"

Ben handed her the paperwork with as much medical history as he knew about. He was explaining Maya's cancer treatments to the nurse when the doctor walked in.

"What have we got?" the doctor asked the nurse, immediately moving to Maya's side.

The nurse rattled off vital signs and other medical jargon Ben barely understood. He kept his eyes on Maya, feeling hollow and useless. The doctor gave the nurse some instructions and turned to Ben for the first time. "I'm Dr. Wilson."

"Ben Evans."

"You're her husband?"

"That's right," Ben answered, struck by his automatic admission as much as he was by the thought that his wife was the most important thing in his world right now. "Is she going to be okay?"

The doctor answered Ben's question with a question of his own. "You said she's undergoing cancer treatments. What is her prognosis?"

"She's in a clinical trial at George Washington University Hospital."

"Is there any chance she might have deliberately overdosed?"

The question and the straightforward manner in which it was asked stunned Ben. "You mean, try to commit suicide? No way. Maya's determined to fight this cancer, and her doctor thinks the treatments are working." Ben pulled her pill dispenser out of his pocket and handed it to the doctor. "She uses this to keep track of her pills. It looks like she hasn't taken the last few doses."

"Do you know when she last took any medications?"

"My sister said she remembered her taking her pain meds yesterday at dinner, but as for the others, the last time I'm sure she took them was Christmas Eve."

"That could definitely cause a problem." The doctor turned back to the nurse and ordered a rush on Maya's blood work.

"Is she going to be okay?" Ben asked again, silently praying for the answer he wanted to hear.

"Her vital signs are pretty good. We'll get an IV in her and see what we can do about getting her back on track," the doctor told him. "I'd like to talk to her oncologist, but at this hour, it may take a little while to get ahold of him. I'd like to admit her so we can keep her under observation for the next day or so."

Despite the doctor's straightforward answer, worry pulsed through Ben. He stepped aside when the nurse arrived to draw blood and set up an IV, and he wished there was something he could do besides watch helplessly. As soon as the nurse finished, she said, "I'll be back in to check on you in a little while. Let me know if you need anything."

"Thanks." Ben watched her go. Then he shifted closer, took Maya's hand in his, and decided it couldn't hurt to pray.

Chapter 33

MAYA CRACKED HER EYES AND saw the room spinning for several seconds before it finally settled and the image of her hospital room sharpened.

"Maya?" Ben's voice sounded through the cotton in her brain, and she felt him take her hand. "Hey. How are you feeling?"

"What happened?"

"You gave us quite a scare." When she did nothing more than stare at him, he added, "I guess your body doesn't like it when you forget to take your medicine."

She noticed the IV line running into her arm and asked, "How long have I been here?"

"Since early this morning. The doctor said he's waiting on one more test result, but so far, everything is looking good. He wants to admit you overnight, but he thinks you'll be able to go home tomorrow."

Maya let her eyes droop back closed for a moment, her hand still in Ben's. When she heard someone enter the room, she forced her eyes open again to see a nurse in green scrubs approaching her bedside.

"Oh, good. You're awake," she said before addressing Ben. "An orderly should be here any minute to transfer her to her room."

"Did the doctor get the last test results?"

"Yes. It confirmed what we suspected, that the combination of stopping her regular treatments and forgetting to take her medication caused the problem. He spoke with Dr. Schuster in Washington, and they agreed that we should keep her overnight to make sure she's stabilized before we send her home."

Maya wasn't sure she heard Ben right when he asked, "Can I stay here with her?"

"That depends. What's your relationship to her?"

A man who looked to be in his early twenties pulled back the curtain, revealing several people standing close by. Ben kept his focus on the nurse and answered, "I'm her husband."

The orderly, who had just come in, pushed a gurney toward Maya. Then he looked over at Ben, and his eyes lit up. "Ben Evans? Oh my gosh! It is you!"

Maya watched as recognition dawned and Ben's face lit up too. "Russell! How are you?"

"I'm doing good." Russell shifted his attention to Maya. "Did I just hear you say you're married?"

Maya expected to see some kind of negative reaction to the question, but Ben took it in stride, lowering his voice when he said, "We've been keeping it pretty quiet."

"Well, congratulations." Russell stepped farther into the room and let the curtain close behind him. "Let's get your wife moved to her room."

Maya tried to help shift her weight onto the gurney, and then she listened to the conversation between Ben and Russell as they discussed the changes in their lives since high school.

While the nurses helped Maya settle into her room, Ben called Kari to give her the latest update. Then he took the seat beside Maya, and she found comfort in knowing he was going to stay.

* * *

Kari opened the front door, her eyes narrowing in confusion when she saw the man standing on the doorstep, a long black overcoat buttoned over his business suit, a briefcase in his hand.

The man in front of her pushed his round glasses farther back up on his nose. Kari guessed him to be in his midthirties, and she was quite certain she had never seen him before.

"Can I help you?"

"I'm looking for Maya Evans."

Kari stiffened. "I'm sorry, who are you?"

"Colin Magnor." He reached under the bulk of his coat and dug a business card out of his suit jacket pocket. "Immigration and Naturalization Service."

Dozens of thoughts raced through her mind, none of them good. "What do you want with Maya?"

"I'm sorry. I'm not at liberty to discuss that. May I speak with Mrs. Evans, please?"

"I'm afraid she isn't here right now."

"Do you know when you expect her back?"

"Actually, I don't."

Irritation crossed Colin's brow. "Keeping me from seeing her is not going to help her case."

"I'm not lying to you." Kari struggled for a moment, debating whether she should give this man any information about her friend. "But unless you want to tell me about this case of yours, I can't say that I'm inclined to help you either."

Before the man could respond, Kari's father stepped up behind her. "Kari, is everything okay?"

"This is Colin Magnor from immigration. He wants to talk to Maya Evans," Kari said, repeating the last name the man had used to make sure her father comprehended the possible implications of his presence.

Kari saw the understanding in her father's expression, but she was surprised when he pulled the door open wider and motioned the man inside. "Please come in. I'm sure it will be more comfortable to talk when we're out of the cold."

Colin hesitated briefly before giving an assenting nod and stepping over the threshold. Steve introduced himself and led the way into the living room, motioning for everyone to sit down. "Can you tell us what this is all about? We've never known Maya to have any issues with immigration."

"Mr. Evans, as her father-in-law, surely you understand that she should have informed us of her change in marital status."

"That status changed only a few weeks ago, and from what I understand, it didn't impact her residential status. She's already a permanent resident."

"Yes, but she could use her new status as the spouse of a US citizen to apply for citizenship earlier than she would have otherwise been eligible."

"Has she applied for citizenship?"

"Not yet."

"And have you received any indication that she is going to?"

"We received a call that a citizenship application could be pending shortly."

"Forgive me, but I don't understand why immigration would bother themselves with a foreign national who is living here legally and has not broken any laws."

"Yet."

"Just because I own a car, it doesn't mean I should get a ticket because I *might* speed. Why don't you tell us what's really going on here," Steve suggested. "Maya's health is not good, and I am not going to sit by and have her stressed over a bunch of innuendos."

Colin tensed and seemed to contemplate for a moment. "The state department received a request from the Indian ambassador that we investigate a possibly fraudulent marriage for one Maya Gupta, aka Maya Evans."

"As we just discussed, Maya was already a permanent resident. How could her marriage be fraudulent?"

"Because the Indian embassy processed the request to revoke her visa three days before her marriage."

"On what grounds?"

Colin shifted uneasily. "The ambassador wasn't willing to share that information with us."

"Then let me enlighten you," Steve said calmly. "According to my son, this whole situation stems from a jealous Indian man who is having a temper tantrum because the woman he planned to marry refused to marry him, a man, I might add, who tried to marry Maya when she was only thirteen, well under the legal age, even in India."

The formality that Colin had been wearing like a shield softened. "I thought it might be something like that. The accusation still remains valid, however, that your son could have married Maya to keep her from being deported."

"As I mentioned before, they were married several weeks ago. Why is this coming up now?"

"Our original investigation indicated that Maya had a prior connection to Ben Evans through his sister here. Our report seemed to satisfy the state department." He hesitated. "Then the complaint was reinstated when some photographs of Ben Evans and a woman named Cassie Birchfield circulated on several social media sites. We were able to confirm that the photos were taken three days ago."

"That can't be right," Steve insisted. "Ben has hardly left the house since he's been home."

"His credit card activity verifies he was at the mall when the photograph with Miss Birchfield was taken. I'm sorry, but I don't have a choice but to proceed with this investigation."

* * *

Ben dozed in the chair beside Maya's bed, no longer sure how many hours he had been in that same position. The hands on the wall clock hadn't moved since they'd arrived, and it was in obvious need of repair. His cell phone had died sometime during the night, so he had also lost his normal way of keeping time.

Earlier in the morning, the doctor had stopped by and determined that Maya's medication levels were back to normal. Even though she was well enough to go home, he had insisted on monitoring her for several more hours just to be safe. Ben hadn't argued.

Maya's hand fisted beneath his, and he recognized the gesture, knowing she must be in pain. He opened his eyes and shifted to find Maya watching him. "I'll call the nurse. She said to let her know if you needed something for pain."

Ben reached over the edge of the bed and pressed the call button. He watched Maya close her eyes again, and Ben guessed by the little wrinkle in the center of her forehead that she was trying to block out the pain.

He waited impatiently for the nurse to arrive and then for the medicine to take effect. When Maya finally appeared to be comfortable again, Ben leaned back in his chair.

"I'm glad you're here," Maya said, her voice raspy.

Ben sat up again to see her staring at him. "Where else would I be? Like it or not, you're stuck with me."

Her lips curved slightly.

"I had Kari take the car when she and Mom came to visit yesterday, but she'll pick us up when you get released this afternoon."

"I'm so sorry about all of this."

"What happened?" Ben asked, his voice holding concern rather than accusation. "It's not like you to forget your medicine."

"I don't know. I think it must have been a combination of not being in my normal routine and letting myself get wrapped up in getting ready for Christmas."

Realizing that most of her Christmas preparations were likely spent making his present, he kept his voice light. "At least the doctors said everything will be okay. In fact, if all goes well, we'll be home in time for dinner."

"I hope so. I'm tired of hospitals."

Ben looked around the room with distaste. He put his hand over hers and squeezed. "I don't blame you."

* * *

"Were you able to get ahold of Ben?" Kari asked her dad.

"No. His cell phone is going straight to voice mail, and when I tried calling Maya's room, there wasn't an answer."

"What are we going to do? You don't really think Maya will get deported, do you?"

"I don't think she'll get deported, but I am worried about what this investigation might do to both her and your brother."

"What do you mean?"

"Maya's health is fragile enough as it is. Like I told Mr. Magnor, I'm worried about what the stress of an investigation might do to her. As for Ben, this isn't the kind of publicity he's looking for."

"This is all my fault," Kari said, her voice guilt-ridden. "If I hadn't tricked Ben into letting Maya stay in his apartment, none of this ever would have happened."

"Ben didn't have to marry her. That was his choice," Steve reminded her. "For now, all we can do is pray that Cassie will tell the truth when Mr. Magnor interviews her. If she admits that she and Ben broke up months ago, this investigation should go away before it can do any real damage."

"I hope so."

"Regardless, I suggest we don't bring this up until after Ben and Maya are home from the hospital."

"Agreed."

Chapter 34

BEN FOLLOWED THE ORDERLY AS the man pushed Maya in the wheelchair toward the hospital exit. He looked down at Maya now, amazed that she could transform so quickly. Yesterday morning she had been lethargic and unresponsive, and today she looked completely normal again. Even though she seemed perfectly fine, Ben couldn't quite chase away the image of her in Kari's room when he couldn't fully wake her.

The orderly continued down a long hall, and Ben asked, "Is it strange being pushed in a wheelchair when it isn't Henry standing behind you?"

"Actually, it is," Maya admitted.

They turned the corner toward the main entrance to find a crowd of what appeared to be reporters clustered in the main lobby. Ben started to ask what was going on, but before he could voice the words, a tall man on the edge of the crowd noticed them and pointed. "There he is!"

Cameras immediately flashed, and the crowd moved toward them.

Stunned that he would garner such attention during the off-season, Ben continued forward, thinking that maybe if he walked away from Maya, the reporters would leave her alone.

Then the questions started. "How long have you been married? Where did you meet? Why the secrecy? What's going on with Cassie Birchfield?"

Ben froze, disgusted that the press was trying to get a rise out of him by bringing up an old girlfriend. Resentment bubbled when he looked back at Maya and the dazed look on her face.

The orderly kept moving forward, hesitating only long enough to wave at the nearest security guard.

The guard stepped forward, trying to make a path for them. "Hey, let these people through."

A reporter pushed past Ben and stepped right in front of the wheelchair. "What's your name, sweetheart?"

Maya didn't speak but instead shifted to look at Ben.

The fear in her eyes was enough to heat his temper and make his blood boil. He stepped forward. "Hey, back off."

"Did you start dating before you and Heather Wallenberg broke up? Is that why you kept your marriage secret?" another reporter asked. "What about Cassie Birchfield? She said you were going out with her after you got married."

Ben clamped his teeth together, refusing to answer. Instead, he pushed through the crowd in the hope of shielding Maya from the cameras and the questions.

The next few minutes passed in a blur of security guards pushing reporters out of their path and the orderly trying to weave the wheelchair past them while questions continued to punctuate the air.

When they finally made it outside, Kari was waiting for them.

Ben opened the front door and helped Maya into the car. Then he climbed into the backseat behind her.

"What is going on?" Kari asked the minute they were all inside their mother's car. "Is this because of Cassie?"

"Cassie? Why would the press be asking about her?"

Kari looked at him sheepishly. "Because she posted a photo of the two of you on Twitter and Facebook and said you were back together."

"She *what*?"

Ben saw the look pass between Kari and Maya, the one that clearly said Maya had known all about it. He turned from his sister and aimed his question at Maya. "You knew about this?"

Kari didn't let her answer. "I'm the one who saw it, but it was on Christmas Eve. Maya didn't want it to ruin your holiday, so we didn't say anything." She started the car and looked back at Ben, confused. "If this isn't about Cassie, then what are the reporters doing here?"

"Someone found out that Maya and I are married." Ben leaned forward between the two front seats and jerked a thumb toward the reporters. "They all want the inside scoop."

"Oh man." Kari started the car and pulled away from the curb. "How could this have happened?"

"Someone must have overheard me talking at the hospital," Ben said with a shake of his head. "Every time I turned around, someone was asking what my relationship was to Maya."

Kari's eyes widened. "And you told them?"

"Well, yeah. How else was I going to stay with her?"

"This is all my fault," Maya said softly.

Ben put his hand on her shoulder. "It's not your fault."

"I'm so sorry," she continued as though he hadn't spoken. "If I hadn't forgotten to take my medicine, this never would have happened."

"Maya, don't worry about any of this right now," Ben told her. "For now, let's just try to enjoy the rest of our visit here. It will only be a matter of time before this all blows over."

* * *

Ben helped Maya to the living room couch, but before he could sit down beside her, his father called him into the kitchen.

"I'll be right back," Ben told her. "Do you need anything?"

"No, thanks."

Reluctantly, Ben left her alone and headed into the kitchen, where his parents and Kari were waiting for him. "What's up?"

His father peered through the doorway to check on Maya. Then he motioned for Ben to sit down at the kitchen table with everyone else. "Have a seat."

Anticipating a discussion on the press camped outside, he dropped into a chair. "I'm really sorry about all of this. I'll call the PR guy at work to see if he can figure out a way to call these guys off."

"That's a good idea, but there's something else we need to talk about."

"What's that?"

"A man from immigration showed up looking for Maya this morning. It looks like her former fiancé is still trying to force her to move back to India. Because of the photos of you and Cassie that have been circulating on the Internet this week, they have decided to open an investigation into the validity of your marriage."

"What?" Ben looked around the table, waiting for someone to tell him this was some insane joke. The grim expressions staring back at him told him there was nothing funny about the situation. "How is this possible?"

His father sat beside him and explained what the immigration officer had told them that morning. When he finished, Ben finally said, "Then as soon as he talks to Cassie, this whole thing should resolve itself. I ran into her the other day at the mall, but other than that, we haven't talked since we broke up last January."

"I thought the same thing. Unfortunately, she's the one who posted the photo and a tweet that said, 'Back together again, this time forever.'"

"You've got to be kidding me." Ben dragged a hand over his face. "This is a nightmare."

"Ben, I'm sorry I didn't tell you about it when I first saw it," Kari said. "I had no idea it might be important."

"Don't worry about it. The real question is, what am I going to tell Maya?"

"Tell her not to worry about the press," Jane told him. "We'll do what we can to shield her from it."

"If immigration is insisting on an investigation, Maya is going to find out," Ben reminded her.

"Before you worry her about all of this, call your team and see what they can do to help," Steve suggested.

"First I'm going to call Cassie." Ben retrieved his phone and called, annoyed when she didn't answer. He left a message asking her to take the photos down. Then he turned back to his parents.

Jane glanced at her watch. "It's only five o'clock. Maybe you should call your publicist now to see if he has any suggestions."

Ben nodded. He dialed the number, not bothering to step away from the table as he normally would when making a phone call. Whether he wanted them to or not, his family had clearly decided to stand behind him through whatever he and Maya were about to face.

The phone rang a half dozen times, and Ben was just about to hang up when Trent answered with a breathless, "Hello."

"Hey, Trent. Sorry to bother you, but I need a favor."

"What's up, Ben?"

"Remember when you said that if I ever had any problems with the press I should give you a call?"

"Yeah." Trent sounded hesitant. "What's wrong?"

"At this point, it might be easier to give you a list of what's right. It's probably shorter."

Now resignation sounded through the phone. "Just start at the beginning."

* * *

Maya looked helplessly out the window, feeling very much alone despite the multitude of voices coming from the kitchen. The half dozen cars parked on the street and the photographers clustered on the sidewalk outside Ben's home proved that she wasn't as isolated as she felt.

She thought of the stunned look on Ben's face when he had realized the reporters at the hospital were there because of them. Because of her. He had recovered quickly enough, becoming protective of her as they'd exited the hospital, but that didn't change the facts. The above-reproach reputation he had worked so hard to maintain had been severely damaged, and it was her fault.

The photo with him and his old girlfriend might have garnered some attention when it hit the Internet, but it wouldn't have been much of a story without the additional news that Ben was married and had been at the time the photo was taken.

She felt silly now to have thought Ben had really gone out with Cassie when she'd seen that photo. She should have known he wasn't the type to go behind her back with someone else, even if their relationship was platonic.

"Hey." Ben's voice sounded a moment before his hand came down to rest on her shoulder. "What are you doing?"

She looked at him. "Just wondering how long they will wait for you to come outside."

"Once it gets dark, they'll give up. It's cold out there."

"I'm so sorry. This never would have happened . . ."

Ben sat down and turned her so she was facing him. "Stop apologizing. It will all work out."

"Your publicist can't be happy about this."

"He'll handle it. This is what he gets paid for."

"I imagine he'll want a raise as soon as these stories start hitting the news."

"They already have," Ben said, his voice tight.

Immediately distressed, Maya asked, "What are they saying?"

Ben shrugged. "It's nothing worth stressing over."

"Are you trying to convince me or yourself?"

He didn't respond, but Maya could tell by the look on Ben's face that he was worried.

His mother walked into the living room and said, "Ben, Maya, dinner's ready."

"We'll be right there," Ben told her. Then he took Maya's hand and tugged her toward the dining room. "Don't think about the reporters. Let's just try to enjoy the rest of our time here. Like I said before, this will all blow over."

Chapter 35

"THIS ISN'T GOING TO BLOW over," Trent said with a frustrated shake of his head. Several recent articles about Ben and Maya were spread out on his desk. "Heather has been talking to the press, and she confirmed that the two of you only broke up a week before you got married. Cassie isn't answering my calls, and she hasn't taken down the photo or her comment saying you were dating again."

Ben lowered himself into the chair across from Trent. This was not how he wanted to start his New Year's Eve. "How did they find out when I got married?"

"My guess is that one of the reporters found a source at the courthouse."

"Now what?" Ben asked. "We had reporters camped outside our apartment when we got home yesterday. I had to hire a car to take Maya to the hospital this morning so they would follow me here instead of bothering her. I don't know if she can take this kind of stress. I still haven't told her about the immigration investigation."

"I hate to break it to you, but the easiest way to get the press to go away is to give them what they want."

"Which is?"

"Your story." Trent rested his elbows on his desk and leaned forward. "They want to know how you met, how you fell in love. They want to see you together so they can capture photos of the happy couple."

"And when they ask about Heather and Cassie?"

"Tell them the truth . . ." His voice trailed off, and he gave Ben a quizzical look. "What is the truth anyway?"

Ben stared at him for a moment. How could he explain his relationship with Maya to Trent when he barely understood it himself? "It's a little complicated."

"Why don't you start with telling me how you met her. I assume you met her before you broke up with Heather."

Ben nodded. "I actually met her about a year ago. She's my sister's friend."

"So you met her before you even started dating Heather."

"Yeah, but I was dating Cassie then."

"When did you and Cassie break up?"

"Early January. At the time, Cassie thought I was interested in someone else, but I actually didn't start dating anyone else until I met Heather in May."

"That's good. We can imply that you and Maya were dating last spring, broke up, and then after your breakup with Heather, you realized you were in love and decided to get married." He jotted down some notes on the pad of paper in front of him as he spoke. "The press is still going to jump on the timeline though. Going from dating one girl to marrying another in one week is pretty extreme."

"Heather is exaggerating a bit on when we broke up. I told her I wanted to take a break a week earlier, but she didn't want to hear it. When she followed me to DC, I had to get blunt about it."

"I hate to break it to you, Ben, but two weeks is not exactly a long engagement either," Trent said. "Any explanation of why you married Maya so quickly?"

Ben thought of Rishi. "A couple of reasons, but I'm not sure we want them in the press."

"Her health?"

"That's one thing," Ben admitted. "I guess you could say that I didn't want to see Maya go through her treatments alone."

"Is there something else?"

"In a way, it's the immigration thing." Ben explained Maya's previous engagement and the arrival of her former fiancé.

"Is that the real reason you got married?"

Slowly, Ben shook his head. He tried to think of a way to explain how he had come to the decision, but he still wasn't quite sure he understood it himself. Before he could try to put words together, images of Maya poured through his mind. The way she looked when he took her to his teammate's wedding, the satisfaction he felt when he slipped the ring on her finger Christmas morning, the conviction in her voice when they debated baseball.

After several seconds of silence, Ben straightened his shoulders. He couldn't explain the truth of why he had gotten married, but the reason he wanted to protect his marriage was incredibly simple. "I'm married to Maya because I love her."

Trent studied him in silence for a moment and then nodded. "I guess that says it all."

More than a little shaken, Ben found himself agreeing. "I guess it does."

* * *

Maya looked out the window of the rented car and saw the reporters by the front door of the apartment complex. Using the same ploy she'd used when avoiding Rishi, she asked the driver to drop her off by the elevator in the garage and found, to her dismay, that several more reporters were waiting there as well.

"Do you want me to walk you to the elevator, miss?"

She started to say yes, but then she saw Ben getting out of his car. This group of reporters must have been following him around. Noticing the hired car, Ben crossed to it and opened the back door for Maya.

He offered his thanks to the driver and reached for Maya's hand. "Come on. Let's get out of here before we get cornered."

"I hope that's possible," Maya muttered. Gripping Ben's hand, she climbed out of the car and followed him past the reporters, who immediately started throwing questions at him and snapping photos. Ben's only response was to pull his hand free of Maya's and slip his arm around her shoulders to draw her closer.

To her surprise, instead of heading for the elevator, he steered her to his car and opened the passenger door. She started to ask where they were going, but the presence of the reporters made her bite back the question. Ben helped her into the car and then claimed his own seat, not wasting any time in starting the engine and pulling out of the garage. As soon as they made it past the reporters, they both breathed a sigh of relief.

"Ben, what are we going to do about all of this? You can't keep living this way."

He glanced sideways at her. "I talked to Trent today. His suggestion is to tell the press our story."

"What do you mean, tell our story?"

"He's going to set up a press conference, but basically, he said we need to make it look like we're married for real."

Her eyebrows drew together. "How are we supposed to do that?"

"Just promise not to slap me if I kiss you in public." Immediately, Maya felt her cheeks flush, and she noticed the wry humor in Ben's voice.

Before she could comment, he added, "I also thought that it might be nice if you let me take you out to lunch after we finish with the jewelers."

"What jewelers?"

"Trent thinks it's time I start wearing a wedding ring." When Ben pulled up to a stoplight, he shifted and reached for her left hand, where the emerald ring gleamed from her finger. "We should probably get you some kind of wedding band to go with this too."

"Do you really think it's a good idea for us to be seen ring shopping two months after our wedding?"

"It's part of our story. We chose not to wear wedding rings because we were protecting our privacy. Now that everyone knows about us, it's time to take that next step."

What he said made sense, she supposed, but she wasn't sure about the idea of having the media scrutinizing their marriage or possibly discovering the real reasons Ben had married her. She looked over at him and found herself wondering again about his real motivations. An instant later, she was scrutinizing her own. Why had she married Ben?

Admittedly, she had been lonely, but if company had been all she wanted, she could have married Rishi. Protecting herself from an unwanted marriage was the most logical of the various reasons she could think of, but looking back now, she could admit that Ben had swept her up in a kind of fairy tale and had given her hope for her future. It was the same kind of hope she had grown up expecting she would find when her parents arranged her marriage, right up until she learned her father wasn't going to give her any say in her future.

Hope. Promise. Love. Ben made her feel all of those things. Everything seemed to have happened so naturally, but now she found herself afraid of all three of those cherished feelings. What would she do, she wondered, if they couldn't convince the media that their marriage was real? What would happen if they learned that Ben didn't feel the same way about her as she felt about him?

Before she could pursue that thought, they arrived, and Ben escorted her up a short flight of stairs and into the jewelry store. Thirty minutes later, she had a narrow wedding band on her finger that beautifully complemented the cut of her emerald ring.

Ben had narrowed his choices down to three. He held up a plain platinum band that was a thicker version of her own. "What do you think of this one?"

"All of these will work," Maya reminded him gently. "Do you like it?"

He looked down at it for a moment, then pushed it onto his ring finger. "This is the one. It's almost a perfect match to yours."

Maya stared down at the thick band contrasting against his tanned fingers. She felt a little jolt knowing it was a symbol linking them together—linking them in exactly what, she still wasn't completely sure though.

Ben pulled a credit card free of his wallet and slid it to the clerk, who was standing discreetly behind the counter.

The man stepped forward. "Will this be all, sir?"

"Yes, thank you." Ben signed the credit card slip when it was offered. He placed his left hand on the glass countertop beside Maya's, looking down at both of their hands. "It looks like we're really official now."

"Sir, perhaps you would like to use the rear entrance when you leave."

"What?" Ben asked.

"Your presence has drawn quite a crowd out front." He looked at Ben apologetically. "I'm sorry. I don't know how the press found out you were here."

"It's not your fault. They probably followed us," Ben said without any element of surprise in his voice. He looked at Maya. "Are you ready to face them? We might as well get this over with."

"What if I say the wrong thing?"

"Don't say anything. We'll give them a chance to snap some photos and head for the car. Then we can grab some lunch and pretend we aren't surrounded." Ben gave her hand a squeeze, but it did nothing to settle the nerves warring in her stomach.

Maya forced herself to follow Ben toward the door. She noticed his hesitation when he looked out the glass door and saw the half dozen reporters outside. Then the door opened, and they stepped outside like two sheep entering the wolves' den.

Chapter 36

THE RUMBLE OF QUESTIONS STARTED the moment they stepped outside. Rather than answer, Ben simply drew Maya to his side, stood at the store entrance for several seconds while cameras flashed, and then led Maya past the reporters and out onto the street to his car.

Feeling crowded, he helped Maya into the passenger's seat and struggled to keep quiet as reporters continued to throw insulting questions at him. He knew Trent wanted him to wait to address the press until he could set up a press conference, but when several people accused him of abandoning his moral values, his temper flared.

Barely holding on to a thread of reason, he turned to face the cameras and the people standing behind them. Drawing a steadying breath, Ben spoke clearly, despite the anger raging through him. "You are all making a lot of assumptions with very few facts."

"Why don't you give us the facts?" one man asked snidely.

"At the moment, I need to get my wife home, but a press conference is being set up, and at that time, I will gladly set the record straight." Ben pushed his way past two reporters so he could circle the car. Without another word, he climbed in and gratefully pulled away from the curb.

* * *

Maya knew Ben had hoped the press would back off after he told them about the impending press conference, but it seemed to have only piqued their interest. They decided against going out to lunch, instead heading straight back home. When they pulled into the apartment parking garage, the number of reporters seemed to have increased.

Protectively, Ben helped her out of the car and through the crowd to the elevator. Even though the elevator was empty, neither of them spoke until they were safely inside their apartment.

"I really am sorry you weren't able to keep all of this a secret," Maya began as soon as Ben closed the door behind them. Before she could continue farther into the apartment, Ben stopped, his hand still grasping hers. When she looked up at him, she was surprised by the serious expression on his face.

"I'll admit I was worried about word getting out that we got married so soon after I broke up with Heather." He paused, his eyes staying steady on hers. "But I've never regretted marrying you."

Maya's heart tripped once at his words. It skipped another beat when Ben slid his free hand around her waist and shifted her into his arms. When he lowered his head and brushed his lips across hers, her heart didn't know what to do.

She heard her own sharp intake of breath, felt a shiver across her skin where he brushed his hand over the nape of her neck. When he pulled her closer and deepened the kiss, she marveled that her bones didn't simply dissolve into a puddle with her tangled nerves.

Her body trembled, and she leaned into him. Then her mind simply shut off as she let herself fall into the achingly sweet sensation of being kissed by the man she loved.

* * *

This was what he had always wanted. That thought circled through Ben's mind as his lips moved slow and easy over Maya's. Love, piercing and vital, shot through him. No longer was Maya his sister's best friend or a cancer victim. She wasn't a publicity problem to be solved or the girl without a home. She might have been all of those things once, but right now, in this moment, she was simply the woman he cherished.

Ben's heart filled with emotions he had never before experienced, emotions he couldn't even name. When he drew back, his eyes met hers, searching for some sign that she had been as affected by the kiss as he had.

She stared for a moment, her cheeks flushed, her eyes bright. Then she spoke in a raspy whisper. "We aren't in public."

Realizing she was referring to his earlier comment about kissing her in public, he couldn't help but smile. "Maybe I wanted to practice."

The corner of her lips curved slightly, and Ben took the half smile as a good sign. He leaned down to kiss her again, hesitating when his lips were just a breath away from hers. He lowered his voice and added, "Besides, we are married."

She gave a helpless little nod that gave his ego a healthy boost. Then his lips were on hers again, and his heart felt like it might explode from his overwhelming emotions. He was completely absorbed in her when he felt his phone vibrating in his pocket, an accompanying ring interrupting the private moment. Ben groaned in frustration and shifted so he could silence the phone. Then he noticed it was Trent calling.

"I'm sorry." Ben took a step back but still kept his left hand on Maya's waist as he lifted his phone. "I should get this. It's Trent."

Maya simply watched him as he answered the call, her body leaning limply against his.

"Hey, Trent. What's up?"

"We're all set. Sorry for the short notice, but the press conference is in two hours."

"Two hours?" Ben repeated incredulously. "It's New Year's Eve."

"I know it's quick, but we've got to get these stories turned in our favor before they get any more out of hand. Besides, if we put this behind us, you and Maya can start your new year off right."

"I guess that's one way of looking at it."

"You should also know that the guy from immigration will be there this afternoon. You and Maya will be meeting with him right after the press conference."

"You've been busy."

"You know it. A car will pick you up in an hour and a half to take you to the hotel where we're holding the press conference."

"Okay. I guess we'll see you there." Ben hung up the phone and turned to Maya.

"What was that all about?"

"We are about to become a very public couple." Ben repeated the conversation to her, deliberately leaving out the part about immigration. Knowing that he had to tell her what was really going on, he led her to the couch and gently pulled her down to sit beside him. "There's something else I need to tell you about."

"It sounds serious. What is it?"

"When you were in the hospital in Cincinnati, a man showed up from immigration."

Fear immediately shone in her eyes. "Immigration? Am I being deported?"

"No, but you were right about Rishi trying to get your visa revoked. The process started right before we got married. Now we have to convince immigration that we didn't get married to keep you from getting deported."

"So we have to lie."

Instantly, Ben stiffened. He prided himself on being honest, and he knew he would be telling the truth if he said he was married to Maya because he loved her. He had assumed she felt the same way.

He could admit to himself that the possibility of her being deported had edged him into this situation, but Maya's comment sliced through him as he considered a deeper meaning: that Maya's feelings didn't mirror his own.

His lips still warm from hers, a reminder of how she had responded to his kiss, he looked at her uncertainly. His parents had been so sure that Maya loved him. Had they all misread the signals?

How could he tell her that being married to her was what he truly wanted, that he wouldn't be lying when expressing his feelings about her? How could he explain that sometime over the past two months, he had fallen completely, hopelessly in love with her?

Despite the pain her comment caused him, he knew he wouldn't desert her now, regardless of her reasons. He stood up stiffly. "Maybe you should just let me do the talking."

Chapter 37

BEN LOOKED OUT AT THE sea of reporters in the hotel meeting room, his palms sweating. A portable screen separated them from the rest of the room, which was buzzing with excitement and filled with several dozen reporters, many with additional cameramen, both the still-photo variety as well as the live version. Four television cameras were situated around the room, the crews claiming the clear vantage points of the portable stage.

A linen-draped table sat in the center of the stage, with three cordless microphones lying on top and three padded chairs evenly spaced behind it. Several people were seated off to the side of the stage, and Ben recognized two of his teammates and their wives. His heart lifted a little when he saw Gavin give him a thumbs-up.

Having allies in the audience helped steady his nerves a little, but he could feel his breathing growing shallow and his palms sweating. He couldn't say what worried him more, the prospect of sharing such an important piece of his personal life with so many reporters or the idea of allowing Maya to know his true feelings.

Foolishness and fear had brought him to this point. He had let himself accept his mother's conviction that Maya was in love with him, and wanting it to be true, he had let himself hope for it without daring to do anything to confirm her feelings or declare his own. Could his mother have mistaken Maya's gratitude for love? Had he?

Maya shifted beside him, but Ben kept his eyes on the reporters. Then she slipped her hand into his. His attention immediately shifted to her. Not once in their months together could he remember her ever taking his hand. Always before, he had initiated any kind of physical contact between them. The simple gesture worked wonders on his nerves, and he felt a new spurt of hope.

But his hope was immediately replaced by concern. Her face was alarmingly pale, and he noticed a slight tremor work through her body. "Are you okay?"

"I think so." She gestured with her free hand. "There are so many of them."

"Relax," Ben said, hoping he could take his own advice. "You don't have to say anything. Trent said it would probably be easier on both of us if I do most of the talking."

She swallowed hard. "Okay."

Trent stepped in front of them. "Time to get this over with. Are you ready?"

Ben looked down at her, but she didn't respond, remaining frozen in place. Giving her hand an encouraging squeeze, he spoke to Trent. "Let's do this."

Trent nodded. "Okay. Remember what I told you both. I'll start out by giving the basic details of your marriage. When they start asking questions, if you feel like they're asking something that has already been answered or they touch on something you aren't comfortable answering, just move to the next question."

Ben heard Maya give a shuddering breath before he led her forward. Then they stepped out into the crowded room, everyone's attention instantly on them.

He thought of the press conference immediately following his loss in the play-offs, the way so many in the press had blamed him for the team's loss. On that day, he had struggled to cling to the belief that he was good enough to play in the majors, the seed of doubt always right on the edge of his conscious.

Today, he realized he had finally put that day behind him. He would always remember the disappointment, but standing with Maya by his side, he knew now what was really important.

Though his legs felt like he'd just finished a ten-mile run, he kept Maya's hand in his and followed Trent the short distance from the side entrance to the stage.

He released her hand and pulled out the seat on the end, waiting for Maya to sit before claiming the chair beside her. They were barely seated before Trent picked up one of the three microphones and began. "I'd like to start out by giving a statement. Afterward, we will entertain a few questions."

Trent explained how Ben and Maya met originally, shrewdly outlining the fact that Ben broke up with Cassie shortly after meeting Maya and implying that he'd started dating Maya back then. He went on to detail how Ben and Maya lost touch for a while after he got called up to the majors and relayed the highlights of Ben's relationship with Heather and their ultimate breakup.

While Trent did explain that the breakup happened earlier than publicly recognized, Trent didn't address the question of why Ben married Maya so soon after. Anticipating the question, Trent had already prepped Ben to answer it.

Sure enough, as soon as Trent opened the floor to questions, that was the first one voiced. "Ben, why did you get married so quickly? Were you already dating Maya before your breakup with Heather Wallenberg?"

Trying to exude an air of confidence, Ben shifted forward and picked up his microphone. "As I've said before, I never cheated on anyone." His statement resonated through the room, and he put his hand over Maya's before addressing the more difficult question. "Right after I broke up with Heather, I found out that Maya's family had promised her in marriage to a man she didn't love, a man who was over twice her age. The idea of her marrying someone else helped me realize what was really important in my life."

He paused dramatically, gave Maya's hand a squeeze, and added, "I'm married to my wife because I love her very much. She has helped me find balance in my life, and I treasure every moment we spend together. I'm a better person because I know her. The truth is as simple as that."

Ben could feel the way Maya's hand tensed under his, and he hoped no one else would notice her surprise. Out of his peripheral vision, he could see her staring at him, but he kept his eyes on the crowd, though his thoughts were on Maya. Now that the words had been said, he would have to face her. He would have to face the possibility that he wasn't loved in return, that his feelings would change everything between them.

Another flood of hands came up, and Trent motioned to a heavyset man in the front row.

"Why the big secret?" he asked.

Hesitating, Ben looked at Maya now. They had discussed the possibility of revealing her health issues to the public, but now that the moment was upon them, he hesitated, needing to be sure she was still willing to move forward. She looked confused for a moment, then understanding dawned, and she gave a subtle nod.

Ben straightened his shoulders as though bracing against a strong wind, and he gathered his courage once more. "My wife is currently undergoing treatment for cancer."

A stunned silence enveloped the room, and everyone's attention seemed to shift to Maya. Ben continued, his voice serious. "One of the reasons we agreed to this press conference is to clarify the facts of our relationship and to ask you to respect our privacy while Maya continues to fight this battle."

With the crowd quiet, Ben explained how Cassie was unaware of his marriage when she posted the photo of them together after he had run into her before Christmas. More questions followed about his previous relationships, Ben answering each in turn.

With each question, he gained confidence, appreciating the change in tone as the questions now focused on gaining clarification of facts rather than accusing him of any wrongdoing. He fielded several questions about Maya's cancer, pleased he had learned enough over the past several weeks to feel confident in doing so. Then someone addressed a question to Maya, and Ben stiffened.

"Maya, will you still be going through treatments when baseball season begins?"

Apparently unsure if she should attempt to answer, she looked to Ben. He gave her a subtle nod. He noticed the way her hand shook when she picked up the microphone that, until now, had lain in front of her untouched. Ben shifted and reached his arm behind her, resting his hand on her back.

"My doctors are planning to remove my tumor around the time Ben starts spring training," Maya said, her voice timid.

"What will your recovery time be? Will you be able to travel with Ben at all during the season?"

"I don't know." The crowd quieted as though trying to make sure everyone could hear her. "I guess if I live that long, Ben and I will have some decisions to make."

Once more, the crowd went silent. Several long seconds ticked by before someone dared to ask, "Maya, what is your prognosis?"

Maya swallowed, and Ben could feel her gathering her strength to answer the question without letting her emotions surface. "If I continue to respond well to my current treatment, the doctors think I should have a 50/50 chance of survival."

Not wanting to dwell on a possible negative outcome, Ben spoke before anyone could ask further questions. "As I mentioned before, we ask that we be given privacy over the next few months. While I am certainly preparing for next season the best I can, my main concern right now is for my wife's health and safety."

Ben looked over at Trent, who lifted his microphone. "Okay, folks. That's it for today. Thank you for coming."

With the crowd still buzzing, Trent ushered Ben and Maya off the stage and out a side door. Ben saw the questioning look in Maya's eyes and understood she needed to discuss his public declaration of love. He spoke quietly, leaning down so that only she could hear him. "Not here. We'll talk when we're alone."

Trent motioned to an elevator. "We have a suite reserved for us upstairs." He handed a hotel passkey to Ben and told him the room number. "Go on up. As soon as I find Mr. Magnor, we'll come join you."

Ben took the key, already worried about the upcoming interview. When he looked down and saw Maya's face, immigration became the last of his concerns.

Chapter 38

MAYA STRUGGLED TO FIND THE energy to follow Ben out of the crowded elevator and down the hall. Her energy was sapped, and her mind was whirling. So many times she had dreamed of hearing Ben say the words he had spoken today, but never in a million years had she imagined she would hear them as an outright lie.

One of the things she had grown to love and appreciate about him was his honesty. Now, the first time she'd heard a falsehood come out of his mouth, it was about the one thing that mattered more to her than anything. As much as she wanted to believe his words, she couldn't fathom that there was any truth to them. Just that morning they had talked about how they would have to lie to cover up the real reasons behind their marriage.

They had been married and living together for two months, and not once had he ever expressed such sentiments. The memory of the kisses they had shared just a couple of hours before erupted in her mind, but one private moment didn't mean he really *loved* her.

Her toe caught on the carpet, and she stumbled forward. Ben caught her by the arm before her reflexes managed to kick in. As she straightened, she saw little sparks of light and her vision blurred.

"Are you okay?"

She nodded, but the slight movement of her head sent the hallway spinning.

"I've had you do too much today. I'm sure there's someplace you can lie down for a bit when we get inside."

When they reached their suite, he drew out the passkey and unlocked the door. He pushed it open, motioning for Maya to enter before him. She did so, but not before putting her hand on the doorjamb to steady herself.

His hand on her arm, Ben guided her inside and started across what appeared to be a living room. Vaguely, her mind registered the enormous size of the suite, but the room kept coming in and out of focus. She blinked several times, knowing she wasn't strong enough to make it all the way to the bedroom. She motioned to the nearest couch. "This is fine."

"Okay." Ben helped her sit down, and she immediately let herself sink into the soft cushions.

She took several seconds to gather her strength. Then she spoke softly. "You didn't have to say that."

Ben sat beside her. "Say what? That I love you?"

"I don't want you to have to lie because of our situation." Pressure built behind her forehead. Ignoring her increasing dizziness, she forced herself to say the words. "One of the things I've always admired the most about you is your honesty and integrity. I don't want you to change for all of this."

She felt him shift beside her, his hand lifting to cup her chin. He turned her face so she was looking at him, and despite her currently blurred vision, she couldn't miss the intensity in his eyes.

"Have I ever lied?" The question was direct, and his tone was no-nonsense. "In all the time you've known me, have you ever heard me say anything that wasn't true?"

"No. That's what I'm talking about. I don't want you to start telling lies because of me. I feel sick knowing you would say something that isn't true in front of a room full of people."

His eyes darkened. "Maya, what makes you so sure I'm lying?"

"Because you said . . ." Her voice trailed off, and her mind tried to catch up with Ben's words. "You never said anything before about . . ." Again she trailed off.

"I told you before that I've never regretted marrying you." He shifted her closer and leaned down to press his lips to hers for a tender kiss that left her even dizzier than before. His voice was thick with emotion when he pulled back. "I wasn't lying then, and I'm not lying now." He paused, waiting for her eyes to meet his. "I love you."

The opening lay in front of her, the chance to step into a real marriage by returning those three little words, yet she was utterly speechless. Her heart flooded with emotion as her pulse pounded painfully in her head. Pain and pleasure. She felt them both keenly and tried to fight back the pain.

She opened her mouth, determined to share her love, but found herself overcome by another jolt of pain. Her hands fisted as the throbbing increased, and she searched for the simple words she so desperately wanted to give Ben.

"I . . ." She closed her eyes as pain sliced through her with even greater intensity.

Concern filled Ben's voice, and he seemed to understand something wasn't right. "Where are your pain pills?"

She put a hand on her purse but didn't have the energy to open it and fish out the bottle. A moan escaped her with the next wave of pain. "I can't think. It's too much."

Ben took her purse from her, riffling through it himself until he came up with the correct medication. As soon as Ben stood, Maya swayed dangerously to one side.

"Careful." Ben's hand gripped her shoulder, and he steadied her, shifting her back so she could lean more firmly against the cushions on the couch. "I'll get you some water."

She barely registered the sound of his footsteps across the plush carpet, followed by water splashing into a glass. A moment later, Ben pressed two pills into her hand. "Here you go."

Maya mumbled her thanks, placing the pills in her mouth before accepting the water glass from him. As soon as she managed to wash them down, Ben took the glass and set it on the end table beside her.

"Can I get you anything else?"

The door opened, and Maya was aware of Trent and the immigration officer entering the room. She tried to look at them, to see the face of the man who would determine her future, but their shapes blurred together, blending into the bone-colored walls. She reached for Ben's hand, unable to find it.

Panic shot through her as her vision continued to blur and fade. Apparently sensing her need for contact, Ben put his hand over hers. "Are you going to be okay?"

It took all of her energy to speak. "I don't think I can do this."

"I'll help you into the bedroom, and you can lie down while I talk to Mr. Magnor," Ben suggested.

Unaware of Maya's declining physical condition, the man with Trent spoke brusquely. "I'm sorry, but the interview must be with both of you."

Weakly, Maya tried to respond, but the room continued to darken, the light streaming through the windows fading until everything went black. Fear snaked through her, and she struggled to find her voice. "Ben?" Her grip on his hand tightened, and trepidation filled her words. "Ben, I can't see."

* * *

Alarmed, Ben shifted off the couch, kneeling in front of Maya, concerned as much by her lack of color as by her declaration. "Can you see anything?"

"Everything's gone. It's all black." Her grip tightened on his hand as though she was holding on to a lifeline. Her voice hitched. "Ben, I'm scared."

Realizing Maya needed to keep the physical connection between them, Ben turned to Trent. "Call an ambulance."

"What's wrong?" Trent asked, already retrieving his phone from his pocket and dialing.

"I don't know. This hasn't ever happened before." Ben lifted his hand and put it against Maya's forehead to find her skin cool and clammy. His stomach clutched as he found himself facing the unknown. Unlike the other two times he'd taken her into the hospital, today he had no idea what was causing the problem.

Behind him, he could hear the 9-1-1 operator's voice through the phone asking, "What's your emergency?"

After requesting an ambulance and giving their location, Trent tried to answer the operator's questions. A moment later, he handed the phone to Ben. "The operator wants more details than what I can give her. She told me to go downstairs and wait for the ambulance so I can guide the paramedics up here."

Ben took the phone from Trent with his free hand and watched him disappear from the room. Trying to keep his voice calm, despite the negative thoughts that swirled through his mind, Ben didn't bother with a greeting, instead asking, "What do you need to know?"

The operator asked about Maya's health history, her medications, and any possible injuries. Ben answered one question after another, using his shoulder to hold the phone in place so he could retrieve Maya's wallet from her purse. After the incident in Cincinnati, she had started keeping the list of her prescriptions there for just such an emergency.

Ben explained how quickly her condition had degraded in the past few minutes and gave the operator Maya's doctor's name as well as what pain medication he had just given her. All the while, he kept Maya's hand in his, asking her questions as directed by the emergency operator.

He could see her energy fading, his concern growing with each passing minute. Finally, the door opened, and Trent escorted two paramedics inside.

It didn't take long for them to decide to take Maya to the hospital. Ben issued the request for her to be transported to George Washington University Hospital.

As the paramedics prepared Maya for transport, Mr. Magnor headed for the door.

"I'm really sorry about this," Ben heard Trent say. "Can we call you and reschedule after Maya is better?"

"There's no need for that," Mr. Magnor told him.

Ben stiffened with frustration, his attention now on the man standing across the room. "You can't hold this against her. It's not like she got sick on purpose."

Mr. Magnor held up his hand. "I'm not suggesting she did. The reason it's not necessary to reschedule is that I've already seen everything I need to." He took another step toward the door. "I hope your wife recovers quickly. As for my report, I will document my opinion that this marriage is valid and convey my recommendation to reinstate Maya Evans's permanent resident status."

Ben stared blankly for a moment, barely able to process the words. After several seconds, he managed to find his voice. "Thank you."

When the paramedics started wheeling Maya toward the door, Ben turned his attention back to what was most important: getting Maya better so he could take her home.

Chapter 39

BEN SAT IN THE BACK of the ambulance, watching helplessly as a paramedic continued to monitor Maya's vital signs. Ben kept Maya's hand in his, murmuring reassurances, trying desperately to believe his own words.

He felt a jolt of panic when Maya's hand suddenly went limp in his. That panic heightened when the paramedic immediately relayed the change in her condition to the hospital.

"Patient has lost consciousness. Pulse irregular. BP dropping."

The driver's response was to increase their speed. Ninety seconds later, the ambulance pulled up in front of the hospital, and the paramedics quickly unloaded the gurney and wheeled Maya inside. Ben jogged along behind them. He saw a security guard beside a set of double doors, and for a moment, Ben was afraid the man was there to keep him out of the emergency room.

The paramedic spoke to the guard as they approached. "He's her husband."

With a nod of understanding, the man pushed a button that opened the doors, granting them entrance. As soon as they passed through, Ben found himself in a swirl of unfamiliar chaos. A doctor met Maya before she had made it into an examination room, the thirty-something-year-old man barking out orders as he walked alongside the gurney.

Ben tried to shift out of the way when Maya was lifted from the gurney onto another one of similar size. Straining to see Maya through the bodies of medical personnel now surrounding her, he asked, "Is she going to be okay?"

His question was ignored, and another nurse entered, forcing him farther into the corner of the room near the foot of the bed.

The newest nurse, a petite blonde in her midtwenties, administered some kind of medication into Maya's IV, and the doctor began probing Maya's neck and shoulders. "We've got a lot of inflammation here." He glanced back at Ben briefly. "You said she lost her eyesight? How long ago?"

"Fifteen, twenty minutes ago. It was right before we called 9-1-1."

"The call came in at 4:12."

The doctor glanced at his watch. He ordered another medication and reached his hand out, apparently knowing the nurse was ready to give him Maya's chart. He looked at it for several seconds; Ben hoped desperately that he would find something to help Maya, something to give him the assurance that she'd be okay.

The doctor's next words sent his hopes into a tailspin. "Call and get Dr. Schuster's ETA." He hesitated briefly and then added, "And you'd better call in the surgeon."

"What's wrong?" Ben asked, panic filling his voice. "What's happening to her?"

A nurse was still dialing his number when Dr. Schuster hurried into the room, firing off his own questions that quickly took priority. He began his own examination of Maya, immediately probing her neck, where her tumor was located.

The two doctors spoke in medical jargon that was gibberish to Ben. Then their words rang out clearly, the meaning stabbing through his heart. "Move her up to ICU. We have to get her stabilized before the surgeon gets here. We'll only get one shot at this."

Ben reached out and put his hand on Maya's foot before they could wheel her away. "Will someone tell me what's going on?"

"Take it easy, Ben." Dr. Schuster motioned for two orderlies to take Maya out of the room. Ben watched helplessly as they wheeled her away, panic clawing at his throat and bringing tears to his eyes. "Let them get her to ICU, and I'll explain everything."

Ben blinked several times and struggled against his emotions. The doctor issued several more orders and finally turned back to Ben. He motioned to a chair in the corner of the room, but Ben shook his head. Whatever the news, he wasn't going to take it sitting down, literally or figuratively.

Dr. Schuster didn't press the issue. "The blindness Maya experienced is the result of pressure on the nerves in her neck. Unfortunately, inflammation in the healthy tissue surrounding the tumor is one of the possible side effects of her treatment, and it becomes more common the longer someone is on this regimen."

"But why did she lose consciousness?"

"Either the swelling or the tumor itself is likely pressing on the spinal cord." His expression became even more grim. "Her body is already in a weakened state, and it's trying to shut down. I think we can stabilize her, but if we don't perform surgery soon, we aren't going to get another chance."

Doubts and confusion dominated Ben's thoughts, and he struggled to process the doctor's words. "But I thought the tumor was still too big."

"It's still larger than I'm comfortable with, but we no longer have a choice. If she gets much weaker, she won't survive surgery."

The words hit Ben low in the gut, and he had to catch his breath before he could ask what he needed so desperately to know. "What are her chances?"

"I'm not going to lie. Her survival rate has always hovered around 50/50, and her current condition doesn't help it. Unfortunately, the chance of paralysis is also much higher than it would have been in a perfect scenario." Dr. Schuster paused as though letting Ben process his words before dealing the next blow. "Even if she does survive the surgery, there is a good chance she could come out of this as a quadriplegic."

A whole new set of possibilities raced through Ben's mind and left his hopes stumbling. What would it be like? A baseball player who spent so much of his time trying to stay in shape married to a woman who couldn't use her arms or legs? The internal strife continued to wage, but he found clarity within the depths of the battlefield. "Just keep her alive," Ben managed to say. His voice fell to a whisper when he added, "Please keep her alive."

* * *

Ben stood in the wide hallway, his fingertips brushing along Maya's arm as two orderlies arrived to wheel her away. All night he had sat by her side, waiting, hoping, praying she would wake up. The nurses said her vital signs had stabilized, and the surgeon had arrived at six o'clock that morning to look over her case one last time. Now Maya's fate was in the hands of Dr. Gaunt, one of the top neurosurgeons in the country, a man who had driven in from northern Virginia earlier that morning to spend his New Year's Day trying to save Maya's life.

The moment Ben's hand lost contact with Maya, he felt his heart shudder with a myriad of emotions. Fear, anxiety, anticipation, hope. He stared at his wife's face, praying against all odds that she would survive.

This couldn't be the last time he would see her alive. It just couldn't.

His hand went into his pocket, where Maya's rings were wrapped in a piece of tissue. The nurse had helped him take them off Maya's finger when she was admitted, and now Ben could only hope she would wear them again soon.

Somewhere in the back of his mind, he desperately wanted her to regain her normal life, to be able to do all of the things she had been denied over the past many months of treatment, but right now, in this instant, he was afraid to hope for anything beyond her survival.

If she suffered serious side effects from the surgery, they would face them . . . later.

He stood there, watching Maya get wheeled away down the long hallway until she disappeared around a corner. Tears welled up in his eyes, but he didn't care. Maya was everything to him. The fear of losing her overwhelmed him, swallowing him until he could barely breathe.

A hand came down on his shoulder, and Ben looked to his right to see Henry standing beside him, his weathered face serious, his eyes also damp. Henry cleared his throat and motioned to a door behind them. "Come on. Let's head down to the cafeteria. Rumor has it you haven't eaten anything since you got here yesterday."

"I'm not hungry."

"Oh, no you don't. You're not going to run yourself into the ground right now. That girl is going to need your help while she recovers." Henry spoke with certainty in his voice, leaving no question as to whether Maya would survive. "She'll be in surgery for several hours. We'll be back up here long before the doctor has any news for us."

His words made sense . . . if she survived. But what if . . . He didn't want to finish the thought, but he was also afraid to leave the surgical waiting room. As though reading the reason for his hesitation, Henry added, "The nurses have my pager number. If the doctor needs to find you, they'll call me."

Reluctantly, Ben nodded and let Henry lead him downstairs. He went through the motions of putting some kind of sustenance into his body, and three hours later, he was wearing a path in the carpet in the nearly empty waiting room. Surgery wasn't usually scheduled for the holiday, so other than an emergency appendectomy, the operating rooms had remained quiet today.

The parents of the nine-year-old appendicitis patient left an hour after Ben and Henry returned from the cafeteria. Henry had settled back with a magazine, aware that trying to calm Ben down was a useless venture.

When he heard a door open, Ben whipped around, surprised to see not the doctor but his parents and Kari rushing through the door.

"Any word yet?" Steve asked.

Overwhelmed by their unexpected presence, Ben took a moment to find his voice. After he hugged his sister and mother, he answered his father. "The doctor said the surgery would take at least three hours but that it could take twice that."

"How long has it been?"

"A little over four." Henry answered for him, standing up to stretch his legs.

"This is Henry. He's been a really good friend to Maya and me." Ben introduced Henry to his family, and at his mother's insistence, they all sat in a corner of the waiting room.

Ben only lasted ten minutes before he was up and prowling the room again. At some point, one of Henry's friends brought sandwiches for everyone, but Ben could eat only a few bites. The nervous energy building up in him was exhausting. He needed to *do* something, and he needed answers.

The thought had barely crossed his mind when the door opened and the doctor walked in.

Ben hurried across the room, desperate to know Maya's fate. "Well?"

Dr. Schuster dragged a hand over his face and let out a relieved sigh. "It's a miracle; she's alive."

Chapter 40

MAYA KEPT HER EYES CLOSED and listened to the squeaking sound of footsteps on the hallway floor, the low hum of hospital equipment, and the constant murmur of voices. The scent of someone's overly floral perfume almost hid the underlying scents common to the hospital she had come to know so well.

Her mind was a haze of confusion, and she felt herself drift in and out of sleep. Once, she vaguely remembered someone trying to wake her up, but she couldn't quite bring herself out of the fog.

She knew she was in the hospital, but her thoughts were too scattered for her to piece together how she got here. She felt a hand holding hers and knew instantly it was Ben's. His thumb rubbed back and forth over the back of her hand as though he couldn't quite manage to stay still.

She tried to move and felt resistance when she tried to turn her head. Some bandage pressed against her forehead, but she didn't have the clarity of thought to question why.

Slowly, her mind started to pull together the events that had brought her here. Thoughts drifted through her mind as she faded in and out of consciousness, the steady grip of Ben's hand constant on hers. Even through her drug-induced haze, she found comfort in the solidity of the gesture. Her dreams mingled with reality, and she found herself hoping this warm, steady, loving feeling could last forever.

A door opened, and she heard her doctor's voice. "How's our patient?"

The sound of Dr. Schuster's voice sent her nerves scrambling. If he was here on New Year's Eve, her condition must be serious.

"I don't know. She still hasn't woken up," Ben answered, his voice low.

"Let's take a closer look," Dr. Schuster's footsteps sounded as he crossed the hard floor. "Maya? Can you open your eyes for me?"

She heard the request, but she hesitated, knowing that if she opened her eyes to the terrifying nothingness in front of her, terror would take over. She wanted to pretend everything was normal, that she could find a happily ever after with Ben. He had already said he loved her. If that was true, maybe she could find another miracle in her life. Or more specifically, she could *have* a life.

When she didn't comply right away, Ben squeezed her hand. "Maya? Are you awake?" She stirred slightly, but still, she couldn't get past her fears and open her eyes. "Come on, honey. Open your eyes. Let the doctor help you."

The steady tone of Ben's voice did what all of her internal assurances couldn't. It gave her hope.

Slowly, she forced her eyelids open, narrowing her eyes against the bright lights overhead. Lights! Her heartbeat quickened, new hope surging through her. Squinting, she tried to look around the room but again felt resistance. The tall shadow at the side of her bed slowly took shape until she recognized it was her husband.

The doctor's calm voice continued. "What can you see?"

"Ben. I see Ben." Her words came out in a hoarse whisper and sounded distant even to her. She summoned her strength and tried to continue, but still, her words were spoken softly. "Everything's a little foggy . . ."

"That's to be expected. It'll take a few minutes to focus."

"What happened?" she managed to ask, Ben's hand gripping hers.

"You're going to be okay," Dr. Schuster assured her.

"Okay?" Maya repeated, confused. Again, she tried to turn her head but found she couldn't.

"Don't try to move. You've already had your surgery. The tumor is gone."

"Gone?" She wanted to ask more, but she felt herself fading. Her eyelids suddenly heavy, she felt them droop closed, and she slid back under.

* * *

Ben sat by her side and rubbed a hand over the stiffness in his neck. The doctor's words echoed through his mind repeatedly. Maya truly was a miracle. According to the surgeon, had the tumor been a fraction larger, Maya wouldn't have survived. A little more to the left and her spinal cord would have been damaged, most certainly causing paralysis. As it was, the doctors were confident that the entire tumor had been removed, and they believed she would recover completely.

Despite the doctors' optimism, Ben couldn't bring himself to leave Maya's side. Through the first few hours after Maya had woken up, he had been overwhelmed with gratitude. Everything he had wished for had come true.

That thought had comforted him during those first long hours by her side, but then, late that night, doubts had started creeping into his mind. Not his doubts about Maya's recovery but about her heart. The scene in the hotel circled through his mind, and one thought continued to surface: Maya hadn't said she loved him.

He had recognized that fact at the time, but so quickly after he had confessed his feelings, her health had spiraled and become his priority. Now, sitting in the dark hospital room, his hand covering Maya's, he let himself remember the moment when he had hoped to hear her respond, but no words had come.

Over and over again, he forced himself to remember, his uncertainty growing with each passing minute.

For the past two months, Maya's whole focus had been on reaching this day—the day after her surgery. Now that she was here, what did she want to do with her tomorrows? They had broached the subject once when they were at his parents' house for Christmas, but that conversation had been in general terms. Never once had he asked what she wanted.

She was his wife. There was no denying that, even if they hadn't gotten married in a traditional sense. With the immigration investigation now behind them, she would be free to apply for her citizenship in a matter of months and wouldn't need him in that regard. Nor was she tied any longer to Washington, DC.

His heart rose into his throat. What would he do if she wanted to leave? He couldn't hold her here. If he tried to persuade her to stay, he'd be no better than Rishi, but the thought of her walking away from him left a hollowness that engulfed his whole being.

By the time the first fingers of sunlight streamed into the room, Ben knew what he had to do. He would help nurse her back to health, make sure she was able to gain her citizenship, and pay off her debts. Then he would give her the freedom to choose—to stay or go.

Ben was still struggling with his decision when Maya finally stirred an hour later. Her leg moved under the blanket, giving Ben a reassurance that Maya had truly avoided paralysis. When she tried to roll over and found she couldn't, Ben stood and spoke in a soothing voice. "Hey, take it easy."

Maya's eyes opened fully now and seemed to take a moment to focus. Ben could tell when she did because her lips curved into a lazy smile. "Hi."

"Hi, yourself." He stood so he could see her more clearly. "How are you feeling?"

"Don't know. Feel loopy."

"Dr. Schuster gave you some pretty heavy-duty pain killers after your surgery."

Her eyes narrowed, and her voice was questioning. "Surgery?"

"That's right." Ben's voice gentled instinctively. "It's the day after, Maya. You made it."

"I don't understand."

Ben explained the sequence of events after she'd lost consciousness—her arrival at the hospital, the decision to proceed with her surgery, and the doctor's assurances that everything had gone perfectly.

She took several minutes to absorb his words and then managed to ask, "It's really over?"

With a shadow of regret, he nodded. "It's really over."

He fought the urge to ask her what she wanted next, trying to keep his promise to himself to let her recover before pushing her to tell him her feelings.

"What's wrong?"

"Nothing. Nothing's wrong," Ben insisted. "I told you. The doctors said you're going to be fine."

"No. What's wrong with you?" Her eyes met his and held. When he didn't immediately respond, she added, "Just tell me."

He drew a deep breath, let it out, and broke the promise to himself. "I'm just wondering, now that you have your life back, what are you going to do with it?"

"What do you mean?"

"You have a future now. I'm asking you how you want to spend it."

He sensed her apprehension and saw the way she seemed to draw up her courage. "I want to spend it with you."

"What?" Ben asked, afraid he hadn't heard her right, praying that he had.

"There's something I've been wanting to tell you for a long time." She shifted her hand in his, linking their fingers. "I love you, Ben."

"What?" Ben repeated, wanting to hear her say the words again, needing to make sure he wasn't dreaming.

Her eyes stayed on his, unwavering. "I love you."

Joy leapt in his heart as shock melted into wonder. Theirs might not have been the most traditional relationship, but seeing the blank pages in front of them, the future they could carve out together any way they chose, he knew he wouldn't want it any other way. He leaned over her bed, gently pressing his lips to hers.

The kiss was sweet and simple, but his stomach jumped with a sense of need and anticipation unlike anything he'd ever experienced. He drew the kiss out, finding unspeakable joy in knowing Maya could be his forever. When he forced himself to draw back, she offered him a timid smile.

Finding new confidence, he reached into his pocket and drew out the wad of tissue he had wrapped around her rings. Slowly, he unwrapped them and held them out for her to see. "Maya, I love you so much. Will you stay married to me?"

She offered him a watery smile, lifting her hand so he could slip the rings into place. "I thought you'd never ask."

About the Author

ORIGINALLY FROM ARIZONA, TRACI HUNTER Abramson has spent most of her adult life in Virginia. She is a graduate of Brigham Young University and a former employee of the Central Intelligence Agency. She enjoys writing what she knows and considers it a bonus when her research includes travel and attending sporting events.

Since leaving the CIA, Traci has written numerous novels, including the Undercurrents trilogy, the Saint Squad series, the Royal series, *Obsession*, *Deep Cover*, and *Code Word*, a Whitney Award–winner.

When she's not writing, Traci enjoys spending time with her family and coaching the local high school swim teams.